Handle
with
Care

GW00362458

Jacinta McDevitt

POOLBEG

Published 2003
Poolbeg Press Ltd.
123 Grange Hill, Baldoyle,
Dublin 13, Ireland
Email: poolbeg@poolbeg.com

© Jacinta McDevitt 2003

The moral right of the author has been asserted.

Copyright for typesetting, layout, design
© Poolbeg Group Services Ltd.

1 3 5 7 9 10 8 6 4 2

A catalogue record for this book is available from the British Library.

ISBN 1-84223 -122-7

Typeset by Patricia Hope in Sabon 10.5/14.5
Printed by
Litografia Rosés S.A., Spain

www.poolbeg.com

About the Author

This is Jacinta McDevitt's second novel. Her first novel, *Sign's On,* was published last year. She has had many short stories and articles published and broadcast. She lives in Dublin and has two grown-up children.

Also by Jacinta McDervitt

Sign's On

Acknowledgements

For all of you who are reading this and all of you who were kind enough to ask "When's the next one coming out?" – well, here it is. I hope you enjoy it. Thanks for reading it.

A huge thanks to everyone at Poolbeg – a really terrific bunch of people; in particular, many thanks to Gaye and Paula for their pearls of wisdom. Also to Anne, Brona and Sarah for their good humour and endless enthusiasm. Thanks too to my agent, Jane Conway Gordon.

Love to all my friends, especially Mildred who's been there from the start and Bethia who tells me I thrive under pressure but is lovely enough never to put me under pressure. Special warm wishes to Eimear, Eoin, Conor and the gang in Spilling Ink. Love to Joe and Lucy.

A big soppy kiss and hugs to all my nieces and nephews: Helen, Sara, Katie, Frank, Ellen, Hannah and Sam. They keep growing in number! Love to Michael, Maeve and Tony who picked great partners.

Lots of love, always, to my wonderful sisters and

brother, Margaret, Lucy, Mary and Frank. Kick one –
we all limp.

Lots of love to my soon-to-be-daughter-in-law
Maire – a treasure. I'll make a terrific mother-in-law.
I promise!

Lots of love and thanks always to Brian – I'm
loving every minute of it.

A huge thank you and lots of love always to my
parents, Frank and Helen. Their love and dedication
to their family and each other is inspirational.

Endless love and happiness always to my son
Alan and my daughter Lucy. Always the light at the
end of any tunnel. Thank you both for making me
so happy and giving me so much encouragement
and love.

Love the bones of you

Now get reading . . .

Once upon a time . .

For
Lucy, Alan and Maire
Mam and Dad
Brian
Margaret, Lucy, Frank, Mary
With all my love

"*This above all: to thine own self be true, and it must follow, as night the day, thou canst not then be false to any man.*"

WILLIAM SHAKESPEARE (Hamlet)
(also my family's motto)

CHAPTER ONE

"Hello!"

"Hi, Kelly. Where are you?"

Did you ever notice that? '*Where are you?*' is the first thing people say to each other on a mobile phone? What difference does it make where you are and what's the obsession people have with wanting to know exactly where you are when you're talking to them?

I mostly have to lie about where I am because I am always somewhere I shouldn't be. I never answer the *Where are you?* question truthfully. I think people have an awful cheek asking the question in the first place, trapping me into a lie. "Stuck in a bastard of a traffic jam. Nearly with you now. Just have to get past this bit of traffic and I'll be with you. Can you believe every bloody light is red? Had to stop for petrol." All lies. Lies I tell to my closest friends just as I'm about to leave my house to meet up with them wherever they are waiting for me and where I should have been already. I am not proud of myself. I'd never lie to them about anything else. I wouldn't lie if they didn't ask. If only they'd stop asking me *Where are you?*. You've no idea of the hassle and guilt trips they cause me . . .

Today I had no need to lie. I was exactly where I should be and I wasn't supposed to be with anyone. I was supposed to be alone. The Divorce Court is a lonely, lonely place. It's like a cattle market except it has none of the fun – no buzz, no atmosphere. Plenty of wheeling and dealing and bargains being stuck. Very few shaking hands. There are people there and you can almost see the daggers sticking out of their backs. Put there by someone they once loved and who once loved the bones of them. People of every ilk and kin gather. All broken people with broken marriages collect there for a quick fix and a fair deal. Fair is a relative thing, you know – it always depends on what slice of the cake you're looking at. Some third party decides what's fair and that's it. It's over. Finito. Fucked. Or never fucked again – it all depends on how strong you are at recovery, how fair you think the judge has been and how much of a gambler you are, to throw your fecked heart into the ring again with someone else who has the potential to pulverise it.

I thought Judge St Clair was very fair. Then again I was looking at a substantial slice of the cake. He'd just given me a house, two children (both young adults so I don't know if that counts as a plus or a minus, time alone will tell) a nice hefty maintenance payment and a lump sum of €10,000 which would ensure I had a well deserved holiday. I still hated the ordeal of it all. The justifying my very existence and the feeling I was begging for what was rightfully mine. It was not a pleasant day's outing and I vowed never to repeat the procedure. I felt a bit like a woman who'd just had a boob-job done – happy with my latest assets, but safe in the knowledge that acquiring them was too painful to repeat.

"Kelly? Are you there? Can you talk?"

"Oh, I'm sorry. Yeah, I can talk, just about. I'm on the verge of tears, but I can talk."

"I was nearly afraid to ring in case you'd still be in there and the phone would ring in the middle of it all and you'd be arrested for contempt of court. You said you'd ring as soon as you got out – why didn't you? Well, is the deed done? Are you a statistic like me?"

"Actually I was just about to ring you and there was a lot of contempt around all right, but nothing to do with phones. I'm just out now. I'm standing on the steps of the Divorce Court as we speak."

My God, I just remembered the last time I'd

3

stood on these steps. It seemed like a lifetime ago. It was a good time. I was a young girl, all innocent and fresh – yeah, it was that long ago! I was wearing a pink tutu and pink ballet shoes, and my blonde hair was piled high into an elaborate little crown on my head. I thought I was terrific. I was terrific. I always wanted to be a ballet dancer. I had the look when I was younger but I didn't have the stamina. Just as well, because I'd be an out-of-work dancer now that I have the stamina but have lost the look. Some things come with age. Others go. I giggled, remembering the ballet I had danced in all that time ago – *The Nutcracker*. Did a bit more nut-cracking today, mind you.

The River Liffey looked the same now as it did back then, just a bit murkier and an extra bridge or two over her. But the building that was once St Anthony's Hall, where concerts and ballet shows and even the bingo was put on, stands beside her, facing her, watching her change with the seasons. It is now the Divorce Court where people from every walk of life ebb and flow in a mixum-gatherum of tears and relief. Everyone's looking to shout "*House!*" – everyone knows their number is up.

I wondered if St Anthony, patron saint for all things lost, still had some sort of a hold over the place. He can't have been there for so long and then evicted without leaving his mark. Would he hear me and respond if I promised him a pound or even a euro and asked him to find my lost marriage? Then again, he probably doesn't deal in euros. Furthermore, he would probably consider that my marriage is not lost at all but broken, broken to bits, smashed in a million, zillion pieces, and not an accident either. St Anthony isn't the man for fixing things – he's only the man for finding things. Maybe he could find me a heart that isn't broken. I wonder who the patron saint of broken things is?

"So you're a free woman then or at least a cheap one?" Phil giggled.

"Yeah, I guess you could call me free. Although my newly-acquired ex mightn't think so."

'Ex' had a nice ring to it. I could get used to it. *Ex*-husband. Yeah, it sounded good. I could live with that.

"So go on then. Don't spare me any details. I want every cringing moment. Did you take him to the cleaner's and did they hang him out to dry?"

I giggled. My best pal Phil is wonderful at cheering me up. Phil is divorced too. It was a clean-cut divorce though. They were adults. They acted like adults. No children or pets to fight over and a house they split right down the middle, fifty-fifty. No blood spilt and no one party wanting to kill the other one. It was all very amicable. It cost very little in either money, blood or tears.

They met one year on holiday in Italy. They fell madly in love with the place and each other. They came home and wanted to keep the romance going. They bought a house together and decorated it Italian-style. Or at least what they remembered of Italian style. White walls, bright coloured tiles and terracotta pots. They had loads of coloured candles stuck into used Italian wine bottles. They had romantic meals of spaghetti bolognese, cheap wine and ciabatta bread. They greeted all their guests with *"Ciao, bella!"* and mourned the fact that the sun never shone in Ireland the way it did in Italy. They lived in their own little world. It was a false little world. We all knew it wouldn't last. But they knew better. Against all our advice, they got married a month later. Phil was convinced it was true love and would last forever.

"This is it, Kelly, this is the real thing – true love. I'm going to bring her back to Italy in years to come to celebrate our twenty-fifth wedding anniversary. Some time in the future I'm going to bring our children over to show them where their mother and I met."

Oh, it was Love's Young Dream all right. But back then I was no fool where love and young dreams were concerned. I knew the only thing the two of them had in common was that they both loved a place they'd be lucky to visit again once a year on a fortnight's holiday. Hardly the stuff of wedded bliss. I knew that even if

6

they did both get to Italy in twenty-five years' time, it wouldn't be as husband and wife. It wouldn't even be as friends. I had a visual image of the two of them travelling all the way to Italy alone. Sitting at two ends of a plane. Sitting alone in candlelight, in two separate restaurants, at either end of some godforsaken Italian village, crying into their respective tortellini.

It was a lonely image, except for the crowds of locals running up and down the cobbled streets peeping in at both restaurants to see what was going on.

But then I did warn them – not on the massing crowds peeping at them, mind you, but on the marriage. I gave them several warnings. I was straight and honest with Phil. "It'll end in tears, Phil," I said. "Cut your losses now," I begged. "For Christ sake, cop on to yourself!" All good sound advice. I am so good at other people's relationships. It's only my own I'm lousy with. I give great advice; I'm lousy at taking advice. Any advice. Mine or anyone else's. So Phil and his little wannabe senorina married in haste and they did what the rest of us knew they would do: repented at leisure. Granted, they didn't spend a lot of leisure time on the repenting. In fact, they spent no time at all on it.

They both knew it was a mistake so they divorced at Christmas. It was their Christmas present to each other. No need of wrapping paper or bows. They haven't seen each other since. They have no need to. It's as if it never happened. It was a perfect divorce. Everything Phil does is perfect. I am not a bit like Phil. It's a wonder we get on together at all.

"I feel a bit peculiar to tell you the truth," I said to Phil. "I'm not sure if I should be laughing or crying."

"Well, when in doubt have a laugh."

"I wish I could – my nerves are gone. To be honest, I wouldn't wish it on my worst enemy."

"Oh, Kelly. I'm so sorry. You were separated that long I thought the divorce would only be a formality."

"It would have been except for The Git I was getting the divorce from. It was really galling. All the things I regarded as sacred were bandied around the court. It made me sick. All my little private details dragged out for everyone to hear. Including The Git. I had to give chapter and verse on all my intimate details. I had to hand over all my financial details. My incomings and my outgoings, my bank statements, my loans and my debts."

"Sure they needed all that to see that The Git had given you feck all. I'm glad they saw the struggle you've had."

"Shag that. No one mentioned the struggle to make ends meet or the robbing Peter to pay Paul and then borrowing off Paul to give a bit back to Peter. I had to lay myself bare financially while everyone just nodded their heads as if they knew for one shaggin' moment what it was like to rob Peter."

"Oh, Kelly. It's over now. All done. You're a free agent. Wasn't it worth it to get rid of him?"

"I know it was worth it. Well, at least in my head I know it was worth it. In the sane part of me. The logical part of me. But I think I left the logical part of me at home this morning in my rush to get here. The heart part of me took over. My illogical part. My emotional part listened as my love life too was pulled asunder. I had to give chapter and verse on my intimate mates. I had to admit that I was still minus a permanent partner and at the moment I was minus even a temporary partner. I was partner-less. I should have hired a Chippendale to come along with me and pose as my partner. No one believed that I was partnerless by choice. They didn't believe that rearing two children on my own had taken all the time and energy I had. They didn't for one moment think that rearing two kids was enough for me to be concentrating on and that having gotten rid of one strange man in my life I didn't want another one around to complicate the issue. They all nodded the slow pitying nods you do when you really pity someone. I guess they couldn't cope with the fact that I was a happy, successful woman without a man? They couldn't come to grips with the fact that I had spent the last ten years (minus the odd fling or two) without a man in my life. I was successful in every way, even emotionally, and because I was in a room full of men they just didn't get it. Why is emotional success measured by whether you are one of a couple or not?"

"It just is, Kelly. Put hey, I'm proud of you."

"Jesus, Phil. I had to lay myself completely bare and listen as they raked over the coals that I extinguished at least ten years ago. They pulled and chucked at my life all over again. They gave the coals a bloody good going-over with a bellows and tried to re-ignite the whole thing. The only thing they fell short of doing was laying me physically bare. It might have been easier to stand in the dock stark naked. I might have preferred it to listening to the endless lies and lack of dignity. I might have preferred it to being exposed and raped by circumstance. Graham had a go at me all those years ago. Today he let his solicitors and barristers join a queue and have another go at me. A team, pack, gang of solicitors – whatever a collection of them is – he let them all loose on me. But I was stronger than the whole bloody lot of them. I had truth on my side."

"Yeah, Kelly, remember you did nothing. Your husband left. He wanted a divorce. It's so awful that it involved you suffering yet again. That's just shows you what a git he really was. He could have made it easy for you. He didn't."

"Thanks, Phil. You're brilliant."

I realised that I was feeling a teeny bit sorry for myself. Well, OK, more than a teeny bit – maybe a whole lot sorry for myself. But, Jesus Christ, wasn't I entitled to the luxury of feeling sorry for myself?

"I know I'm brilliant – we're both brilliant. Sure amn't I always telling you that?"

"Oh look, I've got to go. My solicitor is coming over to me. I'll ring you back in a minute."

"OK, talk to you then."

My solicitor came over to me with his hand outstretched. I shook his hand and nearly gave it a grateful little squeeze. He was a decent man. He had done the decent thing for me in a place that wasn't decent, where only 50 per cent of the people are decent. He had done his very best and we were lucky that his best was very good.

"Well, Kelly," my big decent solicitor said, "you must be very pleased with today's outcome. I think we did our best and all in all it went very well for you."

"Yes, I'm delighted. Sorry I couldn't talk to you inside. I really needed a bit of air. I thought I was going to faint."

"Are you all right now?"

"Yes, fine thanks."

"You did great. The fact that he kept lying to the judge certainly didn't help his case. I think you got the best deal you could . . . considering . . ."

Considering the fact that I had married and lived with a complete git of a mean-spirited bastard and headbanger, I had got a good deal.

"Yeah," I smiled up at him. "I'm delighted, if a bit shaken. Thanks for everything; you were great and don't forget to send me your final bill."

Oh, that was just so typical of me – nice – send me the bill! I'm such a goody-two-shoes. Such a nice person. Yuck! Who the hell else would ask for his bill only me? Well, no more of that kind of talk from this girl. This girl was going to have to toughen up. For someone who had been living in the house of hard knocks for half her life I had learned very little. Now what I should have done with this very handsome, financially secure, single, very eligible, man in his early fifties was pretend to have a little fainting spell. Grab onto his strong arm and lean against his strong body. Then I should have whispered, "You can call me Kelly, now this is all over." But he called me Kelly anyway so that would be a bit foolish. "Can I come in and see you for a follow-up consultation?" wink, wink, nod, nod. But I already had an appointment to make my will; he'd consider that a follow-up. On the other hand, I could go with the direct approach. Get right in there and say, "I suppose a ride is out of the question? And how's your belly for a love-bite? Come up and see me some time when I've nothing on." But, you know, I was only noticing now, after all the months and months of crying on this eligible bachelor's shoulder, that he had indeed a very nice set of shoulders. Broad, strong, muscular, tanned – well, I can imagine, can't I? I bet they were tanned. The rest of him wasn't half bad either – in fact, he was quite cute-looking in a distinguished sort of way. He wore very distinguished clothes. White shirts and smart dark suits and fantastic ties.

You can tell a lot about a man by his tie. A thin tie with a tiny knot doesn't say very much, but a chunky bright-coloured tie with an extra large knot – boy, does that speak volumes! If I have to elaborate here, I feel sorry for you and what you're missing out on in life.

Anyway, he was a chunky-tie guy. As for his hair, I couldn't take my eyes off it. It was dark, dark brown and very shiny and matched his eyes exactly. Not that his eyes were shiny – they were very dark brown and almost twinkled. Just shows you what sort of shock I had been in with the divorce that I never noticed all this before now. This man had been my mentor and salvation for months on end and I was only noticing now what a terrific body he had. What sort of a woman was I? All the opportunities missed and the possible bonks overlooked, all because I was in major trauma. Well, no more of that for this girl! Trauma, major or otherwise, was now a thing of the past. Trauma had been interfering that little bit too much in my life. It would not feature in my new era. Not even by popular demand or for a one-night-only gig. I pulled myself up straight, turned up the fur collar on my bright red wool coat and marched down the rest of the steps. I turned my back on the court. I turned my back on major trauma.

There was a certain smug spring in my step, also a very pained expression on my face. My black, suede, height-of-fashion, kick-ass, knee-high boots were killing me. The heels were too high and the boot part was too tight around the calves of my legs and the blood circulation had ceased over an hour ago. My two knees were starting to swell. The boots were acting as a tourniquet. They would be terrific in any surgical procedure. If I was ever getting my knees replaced I'd ask them could I wear my boots during the operation.

I rang Phil back.

"Hiya, it's me."

"Well? How are ye, now?"

"Great. I think."

"Good. Here, listen, I was just thinking . . ."

"Oh, shit!" I interrupted.

"What? What's wrong?"

"Oh, no! Graham just brushed past me."

"Ah, feck him, sure he's your ex now. Don't mind him."

"Jesus, Phil, you'd want to see the get-up of him. He looks like a gangster."

"Not that you're biased or anything!"

"Most definitely not. I swear to God he has the Al Capone look off to perfection. He even has the white socks on with a pin-stripe suit – now you have to agree that's a no-go area. It's as bad as socks and sandals. When he lived with me he never wore white socks with a suit."

"Well, there were lots of things he never did when he lived with you. Like behave like a married man for one."

"Oh, you'll never believe it. The Floozy is here. She's here. I've never seen her before. It must be her. Well, I'm assuming it's her in the flesh. Well, not in the flesh exactly, she's fully clothed – sure you know what I mean."

"Wow, The Floozy! What does she look like? Come on, gimme the low-down!"

"I can't get a good look at her. I can only see her lower half and she has her back to me. She's surrounded by his entourage of solicitors. She has sheer black stockings on and the highest –"

"How can you tell if they are stockings or tights?"

"They're stockings. Graham has a thing for stockings."

"He has a thing for a lot of things."

"God love her. It'll take her a lifetime to perfect her things. You should see the stilettos. They look like they're killing more than just her feet. Obviously she's starting at the bottom. She'll need to do a bit more work on her ass to keep him. He likes a tight ass."

"He was a bit of a tight-ass himself."

"Oh, God. Graham is furious now. Really raging."

"What's happening? Will you give me the low-down, for God sake – don't leave me hanging on here! What's going on?"

"Well, I have to be careful. I don't want him to know I'm looking. Oh, he's so absolutely furious now."

"What's he doing? How do you know?"

"Well, I just know he's furious because you know the vein he has in his forehead?"

"Yeah, like the one we all have, sort of pumps the blood into all the needy bits of the brain – oh, but hang on, your Graham doesn't have a brain, does he?"

"Here, less of the 'your Graham', please. Anyway, the vein on not-my-Graham's forehead is throbbing and it only throbs when –"

"Oh yeah, I remember – in moments of extreme anger or extreme love and passion. I'm assuming it's the extreme anger were talking about now."

Graham had a vein in his forehead like a thick

blue rope. It throbbed at the smallest provocation. In fact, it throbbed every day for part of the day, particularly when driving. Now we're not talking your ordinary everyday throbbing here. We're talking major throb, throb, throbbing. Building up to a nice crescendo. I used to worry that it would burst one day. Burst all over the windscreen when he was ranting and raving at that "shagger in front" to "put the boot down and stop driving like a ponce!". I lived in fear of his vein bursting all over the inside of the windscreen and the whole windscreen being covered in blood. Bright roaring red. It would block his vision and we'd end up crashing into the back of "the shagger in front".

The throbbing vein was even more frightening when it happened in the throes of mad passion. I used to lie transfixed. Fascinated. Watching and waiting for the vein to take on a life of its own. Spellbound, waiting for the major throbbing to start and we're not talking body parts here, we are talking strictly veins. Of course, Graham thought I was transfixed by the passion of it all. Poor Graham.

"Do you fancy a bit tonight?" he'd say in what he thought was a husky, sexy voice. "What about an early night then?"

As soon as he started talking about "a bit" or "an early night" the vein started popping out of his head. Well, this was foreplay to Graham. He learned nothing in all the years we were married. I, on the other hand, read *Cosmo* with great diligence as if it was compulsory reading for a course on the Open University. I bought it every month without fail. I suffered the nods and winks in the local newsagent's just to get my fix.

"Great recipes in that this month," the guy behind the counter winked and said every time without fail.

But I persevered. I knew everything there was to know about foreplay, play and afterplay. I longed for a man that would sit beside me on the couch and put his arm tightly around me instead of around the remote control. I longed for him to slip his hand into my blouse in the middle of Manchester United v Liverpool rather than waiting for the fifteen minutes at half-time to have a quick grope and at the same time listen to whatever the panel of football experts had to say on ballplay. I knew all the dos and don'ts of a better type of ballplay, but I never got a chance to put it into practice. Whenever I tried to take the initiative he was mortified and said I was insulting his manhood. Jesus, the number of times I faked it to save his manhood!

I'm a natural at sex. It is one of the only things I am a natural at. I think it's what they call a hidden talent. Isn't it a pity all the same that it is something my parents can't be proud of? Can't go around bragging about? They don't even know about it. It's something I have never shared with the group around the table for Sunday lunch. If only they knew.

"We're very proud of our Kelly. She's so good in the sack," my mam could boast to all the neighbours. If only my mam knew how good I was in the sack.

"Well, my Kelly is terrific in bed. She's an expert on eh, eh, well, you know yourself," my da could boast down at the football grounds. If only I was brave enough to inform either of my poor parents how good I was.

I never told them. I was afraid they'd have a heart attack if I told them. I am always afraid my parents will have a heart attack if I tell them something they don't want to hear. So, the pity of it is that my talent went unrecognised. I was like the unsung hero. My poor parents thought they only had a mediocre child whereas the very opposite was true. I was fantastic.

"*Oh, my God!*" I was quickly brought back to the scene in front of me. Graham The Git.

"What? What's happening?" Phil was frustrated.

"I think he just told the tart about the judge's decree."

"Oh, I wish you'd let me come there with you like I wanted to – I'm missing all the fun."

"Ooooops! Now she's furious."

"Is she effing and blinding? Shouting obscenities?

19

Tell me she's making a show of herself. Please tell me there is a just God in heaven and that The Floozy has fallen flat on her face in the middle of the street and her skirt has gone up her legs and everyone can see her stockings and her knickers and they're not her best pair. Please tell me!"

"Sorry to disappoint you, but you still won't believe what's happening. In fact, only I'm standing here and seeing it with my own eyes I'd never believe it myself. She just turned around. God, whoever does her hair should be shot! It's dyed off her. Tarty blonde, cut in a bob. You can see all the dark roots. Oh, my God!"

"What? What is it? Shoot me or tell me. Put me out of my misery."

"Well, I declare to God, the vein in her forehead is popping too and turning bright red. It's throbbing. She looks like she might explode, right here on the steps of the Divorce Court in full view of all the lovely barristers and solicitors – the place will be destroyed."

"Oh, I just had a thought – suppose they decide to explode together?"

"A simultaneous explosion."

"Oh, how exciting! I'm not sure I can take much more excitement."

"Poor aul' Graham will be mortified if he explodes before her and from where I'm standing it looks as though he might. But she'll be quick to follow. No faking it here, Phil – you should see it."

"I'd give anything to be there to see the little pipsqueak."

"Ah! To hell with him! He deserves all he gets and I deserve all the very kind judge gave me. It feels a bit weird all the same. Divorced. Hey, I'm a divorced woman!"

"Yeah, you're your own woman now – make the most of it. Listen, I'll see you later on tonight – we're still all meeting up at your place, aren't we?"

"Yeah, talk to you then. I'm meeting Eve and Becca shortly to give them all the gory details."

"That should be fun. I'll let you go, but if you need me just give me a shout."

"Thanks, I'll see you later."

"I'll bring a large bottle of vodka and you can forget all about the day that's in it."

"Yeah right. I've got two chances of forgetting about this for a while, but I'll give it a bloody good try. I'll see you later."

"Bye."

That's the marvellous thing about having a bloke for a best friend. A woman would have said she'd meet me to discuss the whole situation. Phil was meeting me to help me forget about it. I needed to forget – big-time.

It was then I noticed all the flowers. Everyone was

21

walking along carrying beautiful flowers. Roses, dozens of them – bright red ones – and little white flowers that I knew were called Babies' Breath. Graham, that git of a husband of mine, had brought some in to me when I was in hospital, years ago, giving birth to our first-born. She was nearly the lastborn. Only my conscience got the better of me; she would have been an only child. Only for the fact that I got a major attack of the guilts and felt so sorry for her all alone with no little sister or brother to fight with or conspire against her parents with, I'd never have gone through the whole bloodcurdling experience for a second time. I got it over with quickly. And had my second-born before I had a second thought or a change of mind. The second bloodcurdling experience was as bad as the first.

All the other new mothers had vases of multi-coloured, wonderfully perfumed flowers sitting alongside their Lucozade, adorning the grey metal lockers beside their beds. Their husbands had bought them flowers with big blue or pink bows depending on the sex of the new arrival and showered them with kisses in appreciation of the pain they had endured popping out the next generation. It was heartwarming to see all the young fresh-faced men congratulating their darling wives on all the effort of the pushing and screaming they had to endure when their babies were being born.

The mothers pushed, the fathers screamed "PUSH!".

Graham brought me in flowers too. Lovely roses and lots of Babies' Breath. His were to say sorry he had missed the birth, missed all the pushing and shoving.

"I'm so sorry I wasn't here, Kelly. I'm raging I missed the whole thing. I'd never have gone out with the lads if I'd known she'd be born so soon. I thought it would take ages. She's a beauty all the same. It was just that I had the house to myself – and the excitement that I was going to be a dad. I only went out with the lads on sufferance. I didn't enjoy it at all. We had a few drinks in the house and then went on to the pub which was mega-packed. It was all pushing and shoving, to be honest with you. We went to the take-away on the way home and got curry. The lads had the music on so loud I never heard the phone when it rang. I didn't know the hospital had been looking for me until I was going to bed and rang them to see how you were doing. I'm so sorry. I legged it over here as soon as I could. All the lads said to say congratulations. I rang them and told them we had a baby girl. They're all getting together tonight to celebrate. I feel obliged to go. You know the way it is. You understand, don't you?"

Oh, I understood all right. He didn't feel obliged to be with me, only with the lads. Sort of sums it all up. Now why didn't I see that back then?

23

Jacinta McDevitt

Anyway, while I was up in the hospital, having pushed the most beautiful baby girl out from my innards, I came out all over in hives. I thought it was because I had suddenly developed a sickening allergy to Graham. The nurses and doctors thought it was something to do with the epidural. I wanted them to overdose me with epidural. To numb me from head to toe. To stop the itching. I swear, I had so many hives all over my poor body I was all purple and swollen. My little baby was delighted every time she looked up at me; she thought her mother was Barney, the big purple dinosaur. Imagine her joy! Every kid's dream comes true. Imagine her disappointment when she discovered she wasn't quite so lucky and all she'd gotten was ordinary aul' me for a mam!

All was saved when my mother, wise woman that she was, breezed into the hospital room. She opened the window, grabbed my flowers and flung them out the self-same window. She just missed targeting an innocent, defenceless woman standing below doing nobody any harm, just selling fruit, shouting: *"Bananits, ripe bananits!"* The woman was dressed in a mixum-gatherum of bright colours. Red, yellow and orange. She had a pramful of bananas. She was swinging a huge bunch of them backwards and forwards around her body with terrific rhythm as if she had just plucked them from the nearest tropical tree.

24

"Now, then," my mother said, completely ignoring the mayhem that she had created below as the woman tried to remove the flowers from the pram and her hair. I could hear the poor unfortunate woman shouting up at the window something about post-natal insanity, afterbirth, aftershock and fucking hormones, as she dusted herself off. My mother was blissfully oblivious to it all as she ran her finger along the windowsill of my semi-private room and rubbed the dust she imagined she found between her fingers. "The hives will be gone in no time," she added as she straightened the covers and puffed up the pillows and tucked the sheet in tightly under the mattress. I had spent hours pulling the same sheet out from under the same mattress earlier in the day. I had nearly burst all my stitches in the effort. I was now strapped tightly into the bed. I couldn't move. My mother loves a captive audience.

"The sooner you get out of this place the better. Now where's my first grandchild till I give her a cuddle and spoil her!"

My mother was right. Mothers are always right. Isn't that the wonderful thing about mothers? Even when we're wrong, we're right. The hives were gone that evening and my darling daughter was showing no disappointment at all, sucking away to her heart's content on my boobs. My mother bought a big bunch of bananas from the colourful character on her way home. And she was true to her word; she certainly spoilt her first and, indeed, all her grandchildren to bits. She excused it by saying that it was what she was there for.

"Being a grandmother is a wonderful thing, Kelly," she said as I waddled around the ward with my most tender bits held together with catgut. "It's all gain and no pain."

She never tired of telling Graham that it was only one type of flower I had an allergy to. She was killed telling him about the hundreds of other flowers I would love. She bought me endless bunches of freesias, my favourites. She told Graham all about all the other variety of flowers I loved: daffodils, roses, carnations, petunias and flox. The list was endless. She mentioned them all. But Graham, give him his due, was so thoughtful, he said he'd never buy me any type of flower, as he didn't want to take the risk and have me suffer with a dose of unnecessary hives. Graham, fair play to him, was true to his word. I never got any flowers of any sort from him again. Wasn't The Git so kind and thoughtful all the same?

Anyway, so much for my allergy, it still didn't explain why everyone was going around carrying bunches of flowers today. Unless my ex had hired all these people to walk around near me with flowers and give me a crop of hives.

But there was something else. Like a certain air of

26

anticipation about the place. Romance oozed from everywhere and in Dublin on a nippy February day that's just not normal. Sometimes, Dublin is full of romance. On a hot balmy evening when the Irish soccer team have excelled themselves in the World Cup – there is loads of romance on the streets that night. Or am I confusing it with raw animal passion? Anyway, it was good whatever it was, and you were always guaranteed a snog or two on such a night. But nothing extraordinary had happened lately. No team had won anything for a while and Christmas was just a forgotten week of pleasure in the distant past. It was a dreary February. God – February! The 14th of February – of course! It was St Valentine's Day. I had completely forgotten. Way to go, Kelly! When the world is soaking up the romance, I'm getting divorced. Eradicating any chance of romance on the most romantic day of the year. Grant it, The Git I married was about as romantic as a stuffed marrow, or am I being cruel to marrow just because I don't eat them? Anyway, romance and The Git were not a double act. He wasn't always a git, though – or maybe he was and it just took me a while to notice it.

I made my way through millions of blokes carrying masses of flowers and chocolates. Well, OK, that's an exaggeration, but a very slight one. There were masses of men carrying millions of flowers and chocolates. Probably the only day in the year the gits bought chocolates or flowers. Today it was OK to do the flowers and chocolate routine. In fact, today it was compulsory for it was a show of manhood.

"Yes, I have a woman in my life." Loud thumping of the chest here.

"Yes, I am having regular sex." Jingle of small change in pocket.

"Yes, I treat my women well." A slight rub of the chin with the backs of the fingers. Feeling for fresh growth.

"Look at me! I'm buying her flowers and chocolates. What more can she want?" A full sweep of the hand through the hair with an ever so forlorn look of bewilderment.

Yuck! But, oh, I wished someone had bought me flowers and chocolates or even a soppy card. Even if it was an empty gesture I'd still have liked it. I was not proud, nor was I opposed to the odd gesture, albeit empty, from a man, any man.

Men! I thought. How come each and every woman at some stage in her life fools herself into thinking that she has finally got a handle on them? But history has taught us that we never really get a handle on them. They find it easy to sleep with our best friends; they even rationalise that while they are keeping our best friend happy she will be in a better mood when she is talking to us so they are, in fact, doing us a big favour. They aren't into dates either. Oh, they're into the let's-get-in-between-the-sheets-and-get-to-know-each-other's-bits-better sorts of dates; but I mean dates like remembering birthdays and anniversaries and God help you if you forget theirs.

It's about time we faced the hard facts, I said to myself as I wended my way through all the flower-bearing gits: Men Are a Peculiar Breed. Now, I was not one of those women who had been crushed, bruised, trodden on, walked all over and bitterly used and abused by a man . . . Hey, wait, I *was* one of those women!

But where I liked to think I was different, maybe even bordering on being a bit of a gobshite, is that even though I had all of the above happen to me – and more, I hasten to add – I didn't blame the whole race of men. No, I was nothing if not fair. I blamed only one man for what he did to me. I was not a hater of men. On the contrary, I loved men dearly. I especially loved some of the peculiar things they did to me. In fact, men were very exciting and endearing to me. Wasn't Phil, my best pal, a man? But what a man! He was just the best man ever. He was my idea of a real man. Oh yes, I just loved men and all their bits and pieces.

Now, that being said, I also had to say that they, as a breed – and I knew I was generalising here, but I think on this occasion I was entitled to indulge for a little while – after all, I had just got divorced from

a man – anyway, I felt that as a breed they knew very
little about women. Wouldn't you imagine they
would do their very best to get to know everything
about us, us being the ones they end up spending
most of their lives with? They sat watching nature
programmes about every type on animal on the
planet. If they wanted to go shooting they learned all
about what they are intending to shoot. Fishing, they
learned about fish. Golfing, they learned about the
stick, the ball and the relationship between the two.
Why did they not apply the same methodology to
women?

Men as a race have learned nothing, I reflected.
They must have the attention-span and learning-
capacity of worms. Worms have a very low attention-
span; I have it on very good authority. You cannot
teach a worm tricks. Well, when was the last time
you saw a worm riding a little bike or jumping
through a hoop? Dogs, parrots and seals can do it.
Dogs, parrots and seals pay attention. Worms and
men don't. It has been drilled into men over and
over again, ad infinitum, ad nauseam and from time
immemorial what us women want. How to handle
us. But, my God, they have learned nothing. Zilch.
Nada. Zero. Feck all. Nor do I believe that they are
from another planet – no, I think they are from the
same planet as our good selves and saying they are
alien is only letting them off the hook.

My God, did all those women burn their bras and chain themselves to railings in vain? The countless trees that have been felled for the countless books that have been written on how to treat women, all in vain. The gorgeous Richard Harris would always be remembered with great fondness by me for singing at the top of his wonderful voice in *Camelot* about 'How to Handle a Woman' – he spelt it out. *"Love her, simply love her,"* he sang. Wouldn't you imagine they'd have listened to one of their own and one that had such great success with women? Why have they not gotten the message yet?

If only I could find a man capable of doing that, I thought, then I would have found myself a real gem, a charming Prince.

But would Fate be that kind to me and allow me to find such a man? Well, shag Fate! Why should Fate decide my life for me? No. It was up to me to decide what the future held. Yeah, it was all up to me. The ball was firmly in my court and there is nothing I like better than a firm ball.

I would approach the task like a military operation. I would draw up a plan and a scheme to catch the perfect man and when I caught him I would not let him know for one tiny, winy little minute that he was perfect. For thereon was the rock on which I would perish.

So first of all I knew I must remember the law of

the jungle – know thine enemy or thine prey or whatever thine they have in the jungle. I'd better know mine prey or at least the prey mine wants. After all, it would be a bugger to go to all this trouble and discover I had caught another useless good-for-nothing prey. I had lived for long enough with what I didn't want, so it should be easy enough for me to identify what exactly I did want.

I felt a little list coming on. I am brilliant at lists. I excel at them. Holiday lists, Christmas lists, shopping lists, to do lists, to ignore lists – the lists are endless. List-making is one of the most therapeutic things of all to do. Combine it with a bath and you could slip into a major coma of relaxation.

Today's List

Not to do
1. *Don't ever get divorced again.*

To do
1. *Stop being nice – it's not getting me anywhere.*
2. *Look for a pair of boots that fit.*
3. *Find out the patron saint of broken things – I might need him/her in the future.*
4. *Keep a closer eye out for love opportunities – missed a few last week.*

5. *Send cheque to solicitor – I promised to send it so I will.*
6. *Start ignoring bills and paying them late from now on.*

To ignore

1. *Phone bill – pay it next week.*
2. *Ignore the fact that I didn't get one card, one flower or one bloody chocolate for Valentine's Day – but don't let the same thing happen next year.*

CHAPTER TWO

I was too early for Becca and Eve. I wished one of them was there. I felt alone with my thoughts which can be a very frightening experience if you have my thoughts. The coffee shop was painted in strong bold colours. Very continental. Reds and bright blues. It was a sharp contrast to where I'd just come from. The innards of the Divorce Court are painted in soft shades, all pastel colours – soft pink and apple-green. The wood is light pine. It should be a comfortable place but it's not. Someone, somewhere must've thought it should be all soft and gentle to disguise the bitter blow to the ego you get when you're there. Give you a false sense of security. Make you believe everyone will be as gentle to you as the colours. Some big Llewelyn Bowen-type probably spent ages drooling over all sorts of colour cards to come up with the sickly colour scheme. The toilets are downstairs and around the corner – they are always in use. There is nothing like a good divorce hearing to loosen the bowels and bring on the projectile vomiting in you. I felt the tears in my eyes, again remembering everything. God, I was becoming a snivelling wreck. But I didn't want Becca and Eve to see me like this. They'd be upset. It was difficult enough for them. I'd have to put on a brave face before they appeared. I took out my make-up bag and was surprised that my make-up was still hanging on in there. I only needed a touch-up of my lipstick. I wanted to look nice for my two girls.

I wanted to look nice for everyone today. If I'm to be honest, and I am always honest, I wanted to look drop-down-dead stunning today when I got my divorce. I wanted my ex to look over at me and drool – "Wow! Would you look at Kelly? How could I have walked away from that woman? Look what she's done with her life! She's so stunningly beautiful and so together! How could I have left that vision of loveliness? What a fool I've been!" Instead he probably took one look at me and said, "Jesus, she's still wearing her boots too tight!" My fucking boots were really killing me.

I could say here that I was a young sexy, nubile, firm size ten with the gait and height of Kate Moss. I could say I was a stunner in the looks department, with bone structure like Naomi Campbell. I could say I was truly drop-down-dead gorgeous, but it would all be a lie and I never lie. Well, nearly never. Only when asked where I am on a mobile phone. I had, however, made an all-out effort with myself that morning and maybe I did look good, but I'd be the first to admit I didn't look drop-down-dead anything. It wasn't entirely my fault. I can sometimes look great. I mean, with a lot of effort and a lot of make-up and very little light I sometimes look better than great. But I hadn't slept a wink last night. I had tossed and turned like a well-made salad all night. Well, you try sleeping when all you have to wake up to is a divorce hearing. You try having sweet dreams when you know that the one bastard in the world you don't want to meet ever again is going to be in the same room as you for hours listening to every tiny little thing about your life since the day the big bastard left.

Anyway, between the angst, the suffering and the throes of self-pity I didn't get a wink of sleep, so I looked shite. Sleepless nights don't agree with me unless they are accompanied by a large bottle of vodka. I can cope with them then. There is something about big dark circles under your eyes that tends to take from the whole beauty routine. Bags under the eyes are unfortunately not the latest trend. A good leather bag under your oxter is perfectly acceptable.

Tula, or Jane Shilton. But two moon-shaped bags bearing no major label of recognition under your eyes are just a fashion no-no. I was sporting two puffy, cheap, chain-store types of bags balancing just above the dark circles. But at least the hundreds of tiny lines at the corners of my eyes that I liked to call laughter-lines (I must have laughed a whole lot in my life) distracted from the bags and made the 'Panda look' less frightening. I had, in the face of major obstacles, not the least being my face, done my very best. Sometimes your best isn't quite good enough.

I had my hair cut in a kind of a pixie-meets-punk type of cut – it's a combination of colours at the moment, but predominately blonde with dark-brown streaks. It's spiky. My make-up was superb, though I say so myself. It was so perfect you'd wonder if I had any on at all. I'd spent a fortune on creams and foundation to achieve the natural look. God had been very kind to me in the eyelash department. They are long and curvy. Very Bambi-like. I sometimes think I got someone else's eyelashes. I'm always waiting for some fantastic skinny model type with dumpy little eyelashes to come up to me and say: "Hey, you! You with the Bambi eyelashes! What do you think the likes of you is doing with those eyelashes? They must be mine. You got my eyelashes and, as for your bloody nails, they must definitely be mine. No one like you can have nails like that!"

I do have great nails. They look false. I get no credit for having nice nails as everyone just assumes I stick them on. I love wearing nail varnish, all colours. On my toe and fingernails. Always matching. It is one of my little weaknesses. My eyelashes and nails compensate for a lot of deficiencies in all the other areas. My body is one of those areas.

Ah yes, my body. I was wondering when we'd get around to that. Well, to be honest, and amn't I always, my body is just a little bit flabby around the edges, but isn't that what life and gravity does to us all? Well, nearly all of us. There are two ways of looking at my body: blindfold is one of them.

You could class it as a bit overweight, a bit under-tall, a bit neglected and horizontally challenged, a bit wrinkly and maybe even a bit dimply. But I prefer to look on it as voluptuous, curvaceous, shapely and experienced. This is in the interests of keeping my self-confidence at its highest at all possible times. I rarely analyse my body. That's a dark place where only the bravest women can go. All of them coincidentally are a perfect size ten or less. I leave it to all the body-beautifuls of this world to examine their own bodies. I expect them to leave mine alone. I just accept mine for what it is, not quite perfect but not totally repulsive either.

Well, not all the time anyway. Only first thing in the morning when I wake up naked and the duvet has spent the night on the floor and I've forgotten to shave my legs or my oxters or take off my make-up and my hair stands up perpendicular to my head – not with the shock of my neglect – it just always stands up perpendicular to my head first thing in the morning. But, even the perfect size tens and less have those types of mornings, don't they? Well, I hope they do. It'd be just so unfair if they don't. It would make me question if there is a God or not. Being a perfect size ten should be enough for any woman – wanting to look perfect first thing in the morning too was just plain greedy.

Anyway, maybe today I wasn't repulsive. I had beaten all wanted hair into submission with a lot of gel and a straightener and I had removed all unwanted hair with slightly too sharp a razor and no foam. The resulting little cuts bled little red dots for a while but were OK. I had painted my nails bright red to match my coat and my bloody dots. Today I had put on an all-out effort and I hoped it had worked.

So all in all I guess that, barring major surgery, I was looking as good as I could be on a good day. But then this wasn't a good day or was it? I just couldn't make up my mind.

"Have you decided yet?"

"Nah, I think it might be a good one."

"What?" The waitress stood staring at me. Notebook

in one hand, pencil in the other. I imagined she had shoved the tip of the pencil into her mouth a few seconds earlier. The black spot on her lips was a dead giveaway. It was the first time I had ever seen anyone hold a notebook like a weapon. I was afraid to order nothing. She might hit me around the head with the weapon.

"Three cappuccinos, please."

"Thirsty, are we?" she said as she wrote in the offensive weapon.

I was in no humour for humour.

"Look, I'm waiting for my two daughters if that's OK with you. And while I'm at it would you please point that notebook somewhere else. It is very dangerous to point it like that. Someone might get hurt."

"Whatever you say, Madam." The madam was a definite threat.

"Hi, Ma. What's her problem?"

All heads turned as my daughter Becca came into the coffee shop.

"Hi, petal, don't mind her. She's having a bad day."

I hugged Becca, maybe a bit too tightly. I was so glad she had come to save me from my innermost thoughts. Sometimes my innermost thoughts should be left alone and never brought to the surface.

She was dressed in blue, baggy trousers, tight

cropped tee-shirt and a blue denim jacket. She had matching blue suede boots on. She had a long, soft, blue, knit scarf wrapped around her neck to keep her warm. She was a poor student and everything she wore had designer labels. She had a designer bag flung over her shoulder. She dumped it on the floor. Then she pulled off the blue knit hat she was wearing. It advertised some drink or other. She shook her head and her long curly hair loosened and sat perfectly. You'd wonder how she got the mass of curls to stay up under the hat in the first place. She kissed me on the cheek and sat down.

"Well, how did your presentation go?" It was probably the worst day for her to have to give a major presentation and the fact that it would count for 35 per cent of her exam mark was another pressure she could do without. I'd been storming heaven for her all morning. In between storming heaven for myself.

"Ah you know, the usual – the lecturer said it was good though and one or two of the points I raised were different to the rest of the class so I was happy enough with that. Anyway, come on, less about me and more about you – how did it go?"

"Will we wait for Eve and then I won't have to repeat myself?"

Speak of the divil. Eve swept into the coffee shop and all heads turned again.

"Hi, sorry I'm late, are you here long?"

"Hi, pet. No, not too long. Becca just got here ahead of you." I squeezed her to me and patted the chair. "Sit down. I ordered you a cappuccino."

She was dressed almost exactly like her sister except she was wearing a pale pink tee-shirt, baggy pink trousers and pink suede boots. She was also sporting the compulsory denim jacket. When she took off her peaked cap, a mass of curly pitch-black hair escaped. She was identical to her sister but she was younger by ten months and brunette, where Becca was blonde. Also, Becca had sky-blue eyes and Eve's were chocolaty brown. They looked like identical twins gone wrong. At least that was one thing Graham and I had got right – our gene mix must've been perfect, for between us we had made two stunningly beautiful women. I like to think more of my genes than Graham's are in them and on this issue I think I'm right even if I'm wrong.

Eve hugged Becca and myself and collapsed down into the seat.

"Boy, I'm wrecked! College is mad, isn't it, Becca?" She opened a packet of cigarettes and lit one. I hated the fact that she smoked, but at her age there was very little I could say and she did keep it down to under ten a day, or so she told me. I convinced myself it was the truth just to make myself feel better.

They were both loving first year in college and I sometimes wondered if they were enjoying the social side of it just that little bit too much. They were lucky in that they were clever and didn't need to slog away at the books the way some kids do. But they both worked hard and had a very healthy competitive streak. It meant I didn't have to nag about studying too much. Becca was doing engineering and loved it. I think she loved the feeling of being a woman in a man's world. Eve was doing veterinary science. From the time she could talk she said she was going to be a vet. I thought the blood and guts would put her off. Becca thought the knowledge that she would end up having to shove her arm up the same compartment of a cow that large cow-pats came from would put her sister off. It hadn't.

Sometimes I looked at the two of them and marvelled at what they had become. If it all fell apart tomorrow, for today at least they were doing OK. I was happy with that. Both of them wanted to take a year out when they finished college and explore the world together. They thought I'd go with them. I loved it that they included me, but I guessed I'd only cramp their style. I'd miss the two of them dreadfully if they ever went. Maybe they never would. Life has a funny way of taking over and the plans we make today often become the "if onlys" of tomorrow. I hoped Becca and Eve didn't have too many "if onlys" and just had lots of happy memories when they got to be my ripe old age.

"So? Hey, come on, spill your guts. What happened? Was The Git there?"

"Jesus, where is your woman with the cappuccino? I'm wall-falling. Oh, yeah, was Graham there? Did he ask how we were?"

"Yeah, I hope you told him I'm a genius and gifted in every way," said Becca.

"Me too – did you say we were gifted and he'd missed out on rearing two geniuses or should that be genii?"

"Yeah right! I said the two of you were gifted in spoofing and full of your own importance." I secretly loved it when they ganged up on me.

"You never betrayed us like that, did you? Do I or do I not get an A in every exam I ever sit?" Becca smiled smugly

"Oh, Cruelty, thy name is Mother. Did you let us down, Ma? Ah, Bec, give over with your As! Do we have to hear about them every friggin' minute of the day? I always get a B and you don't hear me go on ad infinitum about it, do you?"

"Of course not! Who in their right mind would brag over a B? Plleeeuz."

"Well, brains aren't everything, you know, Bec."

"I know – that's why I'm so lucky that I am gifted in every department." And there was that smug little smile back on her face.

But there was no denying it, Becca was a very

clever young woman. For all of her nineteen years she could buy and sell most people. She excelled at everything. In another family, Eve would have been considered a genius. B would have been for brilliant and beautiful and bounding with personality, but unfortunately in our family she was competing with an A.

I sat back and watched the two of them, so animated and full of zest, and not for the first time I marvelled at how in the name of God I had managed to rear the two of them on my own for the past ten years. I had to admit they hadn't turned out too bad. So, even if I was tempting Fate – a thing I rarely do because Fate is a bitch for picking up a challenge – like the time Graham and myself were out having a few drinks with the golf crowd and after my third Pina Colada I started waxing poetic about my wonderful husband. I was all smug, like the cat who got the double cream. I went on and on ad nauseam about my terrific marriage and how I couldn't understand anyone staying in a crap marriage.

"Why don't the poor miserable bastards just leave? Get out of the shitty relationship and grab a bit of happiness?"

I was emphatic. I was shouting. Fate heard me. By God, did Fate hear me! In fact, I think I even heard Fate laughing uncontrollably, bordering-on-the-hysterical laughing. A bit OTT, if you ask me.

"Do you hear her? Do you hear the cocky bitch?" Fate was saying. "Now, watch this! See what I can do! See what great power I have! Just watch me while I put her in her place."

Graham The Git also heard me and so he and Fate conspired together. They were both to blame for what happened, but Graham was more to blame – after all, I wasn't married to Fate. I had never bedded Fate. Fate hadn't vowed to love and cherish me till death us did part. Which is just as well because if good old Fate got fed up with me and wanted rid of me he could have organised a few terribly nasty accidents to happen to me to make death us do part prematurely. Bad as Graham was, he wasn't capable of physical violence and fair play to him he always told everyone: "I'd never hit a woman – only cowards hit women."

Yeah, fair play to the big brave Graham. He decided to listen to my pearls of wisdom on shitty relationships and he left our shitty marriage and grabbed a bit. I'm not sure if the bit he grabbed was exactly a bit of happiness or not, but she seemed to do it for Graham for a couple of weeks anyway.

But one thing was for sure: both Becca and Eve seemed like very happy people despite all the ups and downs of their young lives.

"Hey, enough, you two! You're both brilliant."

"OK."

"Yeah, but I'm just that little bit more brilliant that she is!" Becca couldn't resist a final snipe at her sister.

"Oh yeah? Go on, rub it in!" Eve feigned annoyance but she was really enjoying the banter.

"Well, we have to be honest at all times. Right, Ma?"

The waitress finally arrived with the cappuccino. We were delighted to see that there were two luscious chocolates on each saucer. Becca's were plain chocolate. Eve and I had praline. Becca's favourite is praline. She grabbed one of Eve's. Eve grabbed it back. Becca made a grab for it again.

"Look! Take mine, Becca." I shoved my chocolates over at her. She looked smugly at Eve and then down at the four chocolates she now had.

"Give Mam the two plain ones. It's not fair."

"Keep your hair on. I'm giving them to her."

She gave me the chocolates and to save further squabbling I took them.

"Do you want to know what happened in court today or do you want to sit here squabbling with each other?"

"Na – go on, tell us."

"Ah, sorry, go on."

"Right. Well, it's all very good news. You both get to keep your bedrooms, but then we knew that. No one else would want them in the state you two

47

have them. Also, as I'm the only one who's been paying the mortgage for the past ten years the judge really had to give the house to me. Oh yeah, there is one condition."

Their faces fell.

"You have to get rid of the pet mice. The judge said so. He's put a barring order on them. If they come within a one-mile radius of the house they're dead meat. I'm sorry. I tried my best to save them. Flung myself on the mercy of the court. Prostrated myself in front of the judge. He nearly arrested me for prosteration. Anyway, in the end it came down to a choice between the microwave or the mice and you know how much we depend on the microwave. So in order that we might eat from time to time I did the decent thing and hung the mice out to dry. I told the judge that your father could have custody of them."

"You never liked our mice," said Becca. "Ever since our so-called father bought them for us. You said it was his way of getting at you because he knew you were terrified of all things furry. Particularly small and furry. Well, I will not let this go without a fight. I will appeal the decision of the judge. The mice have done nothing so cruel as to be incarcerated with The Git."

Becca and Eve rarely called their dad 'Dad'. It was one of their ways of coping. In fact, I cannot remember a time since he left that they have used the term. Becca always called him The Git. It was she who coined the phrase in the first place: Graham The Git. Eve always referred to him as Graham, unless she was very annoyed. When they were younger I used to give out to them about it. Now they were older I let them use whatever name they liked. It's easy to fool young children into thinking someone cares about them even when they don't. It's much harder as children get older. Becca and Eve knew a git when they saw one. It would have been a farce for them to call him 'Dad'.

"I will appeal to the RSPCA," said Eve. "If he can't look after his own children what hope do the shaggin' mice have? They'll be dead within a week from neglect and lack of love." Eve had a sharpness to her voice now.

"So, go on, Ma, we got the house, what else? All the same, you have to admit, it was decent of The Git not to put up a fight for it."

The use of the royal we amused me no end. "We" got the house but funny thing is "we" never got a bill. "I" always got the bills. I longed for the day when my children would be working and giving up a few bob out of their hard-earned wages. I probably wouldn't need it by the time the two of them were fully educated, with an alphabet of letters after their names. I would be six foot under. Pushing up the daisies. Not caring about bills or money or diets or hair colour.

"Decent my arse!" I exploded. "He tried to get hold of it, but the judge, fair man that he was, put him right on that one. Seriously though, he was a decent judge and he could spot a liar at fifty paces."

"Did you find out where Graham lives? What does he look like now? I bet I wouldn't even recognise him. Imagine not recognising your own father! Jesus. I don't think we've seen him for about five years, have we, Becca?"

"Yeah, I think it's that long. It was at Granda Jack's funeral, remember? Ma saw him and told him what a gall he had coming to it. That he had been more than responsible for killing the man in the first place."

"Yeah, remember he was all set to come back to the house for the afters and do his 'He was a lovely man – he'll be sorely missed by all that knew him' routine and cue the violins. Remember, we went for a drive with him to get him away from the place and we dragged him into the pet shop to look at the dogs and he ended up buying us the mice."

Graham was a professional funeral-goer. Anyone who died within a fifteen-mile radius was guaranteed at least one person at his or her funeral: Graham. He loved funerals the way some people love weddings. He hated weddings. Everyone thought Graham was a great man for making the effort to attend funerals. Graham got a full day off work every time he attended one. It nearly killed me to see him at my dad's. He had ballyragged the poor man, behind his back, as long as he had known him. Never had a decent word to say about him. My dad taught me all I knew about doing the decent thing. Being able to go to bed at night and sleep easy; safe in the knowledge that, for that particular day at least, I had done my best. It was a good rule of thumb and never let me down. My dad was gentle man and a gentleman. Graham could never figure him out.

"Come on, Ma! What's Graham like now? Has he got old-looking?" Eve's eyes were like saucers and I could see the millions of questions she had lined up.

"Yeah, would we know him if we saw him?" Becca was thinking again. She was trying to solve the unsolvable. The never-ending puzzle of why her father had up and left her without a backward glance. He didn't even have the guts to say goodbye. He was there one day and the next he was gone. It wasn't as if there was another woman on the scene at the time. He just wanted to be single again. Moved out and moved on. Leaving a whole shitload of misery behind him. But we were happy in our misery and we got on with it.

"It's a wonder we never bumped into him," Eve

said. "Christ, maybe we did bump into him and didn't know who we were bumping into. Maybe when we said 'Oh sorry' to a complete stranger we bumped into we should have said 'Oh sorry, Daddy!'."

"Who's he with now?" Becca wanted to know.

"I don't know. I barely got a look at her, except outside for a few minutes, and I was trying not to stare to tell you the truth. Some floozy or other, I reckon."

Graham was a serial partner. He was never alone. He went from woman to woman. He was the type who got back on the horse immediately after falling. I suppose you'd have to admire him. If you were feeling generous and kind. I was feeling neither. He started dating immediately after our marriage fell apart. Only a gobshite would go from the frying-pan into the fire and start dating again. Only an even bigger gobshite would go directly head-first into the furnace and move in together. Graham was like a nomad moving from house to house. Always finding a woman to keep him in style. I marvelled at the power he had over these poor unsuspecting women. But they were foolish enough to be taken in and take him in. I'd never take a man in without knowing his full pedigree. I was the cautious type. Maybe even cowardly. But I was not the type that would never take a chance again, the ones so badly wounded that they never get the courage to give their heart to anyone unless there are strings attached. Maybe they are the real survivors.

"Honestly, I wouldn't know her again if she came in here this minute, sat down with us and told us her life story. I barely got a look at her. I don't like her."

We all nodded, in sympathy.

The door to the coffee shop opened. We turned to look at who had come in. It was a lovely old lady with silver hair. She was so muffled up against the sharp February evening that you could barely see her little face. She was tiny but roundy.

Eve and Becca raised their eyebrows and looked questioningly at me. I shook my head and laughed. "Well, I do know it's definitely not her. I'd say she's around his own age and he's living with her and it's her house. I expect they'll get married now. That's the only reason he wanted the divorce. Wonder will we be invited? Now there'd be a thing."

"Would you say they're getting married so they can have kids?" asked Becca.

"Jesus, Becca! Are you mad?" said Eve. "They're too old to have kids. We're too old to have stepsisters or brothers. I'm not getting involved in any extended family crap, Ma, do you hear me? If Graham does end up being a born-again father, I'm not joining in the farce."

"Me neither, Ma. I'm totally with Eve on this one.

I know it won't be the kid's fault that he or she has a crappy father but we can't be dragged in to do the bloody Brady Bunch routine just because Graham decides he wants another child. Jesus, I nearly feel sorry for the poor unfortunate kid already, and it isn't even born yet!"

"Listen, both of you. There was no mention of him having fathered another child and no mention of him wanting to. He would have poured his guts out to the judge claiming that he wanted another family to make up for what he did to this one. He would have begged the judge to make the maintenance order for a lot less money."

"I'm not going to any wedding of his. If I'm not good enough for him to rear, well then I'm not good enough to go to his wedding either."

"Me neither."

"Anyway, let's forget about him for the moment," I pleaded. "The judge saw right through him. He was a lovely judge. A very fair one. He awarded me €1,500 maintenance a month for the rest of my natural and €1,500 a month for the two of you until you are earning, which, knowing you two, will be for the rest of your naturals as well. Oh yeah, we get a lump sum of €10,000."

"Wow, talk about saving the best wine till last – €1,500 a month! What will I do with that?" Eve was gobsmacked.

"Hey you! Half of it's mine!" Becca was gobsmacked.

I was gobsmacked at them being gobsmacked.

"Hold on! You won't actually be getting €750 a month. That's for necessities and to maintain you and feed you and clothe you. It's not for you to drink and pee down the toilet."

"Well, it had better maintain me in a lifestyle I'd like to become accustomed to. Shopping might become one of my necessities."

I could see the euro-signs light up in Becca's eyes.

"Well, isn't it already your main hobby? Sure the two of you would have to put it on a CV if ever you got around to applying for a job."

"Well, we didn't lick that off the stones now, did we?" said Eve. "We had a brilliant role model. We learned everything we know from the best."

Eve was right; they didn't get their shopping expertise from the dew of the grass. My name is Kelly and I am a shopoholic. There now, I've confessed. I feel better. Nothing like a bit of retail therapy to keep the body and soul alert. But, unlike my two lovely daughters, I am a bargain-hunter. I can sniff out a bargain anywhere. Everything I wear has been reduced. The two poor students go for top of the range.

"So come on, what will we spend the €10,000 on?" Becca was all fired up now. "We badly need a DVD player."

"Yeah, a good one, with surround sound." Eve was all excited too.

"In fact, we badly need a new wide-screen telly."

"Yeah, a good one, with a flat screen."

"And we badly need digital TV."

"Yeah, with the movie channels, not just the basic package."

"I could do with a new Walkperson, a good one – I badly need one."

"Yeah, and I could do with a new pair of boots. I was looking at them the other day and for €250 I'd get a really good pair."

"Would they last you for the rest of your life?" I was shocked into speaking. That was the cost of the monthly mortgage payment. "Because unless you can furnish the same pair of boots, paint them and move into them there is no way I'm forking out €250 on them. And don't think it hasn't been done. I recall an old woman with an awful lot of children who used to live in a shoe once."

"We could badly do with changing the computer," Becca continued. My words were falling on deaf ears. "The one we have is like the one Fred Flintstone used only it's not as cute-looking. Actually, I'm embarrassed at our computer."

"Yeah, we could get a good one with a whole rake of additional packages. What about us both getting a laptop. They'd be dead handy for college."

"Here! Becca!" Eve jumped up and was pointing her long, French-polished finger at Becca. "That's my top you're wearing!" She had only just noticed that Becca was wearing her new tee-shirt. I knew that any minute now I'd be dragged in to referee a fight between my two most favourite people in the world. I'd sooner ref a Mohammed Ali fight in his heyday than these two. Actually, reffing Mohammed Ali could be a delightful way to spend an evening. I'd get to blow my whistle and put him into the corner for a quick sponge-down whenever I got the urge.

"Ma, she's wearing my top!"

"I only borrowed it, for God's sake!"

"But I wanted to wear it tonight!"

"So! I'll wash it when I get home."

"It'll never be dry! Ma, look, she's wearing my new top. The one you bought me the other day to wear to the Valentine's dance. I was all set to wear it tonight with my little pink skirt. It's not fair. She already wore her one. Are you looking, Ma? She's stretching all the hearts all over her boobs and her boobs are bigger than mine!"

"We can wash it when we go home and it'll go back into shape. Eve, sit down and stop shouting. People are looking at us. Becca, you shouldn't have taken it – you know that was mean."

"It'll never be dry." Eve scowled.

"Yeah, it will," Becca replied. "Stop overreacting, Eve."

"I'm not and it won't."

"It will!"

"For Chirst's sake, will the two of you ever stop?"

"But, Ma, my top will never be dry, sure it won't?"

"Yes, it will, even if I have to shaggin' well blow on the shaggin' tee shirt myself for a shaggin' hour with my last shaggin' breath! The shaggin' top will be dry and I'll die happy. Jesus, who'd be a mother? Does the misery never end?"

"Wait. Wait. Stop. I've got it." Eve's face was puce with excitement. She was waving her hands all over the place.

"What? What's wrong?" I could feel my heart beating in my chest. In fact, I think it was leaving my chest region and slowly heading for my neck region. I could feel it in my throat. Pounding away at a terrific pace and to a very irregular beat. I knew my neck was swelling and contracting to the beat. I could even hear it. It was deafening. I knew everyone in the coffee shop was looking at my neck wondering what in the name of God I had ordered. Searching the menu for whatever live beast I had swallowed and was now stuck in my throat. Woman on the verge of panic attack.

"Eve! What the fuck is wrong with you? Have you a pain? What is it?" I was shouting in a whisper and trying to keep my mouth half-closed. I looked like a ventriloquist minus the dummy. I was afraid if I opened my mouth wide my heart would decide to lep from my throat and just lie there on the table all messy and noisy. I didn't want a fuss made. I tried to keep my mouth closed. Holding everything in place.

"There is nothing wrong. God, you panic over everything, Ma. But this might be the best idea I ever had."

I wanted to draw out and beat Eve around the head. *Flip, flap!* I couldn't. Firstly I have never hit either of my children and secondly there were a lot of people watching. I felt my heart return to where it was safest. To give it a bit of a treat I ordered another cappuccino.

"Well, what is it?" Becca was looking around, aware people were staring as Eve shouted again.

"This is the best idea ever – I have the best ever solution to what to do with the money. You'll love it, Ma. Well now, wait for it."

And here it was. I knew it was coming. I knew they wouldn't let me down. The little pets. I sat back in my chair. Waiting. This would be it. This was where they would decide that the best thing to do with the money would be to send their long-suffering mother on the holiday of a lifetime. To be pampered and cosseted. I was nearly moved to tears by it already. I had reared two of the best kids in the whole universe.

"Drum roll please . . . da, da! Ma, you're going to love this."

She beat her fingers on the table like a mock drum.

"Cut out the dramatics, will you, Eve?" Becca hated the dramatics unless it was she was doing them.

"Are you ready, Ma?"

Was I what? Ready, willing and able. Two weeks in the sun. And, what's more, if it was a really, really brilliant idea (and she had said it was, didn't she?) then it might be even a whole month. I was getting very excited. I had one of my large, toothy grins on my face that my kids always tell me looks silly. So what. I felt in a silly mood.

"Well, here goes! *A little car! Ta, da!*" She clapped her hands and stretched one arm forward and one above her head, palm upwards. She was beaming from ear to ear with delight. She looked like a bloody magician's assistant. I was hoping she'd disappear right before my very eyes. "For me and Becca. A runabout, even a banger – then we wouldn't have to borrow your car."

"Brilliant, brilliant, brilliant, Eve! I always said you were the brains of the family, didn't I?" Becca hugged her sister.

"So that's it, we're all agreed. Becca and me will get a car and insurance as well, out of the money."

I felt my heart leave the safety-zone again and this time it plummeted downwards. I was sitting down so there was no escape for it. No danger of me giving birth to it as my knees were tightly crossed. It hovered there in the pit of my belly for a few minutes. It must have upset my stomach in some way, probably something to do with lack of room and an invasion of privacy, because my stomach felt sick. I was so disappointed. Not a mention of a little holiday.

"Here, you two!" Selfish brats, I wanted to say. I didn't. I kept my cool. "Hold on, hold on now. Not so fast! It's an ordinary €10,000, not one made from elastic that will stretch from here to Alaska and back. You can make all the lists you like for the money but the house badly needs to be painted so that's what we'll do. Then we'll pay off my credit card before it self-combusts. OK?"

"Boring, boring, boring!" said Eve. "You'd have had to do all that anyway! Can't you look on this €10,000 as a windfall?"

"Yeah, ma, blow at least some of it. You know you want to!"

"Oh please don't gang up on me – not today of all days."

"OK, we'll gang up on you tomorrow."

"Listen, now that we're here we may as well have our dinner. It'll save me cooking later on and we can have a bottle of wine to celebrate." I wanted to drown my disappointment. I thought sending me on holiday was the best idea of all. Why didn't they think of it?

"Good idea. I'll have a steak." Becca would live on nothing but steak if I could afford it.

"I don't know what I want. Where's the menu?" Eve would spend a half an hour choosing, and then when she finally chose something she would wish she had chosen something else.

"Here now, don't take too long, Eve, I'm starving. I think I'll have salmon and pasta."

I fancied an Italian dish to cry into. There wasn't a dishy Italian man in sight. Where are all the dishy Italian guys when you need them? Anyway, that sort of thing only happens to women in books. The pasta would fill the gap.

"Afterwards can we go and look at some make-up I want?" asked Becca. "And I can show you those boots I love that I was telling you about."

Is there no end to it? The bottomless purse. Ah, well, an odd splurge or two had kept us in good spirits on many a bleak day in the past. Why change the habit of a lifetime now just because I had €10,000? In fact, if the holiday was out I could always make do with the next best thing. Shoes. I could do with a new pair. Shoes are my weakness. I'd seen a purple pair to die for. They matched a skirt I had in my wardrobe. They were reduced. If I was very, very lucky I'd find a nice reduced jacket to go with them.

With thoughts of the hunt, the chase and the final purchase uppermost in our minds we inhaled our food.

I paid the bill, flung my bag over my shoulder and stuck my chest out. It's another of my good assets, God between us and all harm, but I have to admit I do stick it out on occasion. I'm not proud of myself. I am no Dolly Parton but when I concentrate on holding my tummy in and my chest out I can do a bloody good impersonation. I swear, at that very moment, just as Becca opened the door, I thought I could hear Dolly Parton singing. But I was wrong. It wasn't Dolly – it was her pal Tammy. Tammy Wynette. No, no, she wasn't there in person, busking on the street. She was in my head. I was delighted she had come to distract me. I wondered if she was divorced. Maybe she and I could swap notes. We could become friends. We probably had lots in common if she was divorced. She'd be a great one to bring along to a party. Wouldn't she be great craic at a karaoke night? She'd steal the show. I started to sing along with my new pal Tammy. I put my arms around my two girls. They turned to me and we all giggled. It felt great. We made our way up the street and all heads turned to listen as we belted out 'D-I-V-O-R-C-E'.

Today's List

To do

1. Carried forward – find a man.
2. Don't forget to look out for bathroom cabinet 8ft x 2ft x 1? ft.
3. Get house painted.
4. Pay off credit card.
5. Have a little splurge.
6. Becca to doctor for pill – I suspect her and her beau, Charlie, are more than just good friends.
7. Make appointment for hair.

Not to do

1. Don't get pink highlights in my hair again – everyone laughed very unkindly last time.
2. Don't go on a guilt trip and buy the girls a car.
3. Don't get into a panic attack ever again – at least not in public.
4. Don't ever buy boots for €250 – this is not a normal price for any pair of boots.

CHAPTER THREE

By the time we got home from town my two lovely girls had managed to spend a small fortune between them. Not quite all of the €10,000, but close enough. I must admit I felt like blowing the whole lot on something frivolous and foolish myself. Years and years of keeping notebooks accounting for every penny I ever had was taking its toll and I could feel a rebellion well up inside me like a physical pain. There was a need inside me to do something completely out of character.

I stayed in character and picked up the post. I searched for a Valentine card that some poor old soul might have sent me. There was none. Not even one meaningless, one. It was all bills and advertisements. I would even have been happy if Becca and Eve had sent me one the way they used to do when they were little. But we were all big girls now. There were cards for them. I handed them each a little bundle and they ran into the kitchen laughing and giggling, as young girls should.

"How many did you get?"

"Three, I got three!" Eve was hardly able to contain herself.

"Look! I got two. One must be from Charlie, but who can the other one be from?"

"Here, gimme a look at it! Maybe it's from that bloke in college that keeps asking you to go out for a drink with him. He doesn't believe you have a fella, you know. You'll have to bring Charlie to one of the dos in college soon."

I shoved the rest of the post in my bag and went upstairs. I was glad they had been sent cards.

Maybe I really would buy us each a nice piece of jewellery to mark the divorce. A little memento each. But I knew in my heart that all the times of watching the pennies and cents wouldn't allow me the little luxury of buying myself a little luxury. I'd give the girls a few hundred more euros to splurge and enjoy, but when your feet have been grounded for long as mine it's difficult to let fly and go crazy with money or anything else for that matter. I always had one foot on the ground. That's what was wrong. It'd be wonderful to have the freedom and confidence to let fly. To soar above the lack of self-confidence and the lack of money. I had a few bob now but the self-confidence bit was still a bummer.

But one day I would soar above it all and that was a promise.

"Ma, how many of these ham sandwiches am I to make?" Becca shouted up the stairs from the kitchen.

"You can use all the ham. Thanks. I'll be down in a minute."

"Can I eat one? I'm starving again."

"Me too," Eve joined in, "and do you want the apple-tarts heated and the cream whipped?"

"Yes and yes. But don't eat them all," I shouted as I ran for the shower. I'd only time for a quick scrub. I was running late, as usual. I had to tidy the bathroom too. There were bottles everywhere. All dripping. I grabbed a basket and shoved all the make-up and perfumes that were lying around into it. I could sort it all out later. I definitely needed a built-in unit in the bathroom, but it was an awkward shape. Every time I got a quote from some built-in unit crowd I swore to take up carpentry.

"You can't be serious. You have to be joking." You rip-off merchant, I thought as I looked at the outlandish price they quoted me time and time again. "But it's only one unit I want. Just in the bathroom. I don't want units in every single room in the bloody house. I'm sure you're quoting me for hundreds of units. I don't want units coming out of everywhere – sure what would we have to put into them? And another thing, I only want wood. Plain ordinary, even less than ordinary wood. Bog standard type. Not some rare, antique ornate stuff."

"Sorry, ma'm, that's the price for one unit. White melamine."

Well, stick it up your jumper!

I put up lovely glass shelves. But I carried around the measurements of the exact size of the cabinet I wanted in my bathroom. One day I would see it. I was prepared.

In the meantime, the glass shelves really did look lovely. The only drawback was you could only put things at one end of them. Whatever you put at the other end just slipped off. Don't ask me why. I'm not the rich carpenter. I'm only the poor mother. Well, half a shelf is better than no shelf at all. I also had lots of different shapes and sizes of blue baskets scattered artistically around the bathroom. They housed a multitude. With three women in the house there was always a multitude to be housed. The floor had been tiled in a wonderful blue, like a fluorescent blue. Bright, rich cobalt. The walls and bath, toilet and sink were white, virginal. It reminded me of my youth.

The great thing about having short spiky hair is that it only takes a minute to dry. A lash of make-up and a quick change into my purple skirt, cream and purple top and wonderful, delightful new purple shoes and I was anybody's. But there was nobody.

I sat on the double bed and tried my best to be cheerful, but it was Valentine's night and I was on my own. Nothing cheerful about that. I was wearing fabulous, sexy, purple, lacy underwear. All for myself.

"Phil's here, Ma!" Eve came running up the stairs. "What are you doing sitting there in the dark?" She pulled the curtains over and switched on the light. "Come on! All your friends will be here soon!"

I sometimes worry about role reversal.

She went over to the mirror that was in the centre of the fitted wardrobes all along the main wall in my bedroom. The mirror is like a magnet for Eve and Becca. I avoid it at all times. When I was young and a cellulite-free zone I liked looking in it. Young women should look at themselves often so that when they are older they can look back with fondness on how they used to be when they were perfect.

Eve started pulling at little wisps of hair that were escaping from the big clip she had tied her hair up with. Her new tee-shirt had dried quickly and had gone back into shape. It went great with the mini and the boots. She was breathtakingly beautiful and even though people said Becca and her were the very image of each other and both of them were the very image of me, I found it hard to see. Oh, I could see how they both looked alike, but I could never see the likeness between them and me, except in personalities. They both had the most amazing eyes, constantly lit up in wonder and amusement as if they were only here to make you feel good.

"Thanks for doing my top for me, Ma."

"Well, I promised I would, didn't I? You look lovely."

"Thanks."

She stood looking at me for a few minutes. Thinking.

"Are you sad being divorced?" she asked.

"No, I'm not sad. I'm legally separated from him so long now that it really doesn't make that much of a difference. But it is the final ending. I think it's what they call closure. It's good for me. I'm happy. In fact, I'm very happy with my lot. OK, so I might improve on some things. Maybe change a few other things along the way but, in general, I have to admit I'm one very happy lady. What about you, Eve? Are you sad that your parents are divorced? I just want you to be happy. Are you happy?"

We are one of those families that need to hear that everyone is happy. It's a thing you develop when someone you love dearly buggers off and leaves you so sad you think happiness is some far distant memory you will never feel again.

We are constantly asking each other how happy

we are. It isn't just lip service either. We never ask
it without genuinely wanting to know the answer. If
it's the wrong answer we do all in our power to
make things all right again. We have this need not to
make each other sad. A greater need to make each
other happy. It's a terrible burden.

"I love you loads, Ma, and at the moment I'm
really, really happy. Of course I'd be even happier if
you bought me and Becca a car, but –"

"Nice try, but hard luck!"

"Ah well, I had to try, didn't I?"

"Yeah. I'd have been fierce disappointed if you
didn't. So come on now and tell me who's making
you so happy these days? Is it the same one that sent
the lovely flowers today? They're really beautiful. I
love freesias. They have the most wonderful perfume.
It fills the room."

"Yeah. I love them. Did you see the roses Charlie
sent Becca? He really did her proud, didn't he? A
dozen red roses – how romantic!"

"Well, they have been going out together for
almost two years."

Becca had met Charlie when they were still in
school. It was love's young dream. He was a nice
enough young fella. Lately though, I thought they
weren't as close as they used to be. The dozen red
roses were proving me wrong. Either that or else he
had a guilty conscience. There was something not

quite right about Charlie. He was a bit too sweet to me. A bit of a charmer. He reminded me a bit of Graham when he was younger.

"Your flowers are just as beautiful and thoughtful. In fact, maybe even more so as you hardly know this guy at all, do you, and he still sent you flowers? So spill the beans –"

"Well, he's sort of a friend of Charlie's actually. I only really know him a couple of weeks. His name's Hugh – you know him. He was here one night with Charlie and Becca and we started talking and well . . . you know . . . He's the cute one with the blond curls."

"Oh! Is he the one who has the motor bike?" I could feel my heart sink again.

"Yeah. Gift, isn't it?"

"Gift if he has two helmets."

I distracted myself by putting on a bit of lipstick and pulling my skirt straight at my hips. No point in worrying about her on the back of a speeding bike. Flying through the streets of Dublin with a total stranger in control. No point in wringing my hands and pulling my hair out with worry over her being belly to bum with a guy I never met at 60m.p.h. on a bike I hadn't even seen. It could be a clapped-out old bike held together with wire for all I knew. No, no point in my worrying about it at all. But I would. I'd worry about it a lot. But no matter what

I said she'd want to go on it. Maybe if I said nothing at all it would go away.

I am a great addict of the ostrich method of coping. If I can't cure or fix something I stick my head in the sand and hope whatever it is will go away. The OM (ostritch method) always fails me. It never works. The thing needing attention always hangs around multiplying and getting bigger until one day you pull your head up out of the sand only to discover it has taken over your whole bloody life – not your head, thank God, but the thing that needed your urgent attention in the first place. Never, ever rely on the OM of dealing with things.

I pouted my lips. For a woman in her prime I was looking good. I hit my prime early. I hit it at thirty. It was brought on early by severe shock. I intended to compensate for the early arrival of my prime by staying in it until I was at least sixty. I had twenty-one lovely more years of it to enjoy.

"I really like him, Ma, and we're careful on the bike."

"What about when you're off the bike?" Once a mother, always a mother. "I hope you remember all I told you about safe sex. Do you know that I was reading somewhere that condoms are only 95 per cent safe?"

I remember being shocked when I read it and doing an immediate pregnancy test having just spent a night bonking my ass off with a wonderful man sporting a very well-fitting condom. He was a nice guy all the same. One of the good ones. I met him about a month after Graham and I split up. James was his name. Lovely James. The timing was all wrong. It was too soon. I was still raw and brokenhearted. I hadn't fully gotten over Graham The Git leaving me. I was still in the "I can't believe it!" stage; trying to convince myself it was his loss. Every time James and I were together I called him Graham. Well, it came out more like 'Graaah –eh–James'. It wasn't the best way to endear me to him.

I sort of messed up big-time on the endearing-me-to-him bit in lots of ways. I kept telling him the tragic story of Graham's buggering off. I waxed lyrical ad infinitum. Poor James was a nice chap and he listened intently the first time I told him the saga. He nodded and tut–tutted in all the appropriate places. He still pretended to be interested the second and third time I re-ran the whole story – he told me what a great woman I was. It was when I got to the tenth repeat and beyond that his eyes started to glaze over, but fair fecks to him he still said I was a great woman, this time adding that I'd be an even greater woman in a few years' time. There was something about him that really annoyed me. I couldn't remember what exactly, but it was something to do with his voice. I had a faint, far distant memory of a really irritating habit he had. I had obviously buried it deep in my subconscious. I wished I could remember what it was because it would make me feel a whole lot better about him not being around.

We had great sex in between my lamenting. I told him he was a great lover and a great guy and that he should go off and find himself a lovely well-adjusted woman that no one had left in shreds. Some lovely young one with no baggage and certainly not the full matching set I had. I thought he'd tell me not to be so silly, that I was a great woman altogether and that he wanted to hang around and help me get over my trauma. He was still telling me how great I was the day he told me he was going to give me a bit of space to heal. The heel. We promised to keep in touch; we never did. I wondered where he and his condoms were now when I needed him?

My body was telling me that it was in need of a bit of TLC and a bit of sex wouldn't hurt either. God, isn't it cruel all the same that you can be living with a permanent means of pleasure twenty-four seven and never indulge in it and at other times be devoid of any means of pleasure at all and be dying for a bit. I wondered was that why sales of vibrators were on the increase? Were women learning how to have a good time without the hassle of ironing shirts or putting the toilet-seat down all the time?

But then what about all the other bits? The holding hands and the laughing and the way a bloke can put his arm around you and just pull you close to him and you feel as if you're in the safest place in the world. A vibrator would be no use to me. I could never cuddle a vibrator. I want the man behind the machine not just the machine. Ah, isn't Valentine's Day a bugger all the same if you're on your own?

"So? Are you going to deliver the condom lecture?" Eve interrupted my indulging.

I was nearly annoyed with her. Everyone should be left alone to enjoy a bit of self-pity every now and again and I was just ripe for a good aul' dose of it. I was really getting into the "Oh lonesome me!" routine and I was trying my best to enjoy it.

"You must know more about bloody condoms than anyone I know," she added.

Eve was fidgeting with her hair. She was nervous. I thought for one silly moment that she was going to ask me had I got any spare condoms I could lend her! I wonder how she would have reacted if I had said, "Yes, what size? Large, ex-large or ex-ex-large. Sorry, I don't bother with small or medium these days. Any particular colour? Ribbed or not ribbed, that is the question?"

I could open a drawer with a grand gesture and let her see the full display. But, then I would come a cropper. I am not a neatness person. If I did have any condoms anywhere in the house we would have to search for them. I would probably find them eventually in my knicker drawer. Or they could have found a nice home for themselves snuggled up alongside all the odd socks that had lost partners in the Bermuda Triangle that was part of our house. Its exact location was between the washing machine, the line and the tumble dryer. One day I would re-arrange the three items so they no longer formed a triangle. I would line them up in a row. Until then I would have to put up with the fact that ones of everything that was a pair went missing in our house. I felt sorry for the one odd sock of the pair that was left, unwanted and unused. It didn't become odd until it was alone. Then it became socially unacceptable. I empathised with it. What did it ever do to anyone to be left discarded, alone and unloved, in a drawer?

Phil knocked, came in and sat on the bed. As usual his outfit was immaculate, even though it was only a pair of jeans. It was the crisp white shirt with them that really made it. Small grey wisps had grown around the temples of his rich, pitch-black hair, but Phil had announced that to grow old gracefully was the thing for a man to do. The manly thing to do must be done at all times so no dye would touch those tender tresses. It was tied back neatly in a ponytail. It was always tied back in a ponytail with a small black elastic thing. Phil is a neatness person. Rows and rows of black hair elastics are sorted neatly in Phil's bathroom cupboard along with the rows of toothpaste and soap. Everything filed where it should be. It's nearly a pleasure to open a drawer. Only for the fact that it reminds me how lacking in the neatness quality I am myself, I would constantly be opening Phil's drawers. As it is I never go near them.

"Wow, you look great! Where'd you get the purple shoes? They are amazing!" Phil was one of those gentle innocent souls that told you when you looked good. Never held back a compliment and always made me feel good.

"You don't look half bad yourself. I was shopping with Eve and Becca this afternoon. You should see what they got – boots to die for and anything else on the rail between the entrance door and the shoe department. I actually thought I had died when it came to paying for the boots. They had to prise the money out of my hand. It wouldn't open. I thought I had rigor mortis. Honestly, I got an awful fright. My brain kept saying 'too much, too much' and my hand obeyed and wouldn't give up the money. It was very embarrassing. Eventually Eve pinched my hand and I let go of the money and howled in pain. The assistant fully understood the problem when

Becca and Eve explained that I wasn't au fait with the price of anything designer but that they were trying to educate me. She kept nodding in a silly way and half grinning, trying to distract me as she shoved the money in the cash register and pushed a button for her commission. She even had the gall to ask us if we wanted the box. At that price I said we wanted the bloody display stand to see if it would do for a cabinet in the bathroom and her to do all our ironing for the next six months. She was not impressed."

"Ah sure, it's good therapy for you. So how are you now anyway and how did Becca and Eve take it all?"

"They're fine, but then I knew they'd pretend to be even if they weren't. It must hurt them."

"Yeah, but they're great kids, Kelly. You're lucky, you know."

"Yeah, Phil, I do know. I do." And I did.

We sat for a few minutes in silence, which was unusual for Phil and me but not uncomfortable. I was bathing in the milk of human kindness that thoughts of my daughters brought, especially when I wasn't with them and when they were not looking for anything. I knew Phil was thinking that children might never be an option for him. Spending time with mine was as good as it gets.

"Phil, thanks for all you've done for Becca and

Eve over the years. You know they adore you. You're the nearest thing to a dad they have."

"Yeah, and thanks for sharing them with me."

We gave each other a hug and the door burst open. It was Becca.

"Come on, you two! For God's sake, Ma, the rest of your weird friends are downstairs and Charlie and Hugh are here too. Your weirdo friends are telling childhood stories about me and Eve and I'm afraid they'll put the blokes off us completely, so come on, will ye!"

"OK, I'm coming. You look beautiful by the way. Have a nice night tonight."

"Where are you going?" Phil asked.

"Valentine's Day dance. If we ever get going."

She rolled her eyes up to heaven and checked herself in the mirror. She was pleased with what she saw.

"Keep an eye on Eve for me, will you? She doesn't know Hugh that long and you know how emotional she is."

I couldn't help doing the mother-hen bit. How could I change the habit of a lifetime?

"She'll be fine, but don't worry. I will watch out for her. Hugh fancies her no end. He's gorgeous and mad into her."

"Well, be careful and take a key, will you?"

"OK, Ma, love you."

She came over and gave me an extra tight hug.

80

"Yeah, love you too."

Becca ran down and rounded up her pals.

"See you all later, bye," she shouted at my friends.

"Bye all." Eve nearly broke her neck getting out of the house as fast as she could. I think she was afraid I'd corner Hugh and quiz him about the bike.

"Grunt, grunt." Hugh tried to be polite I'm sure, but I only heard the grunting.

I saw them all out the door and turned to Phil.

"Come on and let's see what books Clotilda and Mary have read this week."

"Yeah, I hope it's something a bit juicy."

The meeting of the book club, or the Sad and Lonely Tribe, as we call ourselves, was in my house this week.

Today's List

To do
1. *Carried forward – find a man and a bathroom cabinet – 8ft x 2ft x 1 ? ft – the cabinet not the man.*
2. *Try to become a neatness person.*
3. *Buy a helmet for Eve.*
4. *Find out more about Hugh.*
5. *Have a bit of sex soon to keep me going till I meet my Prince.*

6. *Keep an eye on Charlie.*
7. *Try to find out where James is now. The timing might be right.*

Not to do

1. *Don't become obsessively neat.*
2. *Don't ask too many questions about Charlie – I might not like the answers.*
3. *Never buy boots for €250 again – they were a once-off.*

To ignore

1. *Try my best to ignore that fact that Eve travels on the back of a bike.*
2. *Try to ignore the fact that it's so long since I've had sex my virginity has grown back.*

CHAPTER FOUR

"Hiya, Mary, Tilda."

I put on a brave face even though I wanted to burst out into the most dramatic tears and never stop. You know the type of tears you only engage in maybe five times in your lifetime. The runny nose and the weeping and gnashing and slobbering all over the place type of crying. The type you get great sympathy from your friends and family for type of crying.

I was divorced. The good thing about being divorced is that you can cry forever and just whisper "I'm divorced" by way of an explanation and people just get all embarrassed and tap you on the arm and nod and say "I understand". These are usually the people who are playing happy families and really haven't a bull's notion what you're talking

83

about. The ones to whom "till death us do part" actually means something and it's not "till sick of her I do get".

You'd be surprised how many of those lovey-dovey couples there are still around. It'd do your heart good sometimes, when you're in the humour. Other times it'd give you a pain in your face. At times when you're at your most vulnerable there is nothing like being eye-witness to a public showing of affection and tenderness to really push you over the edge and make you nauseous. I hoped I'd never turn into a begrudger. Then again, what would be so wrong with that? It'd be a good start to a new me. The New Me could do with being a bit of a begrudger. They seem to get along very nicely in life, begrudging all n' sundry. Yes, it could be very good for me. While I'm at it I might also try to develop a large chip on my shoulder – people with large chips on their shoulders always seem to rise to the top, unscathed and in no time at all. It has to be on your shoulder though – being a chip off the old block isn't nearly as good nor is having a large chip on your backside or on any other part of your body.

Now, I'm not talking your thin little McDonald's type chip here either, nice and all as they are. I'm talking more your mega, chunky, deep-fried-in-thousands-and-thousands-of-calories-of-oil type of chip – the made-from-real-potatoes type of chip. Sal' n' vin'gar if you want, it's a matter of taste.

So that was it then: becoming a begrudger with a chip the size of a mini (car not skirt) was a good start. It was time for the New Me to stand up and be counted.

I'm telling you. No more Ms Nice Gal for me. I was sick of being Ms Nice Gal – everyone calling me 'Nice' for short. Nice people always get their comeuppance. I am a nice person and I have got more than my fair share of comeuppances. But today had changed me. I was going to be different. Today was the end of an era of comeuppances and the end of a lot of other things in my life too.

"Hi, Kelly, these are for you," Clotilda said as she glided across the room and handed me the biggest bunch of flowers I had ever seen.

Clotilda is a glider; she glides everywhere. You know the way some people sweep into a room? Well, she glides in as though she were on wheels. I tried doing it once and it was one of those things that I immediately regretted trying. Falling flat on my face on the way up to do a reading at Eve and Becca's confirmation was not a good idea. If the glide had worked I would have been a wonderful mother, but it didn't so I wasn't. Isn't that the way it is with mothers? One day you're flavour of the month and the next you're poison.

I wouldn't mind, but I never even volunteered to do the reading in the first place. I'd sooner have been a human sacrifice on the altar, offered up against any sins the young teenagers already had and any they might have in the future. There were a few in the group I knew could confess to drinking to excess and having the odd impure thought or two. I was sure that in the not-too-distant future they would be turning their impure thoughts into impure actions or was that just me having an impure thought? Anyway, I'm not big into human sacrifice either; I'm more your traditionalist in the religion thing. But I would gladly have been led like a lamb to the slaughter rather than do a reading. But I was up against strong opposition.

Becca and Eve felt sorry for the teacher because she had no parent to do a reading. She played every sympathy card she had. She even told the class her own parents were dead or she'd have asked them to do it, she was so desperate. She was only short of having a séance with the class to get her parents back for the day according to Becca and Eve. But I knew if the parents came back for a day they'd hang around for a lot longer, picking faults and enjoying themselves doing it. That's parents for you. We excel at picking faults. Becca and Eve thought the teacher was on the verge of a nervous breakdown. She cried a river load of tears and came out all over in a dreadful rash from worry. My two suckers fell for it. They were the only two out of a class of forty that fell for it. Does that not say something about how I have reared them or what? I mean all the other kids in the class knew to avoid anything you have to volunteer for. Why would anyone volunteer for anything? The very word volunteer conjures up all sorts of dangers and brushes with death. I suppose it is better to volunteer a third party rather than volunteer yourself so at least my two children had some sense. It's a pity they didn't think about some other gobshite of a third party rather than their poor defenceless mother. The poor woman.

They raised their hands simultaneously and in unison shouted in one loud voice: *"Our ma will do it!"* I'm only grateful it wasn't a surrogate mother the teacher wanted or I'd have been in trouble for at least nine months. Not to mention the getting it into the womb bit and the arduous task of getting it out of it again. Ooooo, it brings me over all cross-legged and wobbly just thinking about it. Sure no money would pay you. At least the normal way you get the few minutes of pleasure if you're lucky and a few seconds if you're not lucky – either way you get some bit of pleasure.

Anyway, when the two of them told the teacher that I'd do the reading she was charmed altogether. Becca and Eve were guaranteed full marks in every exam they ever sat in the woman's class. There was nothing in it for me though. Apparently she was seriously overcome with joy and emotion. Even though I was about twenty miles away at the time I felt a cold shiver all over my body. And then I was overcome myself – but not with joy and emotion. More like an enormous feeling of dread and impending disaster. I didn't realise it was also impending torture.

I'm so used to torture, my kids actually think I enjoy it. They think it is one of my pastimes. They thought, as I was so used to tortuous situations and predicaments, that doing a reading with all those long Latin names of people begetting and begotting in front of everyone would be a cinch for me to do. In true Ms Nice Gal fashion I decided to give it Dixie and do my best for the poor teacher. I even decided to glide instead of plod. I glided up to the pulpit with my fabulous new pink flowing outfit with matching shoes and bag. Matching hair too as the strawberry-blonde streaks I had put in the night before had gone a bit wrong and given me an all over pinkish hue, but the effect was stunning and very different. Becca and Eve wanted me to wear a hat but I didn't. I was glad afterwards that I didn't because halfway through gliding up the isle I just keeled over and fell flat on my face.

Everyone thought I had fainted. I tried to faint. To be oblivious to the crowds gathered around, shaking their heads and tut-tutting to each other, poor Becca and Eve pulling my skirt down to cover the pink matching knickers I had treated myself to for the occasion, never thinking when I was making the purchase that the same knickers would be giving a public performance. At least Becca and Eve only had their own hats to worry about. They were now skew-ways on their heads as they stood weeping and gnashing all over me – not in sorrow or pity as you might think – they were just urging me to get the hell up and end their humiliation. The organist, kind man, as he was, played as loud as he could to try to cover up and drown out the whole catastrophe. 'Fall on your knees' was probably the first thing that came into his mind, aided and abetted by the visual clue I was giving him. So, it wasn't a great choice of hymn and it was a bit out of season, but you could see where he got the inspiration from, God love him. The choir backed him to the hilt and gave it gusto. And through all this, not one word of sympathy, not even a tiny syllable, from the teacher who was responsible for the whole bloody disaster. She just kept crying to herself and muttering how I was spoiling the beautiful day for the Bishop and thank God her poor departed parents weren't alive to see all this mess. No thanks to me for saving the day in the first place.

Let me tell you here and now that proffered service stinks. Volunteer for nothing, do nothing, be selfish, enjoy it. In fact, delight in your selfishness and people will delight in it for you; you get the same thanks in the end. So the same day I took up gliding, I gave up gliding. I went back to plodding. I am a natural plodder. Plodding is safer and less humiliating. It was also the last time my children volunteered me for anything.

But to get back to Clotilda as she glided over beautifully, presented me with the flowers and wrapped her arms around me with the warmest hug.

"To cheer you up." Then she added, "I hope everything went well this morning?"

I nodded. I knew the flowers had come from her garden. Only she would have flowers in bloom in her garden in February.

"Well, congrats then. Is that what we're supposed to say?"

Joan joined in for a group hug. "I left you a nice box of hand-made chocolates on the coffee table. None of that cheap rubbish. You can open them later." So I was getting my chocs and flowers after all. Valentine's Day wasn't a total write-off. Phil, not wanting to be left out, joined in the hug. These were my three best friends in the whole world. All for one and one for all. Kick one, we all limped. We knew everything about each other and in spite of what we knew, we still liked each other.

We had met in odd circumstances and have

remained close ever since. I dated and nearly married Joan's brother, Simon, who was anything but simple, so I got to know Joan in the process. I broke it off with sensible Simon and married The Git, Graham. No prizes for guessing which one of us was in fact simple. The lovely kind, gentle, sensitive Simon married a lovely and kind, gentle, sensitive woman and they bathe in mutual admiration of each other still, even after twenty plus years of marriage. Simon's best friend is Dan and we all hung around together when I was seeing Simon and Dan is Clotilda's husband or Tilda as we call her for short. So of course I got to know Clotilda when Dan and her started living together.

As for Phil, well Phil was always in my life. I can't remember a time without Phil. We started school together and we were best friends all along. We were inseparable. We grazed knees together and grew up together. We had our first drink together at the end of the garden in my parent's house when they were having a party. We both got violently sick afterwards, but it didn't put us off. We got drunk together many's a time and oft since then. We cried buckets on each other's shoulders all through our teens when we both bemoaned the greasy hair and pimply skin stage that nowadays teenagers don't seem to go through. So here we were now in our late thirties still whinging on each other's shoulders. Phil was a permanent fixture in my life and always would be.

"Tell us anyway, how did the divorce go?" Joan had a furrow of worry plastered all over her perfectly made-up face.

I could see she and Clotilda were really concerned for me, which was lovely. They always restored my faith in human nature. So, I launched into the gory details yet again to this captive audience. They had been through all the shitty bits with me step by gory step and the very least they deserved was to hear how it had ended. Clotilda, predictably enough, started to cry. She's a very emotional person, her bladder being so close to her dark brown eyes that you could see it at times. It's a bit scary.

She's a bohemian type, bakes all her own bread and takes everything to heart. We're used to it by now, but at first it was a bit of a culture shock. She has a quiet calm about her that makes you listen intently to what she's saying even if its bullshit. She appears to be an expert on everything earthy and I have seen grown men succumb to her charms. One in particular was the butchiest, sexiest, machoest man you ever saw – Boss by smell and Boss by nature. He was transformed overnight – well, OK, over a few months – from an IT wizard, being head-hunted by top companies all over the world, to an expert on Save the Whales, Save the Rainforest, Save the Ozone layer and most importantly save our own asses. It was like watching a dormant eco-warrior being unleashed with the first flush of love. The animal passion released another passion in Dan, which maybe Tilda saw hidden deep down in him and that attracted him to her. Whatever it was, the world would be a safer place now that Dan was on the case.

It wasn't as if Clotilda bullied or browbeat him into submission. I don't think she's capable of doing either. She's soft-spoken and soft-natured, mesmeric if there is such a word – if not there should be because that's exactly what Clotilda is – mesmeric. She'd mesmerise you. She has long flowing red hair and wears flowing flowery patterned clothes in pastel shades and knitted cardigans that always match something, but they always seem to match something other than what she's wearing at the time. She always wears flat shoes even though she's barely five foot tall – odd shapes and colours. Lots of winkle-pickers and elfinlike booties.

She never wears make-up and to tell you the truth she doesn't need it. She has skin like a newborn's bottom. She looks like an Irish Colleen, but both her parents were French. Her parents were real odd-bods. They kept getting divorced and re-married. It was a strange set-up, but I never asked any questions. Every now and again Dan and herself would head off to France for a wedding. Or indeed, a divorce.

"Oh, Kelly, I feel so awful for you. I hope Dan and I don't get a divorce. Do you think he'll ask for one soon? What'll I do if he does?"

"No way. Clotilda. Dan won't want a divorce," I reassured her.

"Never!" Phil said.

"He'll be back. Just you wait and see," Joan added.

Then we all sat in silence. We all knew that Dan and Clotilda were made for each other. They were real soul mates. In a moment of madness the previous week they had had a row. Tilda flipped and told him to get out of her life and never come back. As this was the first time Tilda had ever flipped Dan reacted very badly. He thought she meant what she said, so he did it. He just upped and left. He was bitterly wounded and hurt to the core.

He was now living with his sister and by all accounts driving her mad advising her on compost heaps and recycling everything in her house. She was reacting very badly to it and had set a match to a whole load of papers he had been putting in a green bag to re-cycle.

"Now re-cycle that!" she shouted venomously, at him pointing at the huge flames and laughing hysterically as the bonfire got totally out of control.

She cried on the fireman's shoulder when they put out the fire. She told him she was driven to starting the fire and Christ only knew what she would do next if she heard the word re-cycle again. She was doing well and had the fireman's total sympathy until she started talking about straitjackets, saying what sort of a country was it when firemen had no power to put a crazy man in a straitjacket and haul him away. She got so frustrated she started pounding the fireman on the chest with her fists. Shouting at him that he was second to useless. He seemed to take exception to this. So she was stuck with Dan for a while longer. That's the bad thing about being a sister and living so conveniently close.

She had rung me and asked me to please do whatever I could to get Dan and Clotilda back together. She said something about my life depending on it and to tell you the truth I think she meant it. She said it through clenched teeth and there was that insane high killer tone in her voice; she sounded like Bette Davis in *Whatever Happened to Baby Jane?*. Dan was happy though. I could hear him singing at the top of his voice in the background. He fancied himself as a bit of a singer, did Dan. He was belting out 'No Regrets', the French version, and with a bit of an overemphasis on the rolled 'r' if you ask me. He was a fluent French speaker. I think that was getting on his sister's nerves too. I think a lot of things were getting on Dan's sister's nerves.

Clotilda and Dan had met in France when he had gone over to that romantic country to drag one of their major banks into the twenty-first century. Some sort of big IT programme or something like that. I'm not really computer literate, but anyway, according to Clotilda, Dan was a big hit over there. If you were to believe her, and I have no reason not to, he was, in fact, *la crème de la crème* of the IT world and the bank gave him *trés bien de la Francs* or *plus, plus francs* for all he did for them.

Clotilda was working in a bakery near the bank at the time and Dan used to frequent it for a bit of a French knot or a hot baguette, or a bit of a how's your father I suppose, depending on the mood. Anyway, at the end of his stay he brought her home with him and up until now they had both lived together very happily. So, I was convinced this row was only a little blip on the horizon.

After all, there was little Gary to consider. Gary was their six-month-old baby. Gary had the best of every natural thing you could think of. Gary was definitely a hand-reared child. The birth was so natural it was bordering on obscene with friends and family hanging around outside to greet the new arrival and welcome him into this miserable world. At least he was male so it wouldn't be quite as arduous for him as it might have been. The wonder was we hadn't all been invited to the conception. Given a big bag of buttered popcorn and a blow-by-blow account of what was happening as "Spermy" and "Eggy", as Dan would say, rushed forward from their safe haven and with arms open wide greeted each other and got stuck in, knowing they were meant for each other.

"Why don't you phone Dan?" I asked for the hundredth time.

"Because – because I'd feel such a fool."

She snivelled and at the same time pulled an absolutely enormous breast out of her blouse. I ducked quickly and for a moment I didn't know where to look. I thought she was aiming it at me. Then in one fell swoop she gathered Gary up from beside her and as he puckered up his lips and rocked his head from side to side in a frantic, jerky movement she pushed him towards the biggest nipple I had ever seen. How the child could miss was beyond me! It must have scared the shit out of him. It was like a missile. Then with a sudden, loud "slurp" he made contact and sucked for all he was worth. He made the exact same noise as an aul' fella downing a pint of Guinness once he got into his stride. From the moment he was born Gary was permanently stuck to Clotilda's ample bosom like a huge ornate brooch. She believed in feeding him when he was hungry and he was permanently hungry. He lurried into it at every available opportunity. We had to shout over the sound.

To tell you the truth, none of us could get over

the fact that Dan had left – because he was besotted with Clotilda and Gary. Every time we were with them he would put his arm around his wife and display her like a trophy, saying what a wondrous thing it was to see a child suckle on its mother's breast – the rest of us thought it was a wondrous thing all right, but the novelty had worn off after we'd seen it for the millionth time. We had a sneaking suspicion that little Gary would grow up to be a real tit man and suck his way through college and beyond. He'd certainly be an expert at it.

"No, don't be daft. I bet you won't feel like a fool at all. Dan'd be glad to hear from you. He's probably sitting by the phone as we speak just waiting for you to call him," Phil shouted, over the tit-sucking noise.

"Well, if he's that near the bloody phone, why doesn't he ring me then?"

"Maybe because you asked him to leave and he thinks you don't want him back. Look, I've known Dan for years, he's probably off licking his wounds and wondering what he did wrong." I really wanted her to ring him. You see, I believed in love. Yeah, I know, silly me and at my age I should have known better, but there you go. I really believed these two were a love match.

"God, Kelly, would you listen to yourself! If you tell me once more that you know Dan longer than me I'll scream. You may know him longer but I know him better. He is in his arse off licking his wounds! He's playing with his computer and here am I with one child like a permanent appendage to my tit and another on the way!"

She took the wind out of all our sails.

"Pregnant again?"

"You're pregnant?"

"Does Dan know?"

"Of course he knows – hasn't he already started the bloody story of 'Spermy' and 'Eggy' joining together and the million to one chance of it and how wondrous it all feckin' well is. I will go mad if I have to listen to it for another nine months."

We all understood. The "Spermy" story had grated on all our nerves.

"Well, look, can't you just give him a ring and talk it through with him? Tell him how you feel and that you hate the 'Spermy' story."

"I already told him. I never meant to be so cruel about it. I was just at the end of my tether and I was trying to feed Gary and everything got on top of me and he started asking me if I had felt 'Spermy' and 'Eggy' move today? I just snapped. I ran around the house like a lunatic and told him I would pull my hair out strand by strand until I was bald if he didn't stop with the bloody biology lessons and that quiet, understanding voice he adopts for nine long months."

"What did he say?"

"Oh, that's the best bit!"

"What?"

"What?"

"Go on, tell us!"

"He said it was my hormones acting up and that was to be expected in my condition and not to get too uptight about it – that he understood. He understood! Can you believe that he actually said that? I told him I was going out to get a vice grip and secure it to his nipple and leave it there for twenty-four hours a day and then give him something to make him vomit every morning and see how he'd like that. Oh, we'd see then how cheerful he'd be! See how many funny little stories he'd come up with then. He said that if I really thought that would give him the feel of motherhood and a perfect understanding of pregnancy then we should try it. I blew my top and told him to feck off and never come back and that me and Gary and 'Spermy' and 'Eggy' would do very well without him.

"Then he had the gall to tell me to lower my voice, that the children would get upset. The children? What about me? All he was worried about was a six-month-old and an unborn. I knew my voice was getting higher and higher and louder and louder. It was the final straw and I could see the bloody straw ever so gently floating down and landing right on my back. 'Screw you and you're being so reasonable all the time!' I exploded at him. Then I took a bundle of disposable nappies and threw them into the middle of the floor and stamped and danced on them. Then I told him to bugger off and I think it was at that stage that he took me seriously."

We were all speechless. Clotilda never normally even raised her voice.

"It'll be OK, Clotilda, I know that Dan says silly things sometimes, but he does it with the best possible intentions." I was trying my best.

"Suppose he was off out whoring about and not bothered about you at all, then you'd have cause to complain. But he adores you."

"Yeah, I know."

"He really does love you, you know. Even if he is a bit irritating at times, not that I ever found him irritating, mind you. Then again I don't have to live with him." Phil was being careful. Treading softly softly.

"Go on, give him a ring." Joan gave her tuppence-halfpenny worth.

"OK. Maybe I will, just to shut you all up."

We all busied ourselves and tried to pretend we weren't having a good aul' earwig.

"No answer," Clotilda said as she put the phone down.

Her eyes met mine. I knew she was lying.

I can spot a lie at fifty paces. I'd had a good teacher. Been lied to by the best.

Clotilda was a novice. She never lied. I wondered why she had now.

"He's probably out or asleep. I'll ring him later."

"OK, now that Clotilda's love life is sorted, or if not quite sorted then in the process of being sorted, let's talk about the books." Joan took the book club very seriously. It had been her brainchild and it was up and running now for eighteen months. She loved that it was going well. I suppose it started because we all used to borrow books from each other all the time, but the meeting up and talking about books was all down to Joan. I loved the sheer escapism of it all. The participation and enjoyment I got from anyone else's life but my own. I loved to go into a world of fiction where everyone had problems. I took comfort from the fact that their problems were sometimes worse than mine and yet they were always solved by the end of the book and all the characters always lived happily ever after. I reasoned that if some people with horrendous lives got everything sorted in the space of a few chapters then surely be to God I would. But it was only fiction.

Then one week I made the mistake of buying a self-help book: *How to Bring Happiness into Your Front Room*. I devoured it in one evening. It was written by a very happy person so I took it to be gospel, never even thinking that the person in the book might never have had a day of crap in his whole life so why wouldn't the lucky bastard be happy? Anyway, his next book was *How to Bring Happiness Into Your Bedroom* and it was a sell-out. He seemed like an even happier person when he was in the bedroom. I started putting his tips into practice: "Whatever you do first thing in the morning, when you get out of bed put a great big smile on your face. Do it the same way you put clothes on your back and wear them every day. Get into the habit of putting on a big cheery, kick-ass smile first thing in the morning." So, apart from the severe pain in my jaw from smiling all the time, I looked like the village idiot. It did work for a while, but I have to be honest and say that sometimes in life you have to appear to be sad. Even if you are all over happy.

Like the time Joan called to my house in bits.

"Oh, Kelly!" she wailed. "My dear, wonderful granny that I loved with all my heart died miserably this afternoon." Or words to that effect. The granny had died anyway.

"Oh, Joan, I'm awfully sorry for you to have to go through such excruciating pain," says I, or something similar, with a smile all over my face. It said in the book always to have a smile on your face.

"For fuck sake! Will you take that stupid smile off your stupid face and cry with me?" Joan was indeed crying, bucketfuls. "That bloody book you're into is going to make you miss out on a lot of things, Kelly – like my friendship for one. You can bugger off if you're going to keep smiling through my every trauma!"

I wiped the smile off my face pronto and all of a sudden it hit me – not the smile, a thought. I often get hit with thoughts. This was one of those times.

Anyway, around the smiley time I had noticed that my boss was a bit short. Well, she's always short, being all of four foot six in her stocking feet. Anyway, this time she was short as in snappy with me. In fact, I felt she was downright rude.

"Kelly, I'm in deep shit. I can't find all the figures that we were sent from head office. I don't know where I've put them. Can you please look for them and bring them to me ASAP." She was in a right state.

I looked high up and low down and then I asked the new temp had she seen them.

"Oh yeah, pages and pages of numbers, do you mean?" She was chewing gum. She constantly chewed gum. It drove me spare.

"Yes, dear, that would be them – you know, numbers, pages of figures – have you seen them anywhere?"

"Yeah, I thought they were useless so I shredded them to see how the shredder worked." She continued chewing.

"For God sake, could you not have asked before

you did a mass murder on the figures and the rest of us into the bargain! I may as well pack my bags and go get my P45. I'll leave you to tell the shredder story to the boss – at least that way I will still be able to walk. You might think of losing the gum before you talk to her."

But instead of packing my bags I did my martyr-for-the-cause routine and went in and told my boss. Before I knocked on her door I remembered the Happy book and how to cope with stress. I put a huge "look at my teeth" smile on my face and went in to break the news.

She blasted me out of it. She lacerated me. I told her I hadn't shredded the lists, that I had no hand act or part in it, in fact, and furthermore that I was only the messenger and I felt I was being shot, big-time.

"Well, with that smug little smile on your face it's clear to see you don't give a hang about me or the lists. Actually, now that I come to mention it, is there something wrong with your face? Have you had a face-lift? If you did, it didn't work too well, did it?"

Now that last bit I thought was so rude. But now I realise it was because I was doing Happy that she was so upset. People react funny to Happy. Some people hate it. You have to be so careful with Happy. Whatever you do don't do it too often.

"Come on, Kelly, stop smiling and tell us what you've been reading," said Joan.

See what I mean? You just can't smile and get away with it.

Joan should have been a schoolteacher. She'd have been a great one. She was a beautician. A lousy beautician. I had been her guinea pig on more than one occasion and my eyebrows are only recovering now. She swore a hole in an iron pot that the permanently surprised look was all the rage. I believed her. It took weeks and months for me to get them back into shape. As for the wax treatment! Joan's idea is to remove the skin and the hair will follow. I walked like John Wayne for weeks after getting the perfect equilateral triangle, which would have been great, only no one got to see it. Between the walk and the eyebrows, I was offered several walk-on parts in Westerns and I even heard a young mother telling her children to stop staring at the funny lady, that it was rude. Maybe the fact that I stuck my tongue out at her for calling me funny didn't help.

"Well, I've been doing a lot of thinking." I decided to come clean and share with the group. "Now that I am a divorced lady."

There was a big cheer from the group. I was moved.

"Yes, I am a divorced lady." I bowed. "I have been thinking about my life. I've been thinking that I don't want to spend the rest of it on my own. I know you'll all groan and say that I'm not on my own, that you're all behind me and with me and there for me and all the rest. Well, much as I appreciate it, and I do really appreciate it, more, in fact, than any of you will ever know, I just want something extra in my life. Now, I love having you all in my life but I think I'd like to have a man in my life too, if that's OK. It's time for me to meet someone. Not just anyone, mind you. Ah, you know what I mean. So what do you think?"

"But you're one of those people that always says how stupid it is for women to feel they need a man to make them feel good."

"Yes and I still believe that. I don't want to meet a man just to make me feel good. I feel good already apart from the need for liposuction, and the crime it is that they don't do it on the National Health. I feel great. I'm happy with my lot."

"So what's the point? Apart from the obvious – sex." Joan always had a knack of cutting to the chase.

"It's not just sex," I said. "Sure you can get that anywhere, although as I get older I suppose that will be sparser and sparser until it's just a faint memory I cherish, and a little tingle every now and again that passes in the night."

"I thought Graham had turned you off men. That's what you said, remember? Something about

107

them all being low life's and not fit to polish your
boots and an infliction Christ put on earth to torture
us or words to that effect if I remember correctly."
Clotilda remembered very correctly indeed.

"Oh, bugger it anyway, I know what I said and, at
the time, I think I meant it, but I was going through a
shitty time. I can't condemn the whole male population
just because of one git, now can I? OK he was a pretty
obnoxious and devious git and he did turn me off men
for a while but I'm back on track now. After all, what
are the chances of there being two obnoxious gits out
there and what are the chances of them both ending up
with me? Oh, shit, am I tempting fate again? I will
seriously have to stop doing that. Anyway, are ye with
me or agin' me on this one? I'm going to need all the
help I can get. Maybe this isn't so much the end of a
shitty era but rather the start of a wonderful, exciting
era. My best era yet. Maybe I should embrace my new
era or better still grab it by the neck and hang onto it.
Or better still, grab it by the short and curlies and make
the most of it." I was on a roll. I nearly convinced
myself that this era would beat all eras. I looked at my
friends' faces staring at me, gobsmacked, speechless. I
moved in for the kill.

"Right," I said.

"Right?" I asked them. "Are you with me?" I
didn't wait for an answer. "We're going to find me a
man. Nay, not just any man but a Prince. A Charming

Prince." I was really going now, my arms were flailing all over the place. "Shag fate and the rest. I'm sick of kissing frogs. I'm getting up off my ass and I'm going to find myself one terrific Prince."

My captive audience burst into a round of applause.

"Way to go Kelly!" Joan was nearly crying.

"I'm with you all the way." Clotilda shouted.

"Wow, fighting words!" Phil was impressed.

I was impressed myself.

"OK were do we start?" asked Phil.

"With a list, of course!" I said.

Today's List

What I want

   A MAN

   1. *Kind – not just to himself.*
   2. *Generous of spirit – well, OK, generous of wallet as well – showering me with little gifts from time to time.*
   3. *Loving – in more ways than one.*
   4. *Not a mammy's boy – not one of the lads.*
   5. *Looks Department – A God.*

To do

   1. *Carried forward – find a man and a bathroom cabinet – 8ft x 2ft x 1 ? ft – the cabinet not the man.*

2. Try and get Dan and Tilda back together.
3. Embrace my new era and anything else that comes along.
4. Keep on the look-out for Prince Charming – make sure he's the genuine article – I don't want just a very good substitute.

Not to do

1. Don't read anymore self-help books – they are no help at all.
2. Don't become dependant on a man – even Prince.

To ignore

My track record with men.

CHAPTER FIVE

I heard the key in the door and said a quiet little thank you to God for bringing my two girls safely home. There are lots of joys to parenting; there is also lots of heartache. I knew I was not alone in waiting for the key in the door every time each of my children went out. Many other parents sat up watching out the window. Lots of parents spend their whole lives pacing the floor trying to get babies to sleep or waiting for teenagers to arrive home. Watching the clock and reassuring each other that their precious children were safe. I had no one to reassure me. I was in fact a lone clock-watcher.

Eve and Becca came up the stairs and bounced into my bedroom full of the joys of spring, regardless of the fact that their mother needed all the beauty sleep she could get.

"We had the best time ever!" Eve was all starry-eyed. Oh, oh, I recognised that look.

"He is just the most wonderful dancer!" she continued. "We were dancing all night. I was wishing it would never end. Ma, can you fall in love this quickly? Isn't Valentine's Day the best day of the year?"

"It depends on who you're with at the time," I said very wisely. I had been thinking how it was the loneliest day of the year up to a few minutes ago.

"Oh, spare me the crap, Eve!" Becca launched at her sister. "You should have seen her, Ma – it was embarrassing. She was flaunting herself all over the place. Cringe factor of ten and more. I wanted to disown her."

Becca and Eve constantly wanted to disown each other. They both constantly wanted to disown me.

"Don't be so mean, Becca."

There were tears in Eve's eyes and I couldn't believe how hurt she was. I guess Becca was hitting hard exactly where it hurt and it looked like it was hurting a lot.

"Ah, leave her alone, Becca," I intervened.

"Well, she's just embarrassing, that's all, and he was as bad as her. Jesus, get a room, girl!"

Eve's face was scarlet.

"Now enough! It's the middle of the night and while you two young nubiles can manage with an hour or two sleep, I need all the help I can get so I'm going to try to get even six of the eight I should be getting. Good night, I love you both."

Becca gave me a peck on the cheek and headed for the bathroom. Eve stayed perched on the end of my bed, safe in the knowledge that Becca would be in the bathroom for ages doing the nocturnal ritual of removing all the war-paint. Applying moisturiser and doing the usual routine that all us women do. She'd be ages brushing and flossing her teeth, which she did with annoying regularity and detail.

"I wasn't that bad, Ma," Eve said quietly. "I just really, really, like him, that's all. He's so nice and kind and thoughtful. It feels great when we're together."

"I know you like him, Eve, and he seems really nice, but you should take it a bit slowly. Don't miss out on the game in your haste to get to the final whistle."

"It's his ma's birthday tomorrow and he's taking her out to lunch. He bought her beautiful earrings. See, that's the sort of guy he is."

"Well, that is nice. He seems to be a lovely fella, Eve. What are his family like?"

"They seem nice. He has a terrific older brother. He's two years older. They get on great. I don't know much about his ma, except that she's divorced, like you, but she met someone else a while back and she's living with him now. They're madly in love, according to Hugh. He says he's happy for her."

"Where did she meet him?" I nearly reached out for my notebook and pencil.

"I don't know."

"Well make it your business to find out, will you?"

"She's getting married in a few months and he wants me to go to the wedding with him. I'll have to get something stunning to wear to it because he's the best man. Him and his brother. She decided to have two best men. She didn't want to leave him or his brother out. Isn't that the best thing you ever heard? That's the sort of thing you'd do."

"Yes. It is lovely. I wonder how it will work though."

"I don't know. I don't see why it won't work. They've decided to do the speech together and make it funny. Should be good. What one leaves out the other can add in. Anyway, before all that he wants me to go to her birthday party. She's having a big party. I can hardly wait; I'm dying to meet her. It'll be nice to see his house too. He keeps asking me to come over to dinner. But I'm not ready to meet his ma and her live-in lover over the dinner table just yet. Hugh and his brother call him 'Lover Boy'." She giggled. "I'll have to get something stunning to wear to the party, take the eye out of their heads. It'll be easier to meet them for the first time in a big crowd at the party. It'll take the pressure off me to make small talk."

"You always look stunning, Eve, and you can hold your own anywhere. Wait until nearer the time of the wedding and see how things are going between you and Hugh before you say you'll go to it. Anyway, get the birthday over with first."

"I know what you're thinking. You think that I'm rushing things, but I'm not. I really do think I'm in love with him."

We heard Becca come out of the bathroom.

"Well, go on now off to bed, Eve, and have sweet dreams. No need to guess who'll be in them."

"Good night, Ma." She bent and gave me a peck on the cheek.

"Goodnight."

Becca came in to say goodnight.

"Did you have a good night tonight, Becca?"

"Ah, it was all right. Bit of the same aul', same aul'. Charlie pissed me off a bit to tell you the truth."

"What did he do?" Eve jumped to her sister's defence. "Did he say something to upset you?"

"Well, it wasn't so much what he said as what he didn't say. Ah, I don't know what it was, but . . . Maybe I'm being silly. Are all men totally insensitive brutes?"

"No, Becca all men certainly aren't totally insensitive brutes." I was quick to reassure her. She was too young to be disillusioned. "Most of them are very sensitive creatures. Sometimes they forget and lapse into Neanderthal man, but if you're with the right man for you he'll be sensitive to your every thought and need. It works both ways though Becca – you have to try to be sensitive to his. It only works if you're with the right man though. You could flog yourself to death doing everything for the wrong man and nothing you could do would make him care. That's why it's so important to be sure he's the one for you."

I was hoping both of them believed what I was saying. It sounded convincing. I nearly believed it myself.

"Were you sure about The Git?"

"I think I fooled myself into thinking I was. I think I wanted the all over thing of being in love. I was head over heels in love with him. I was head over heels in love with the wrong man. I never watched out for the warning signs when we were dating. I didn't pay attention. He never treated me as though I was special and I went along with it. Everyone deserves to be treated as special and loving. You know in your gut, no matter how in love you are, when things aren't right. It just takes a little bit longer to see because you're so starry-eyed. Would you be happy if someone treated Eve or me the way Charlie treats you? That's a good question to ask yourself. As far as I can see he does all the right things, but it's only you who's with him on your own. It's only you who knows what he's really like in private."

"It's all so complicated isn't it?" Eve yawned.

"Yeah, isn't it just? But I'm just being silly. I had a bad night, that's all. Charlie is OK."

"Goodnight, Ma." She kissed me on the cheek.

"Goodnight, love." I kissed her back.

"Goodnight again." Eve gave me another kiss.

"Goodnight, love."

I tossed and turned but couldn't get to sleep. I wished I could reach over and put my arm around someone and tell him that I was worried about my little girls getting hurt. I knew they were young women, but in some ways they were still my little girls. It would be lovely now to turn around and snuggle into someone who'd reassure me and tell me that they were fine and that maybe their hearts wouldn't have to be broken, a broken heart not being compulsory and only visited on the select few of us. But there was no one there for me to off-load on and the only pillow-talk for me was literally between me and the pillow – if that pillow could talk! Imagine all the secrets it would tell!

How I missed the unique feeling between a man and a women! The feeling in your heart as if it's just overflowing and that feeling that you're so happy, even when you're sad, that you could burst. To be honest I missed sex too. I hadn't told anyone that I missed sex. It's a funny thing, isn't it, the way you can tell your friends you're dying for a ham sandwich or a good holiday and they go out of their way to facilitate you but you can't say I'm dying for a bit of the other, now can you? And here's another odd thing – once you get into the habit of having sex it's hard to go without. If you never had it, it'd be fine and you could go without it quite blissfully forever. I'm sure there are lots of things I've never experienced that I don't miss but if I tried, I would love.

I'm a physical person, touchy feely. Being deprived of physical contact was taking its toll. Other areas of my life were benefiting though and I had the best-kept notebooks for miles, lists and lists of things to do, not to do and one mega-large notebook of all the things I wanted done to the house. Repairs and re-vamping. I had started at the top of the house and was working my way down. I wished I could get a team of men in to do it all together but I didn't have the wherewithal for that. Maybe now I had a few bob extra every month I could do it. It'd be great to get a team of men in. I'd be spoiled for choice – I'd only want the ones over the ages of forty who were kind, loving and into spoiling women. I would want all of them to have some experience and if they were good at their trade, well, then that would be a bonus. They could knock down, strip, level, hammer and just as soon as they were finished with me, they could do all the repairs around the place. I know it would have been easy to pick up someone for a night of mad passionate loving but there's always the fallout in the morning and I'm lousy at one-night stands.

I have a problem with anyone seeing my naked body and then heading off into the sunset. It's not so much a moral thing as a major fear of anyone getting that close to me and yet not being close to me at all, if you know what I mean. I'm very fussy about who sees me first thing in the morning with no make-up and my hair at right angles to my head. You have to really love someone to think they look good first thing in the morning. I suppose it's the being-used factor, even if it's two consenting adults using each other. Anyway, it's better if you're in love. No comparison.

I just loved being in love; I wondered if I would ever be in love again. Eve loved being in love too. I could see it all over her face. And Hugh's mother, she must love it too; imagine her meeting someone new all the same. It restored my faith in love for a little while. I was wide awake. Not a chance of drifting off to sleep with warm thoughts of happy ever afters.

I threw on my dressing-gown and went down to the kitchen to make a cup of tea. I was dying for a biscuit, but I hadn't bought any that I liked. I was on another diet. So I had bought the one type of biscuit out of the whole range of biscuits that I hate: chocolate chip cookies. Too much cookie and too little chocolate chip. While the kettle boiled I searched for a bit of chocolate. I was all out of luck. Not even a square. I thought I remembered the remains of a tube of Smarties in my bag. I upended the bag all over the worktop and hit pay dirt. A tube nearly three-quarters full. I upended the tube into my mouth and waited for all the Smarties to melt.

I started to put back all the bits and pieces into my handbag – now was not the time to clean it out – then I saw the post I had thrown into my bag earlier. Gas bill. I opened it with a sick stomach and a dread. Terrific, it was smaller than I had thought it would be. Credit card bill. My stomach churned as I opened it. Shite, it was higher than I thought it would be. Ah well, I supposed I had saved on the gas bill, can't win 'em all. But it would be nice to win a few. There was an advert for aluminium windows and a coupon for some money off a chicken in the local supermarket. One with stuffing and basted and bordering on suicidal – only short of flinging itself into the oven and turning it on. They were giving them away for next to nothing. I put the coupon into my purse and took out all the out-of-date coupons I had forgotten to use. Ones for washing-up liquid and toilet rolls and other even bigger chickens. I opened the last bit of post. It was a lovely blue envelope. There was a letter inside. I pulled out the lovely pale-blue page:

CONGRATULATIONS

was printed all across the middle of the top of the page. It was in huge lettering. I read on. Enraptured. I couldn't remember the last time I had been congratulated by anyone for anything. This was exciting stuff. I was charmed. CONGRATULATIONS. I read it again just to make sure.

Dear Ms Kelly Daniels

Yes, that was me. There was no denying it now. The congratulations were all for me.

We are pleased to advise you that you are the winner . . .

Yes, yes, the winner, I was a winner. I was nearly taking pleasure in their pleasure. What did I win? Did it matter? I had won – that was all that mattered. I had never won anything before in my life. I danced around the kitchen in my worn-out navy dressing-grown, punching the air like a professional boxer. The champion loser was at last a winner.

. . . in our competition.

What competition? I hadn't entered any competition.

Thank you for entering and we hope you enjoy your prize . . .

Prize! Prize! They were going to give me a prize and for nothing. What sort of fools were these people? Sending out prizes in the post and it not even as if it was Christmas. Enjoy it? Enjoy it? Of course I'd enjoy it – what sort of fool did these people take me for? Was I not human? Was I not fickle? Of course I would enjoy any and every prize. In fact I have not met a prize yet that I didn't enjoy. I have even been known to enjoy other people's prizes. I'd enjoy this one even more as it was all mine.

. . . a year's free membership in our gym.

Holy shit! A gym. The fools. It must be a mistake. I couldn't accept such a ridiculous prize. Anyway, I never entered any competition and I most certainly never entered one in a gym. I started to giggle at the thoughts of myself in a gym. What sort of fool did these people take me for?

Your daughters, Eve and Becca, wrote to us and

nominated you for the prize. They also sent us your photograph . . .

I stopped giggling

"*Becca! Eve!*" I shouted to the top of my voice as I ran out into the hall. "*Get the hell down here the two of you!*"

"What? What is it? What's wrong?"

"What's wrong with you, Ma?"

"Don't you 'Ma' me! This. This. This is what's wrong with me." I shook the letter in both their puzzled faces. Which was difficult because they kept ducking. "How could you have done this to me? How could you have gone behind my back? Stand still, will you! You conspired against me and then stuck the knife in deep? How could you have done this to me? You both ganged up on me. Look! Look! Look at what you've done to me now! Have you no regard for me at all?"

"Stop waving that thing in our faces and we'll stand still," said Eve. "You lunatic, what's wrong with you?"

"We did nothing. Whatever it is you're talking about we didn't do it – sure we didn't, Becca? We haven't a clue what you're talking about."

"Honest, we don't know what you're on about, Ma. Calm down. Give me that!"

"Here, let me look too."

"How could you? How could you?" I handed over the letter and watched the two of them read every word. I swear to God I thought I saw them smile at each other. Only that I know they wouldn't be so cruel to me or so stupid to themselves, I could have sworn that I saw them wink at each other.

"Wow! Brilliant. This is great, Ma. Have you any idea how expensive it is to join that gym. There's a fab swimming-pool there too. You'll love it. Well done, you!"

"Well done, my ass!"

"It's fantastic, Ma. I wonder will they give you family membership? I think they should."

"What's so fantastic about it? Will you look at me? I am not gym material. I'd need to lose a couple of stone before I go to that or any other gym!"

"Will you not be so ridiculous, Ma! That's what people go to a gym for!"

"No, they don't. Only skinny people join gyms. I notice neither of you said I don't have to lose any weight."

"But everyone could do with a bit of toning up. Isn't that right, Becca?"

"Yeah, Eve, everyone except me." Becca giggled.

"Well, I'm not going and that's final. I'll ring them in the morning and thank them and apologise profusely. I'll say that my two ninny-hammer daughters lost the run of themselves and not for the

124

first time either, but most certainly for the last time. They can give the membership to some stick-insect who needs it."

"You can't do that. You have to go. Here, give me the letter until I see what the rest of it says." Becca devoured the letter again. "It says here that all you have to do is go down to them and they'll sign you in and give you your membership card. There you see. Nothing to it. It's no big deal."

"Well, it's a big deal to me! I'm definitely not going and I am certain of that. On that I will not be moved. I can't believe you've done this to me."

"For God's sake, Ma, people are queuing up to join gyms and here you're being handed one free of charge and you're not a bit grateful. You should be thanking us for entering you. You never know – you could even meet some really nice bloke there. It's a great place to meet men. Lots of men are members of gyms and this is a really classy gym so you'd meet really classy men."

"Yeah, lots of eligible, muscular men. Oh, go on, Ma!"

"If you think you can use that carrot on me you're greatly mistaken. Nothing you can do or say will persuade me. You could tell me the man of my dreams will ride in on one of those exercise bikes all togged out in his tight Lycra shorts showing off his prowess with the dumbbells and whisk me off, sweatbands and all, and I still won't go. To be totally honest with you both I'm really pissed off with the two of you. I'm thinking it will take me a long time to get over this."

"Ah Ma, we only did it because you're always saying you want to join something where you'll meet new people. Ah, go on, at least give it a try!"

"No way! End of discussion. Now get up to bed the two of you and if you ever pull a stunt like this again, you're dead. This has to be the worst thing you've ever done to me. Goodnight."

"Goodnight. Will you think about it at least?"

"Goodnight. See you tomorrow."

I marched up the stairs and into bed. I snuggled down under the duvet and closed my eyes. I got a frightening image of myself in a track suit. I don't do track suits nor do I do Lycra. Lycra doesn't like me. The mental image of me in the gym included track suits and Lycra. It was the stuff nightmares are made of. I tried to change the images in my head. To think of something nice. It was very difficult.

Today's List

To do

1. *C/fwd. Find man and cabinet – check measurements – the cabinet not the man.*

2. *Find out what's going on with Charlie and Becca – keep an eye on him.*
3. *Try to experience something new, but not a gym.*
4. *Use the money-off coupon for a chicken.*

Not to do
1. *Don't let Becca find out what I'm doing.*
2. *Don't go near the dreaded gym.*

To ignore
1. *Becca and Eve – I should have started ignoring them years ago.*

CHAPTER SIX

We had arranged to meet at Phil's to launch my new
life and plan the man mission, which I must admit
the others had taken on board with great gusto. I
was eager, so I was first to arrive. Also I was trying
to forget about the two traitors at home and how
they had let me down. I was going to ask them
exactly which one of my photos they had sent to the
gym. I was going to ask this a little bit later when I
was sure I was in happy mode and that I wouldn't
kill the two of them once I saw the offending photo.
I was thinking the gym wouldn't have given me the
prize if they thought I already looked svelte and
healthy. I was thinking they wanted it as a 'before'
picture and then after six months in the gym and
doing exactly as I was told they'd take an 'after'
photo and in the speed of the shutter I would be

forever held up as an example of what to do to improve yourself. My 'before' photo, which, let's face it, is me exactly as I am, now, today, would be up for ridicule. I was raging that my kids had volunteered me for ridicule again. I don't do ridicule very well.

So I distracted myself. I had my notebook at the ready and I was on a mission and prepared for all the wonderful suggestions on my new life I was sure the others would have. I had decided to listen to all suggestions and unless they were totally off the wall or involving any form of ridicule I'd give them all a try. I was hoping that they would have been talking about it amongst themselves and would maybe even have a blind date or two set up for me already. I was full of anticipation. I knew they wouldn't let me down.

They were my friends. Between the three of them they must know some eligible, wonderful men. I had never heard any of them talking about any wonderful, eligible men, but then again I was never interested before. Maybe I wasn't listening when they did talk about them. They could have given out vital statistics and telephone numbers and I'd miss it all because I wasn't fully paying attention. So who knows, they could know hundreds of single men. I was hoping Joan was getting all fired up about it. Once Joan sets her mind to anything she's dangerous. She'd leave no stone unturned or no turd unstoned.

I could visualise her in the beauty salon quizzing

her customers about their families and the male members in particular. I knew some people would think this a little bit too personal – others would delight in the telling.

"How many do you have in family? Any brothers? Male cousins? Uncles? Sons? Fathers? Any free and available for my fantastic friend?"

She would probably have a list of ten or more for us to go through tonight. I'd be very selective.

Clotilda would do her best for me too, but in a quieter way. She would probably have included it in the Minutes of Meeting of the Mother and Toddler group she had joined and been roped into being secretary of. Under 'any other business' she would have put:

– If any of you know of any single men please bring them and their cvs to the next meeting for me to check out for my dear, lonely friend –

She would be inundated with replies. In fact she had probably got a few already. Again I would be selective. I certainly didn't want the dregs or the leftovers of the Mother and Toddler group.

Phil would also be doing the rounds. Ringing people and inviting them to the latest, must be seen at, bash, but only if they brought an eligible bachelor with them.

I was so excited I could hardly contain myself.

I noticed no cars in the drive. Except Phil's of course. I was even more excited. The girls would be drinking and left the cars at home. I might even have a few drinks myself. Get a taxi home and leave the car here overnight. This was promising to be a great night. I had a wonderful feeling in my waters that this was a night I would remember for a long time. My waters never let me down. Tonight was the night.

"Hi Kelly, I'm nearly ready! Come on in! Here, come up and I'll finish getting ready and we can talk. Maybe we'll go out for a drink to the pub, then get a takeaway on the way home and come back here to eat it. What do you think?"

"What?"

"Well, it's no problem if you'd prefer to stay here. I have loads of booze. I just thought it might be nice to go out."

"But what about the mission? What about me supposed to be finding my Prince?"

"Oh, yeah. Sorry, we have to put it on hold. Clotilda rang and she can't make it. Gary is acting up and she thinks he might be coming down with something. She's staying at home with him."

"Well, I suppose that can't be helped. What about Joan? Where's she?"

"Joan had to do some woman's hair. Something

131

about her having done it today and when the woman
got home everyone laughed at her. They told her she
looked like a conehead apparently. Joan is gutted.
Joan said it was a masterpiece and what can you do if
people are too ignorant to appreciate a masterpiece
only cut it again and send them out nearly the same
way they came in. Joan said people are lousy with
anything different or creative. Apparently, she did this
style where the hair is swept right back and up in the
air into a point. It's the height of fashion in Paris –
according to Joan. I made the mistake of telling her
that she didn't have her salon in Paris and that she
should stick to what's the height of fashion in Dublin.
Needless to say, she took the face off me and told me
I was as bad as the ignorant clientele she was dealing
with on a daily basis."

"Get to the point – my Prince!"

"She said to tell you that she was working on
your project and that if there was one cross word
out of Conehead the Barbarian tonight that you'd be
fixed up no problem. She'll murder her client and
introduce you to her husband. Although, if he laughed
at his wife's fashionable hair she wondered would
you really want to meet him. He must have no class
at all. So she said."

"Well, I'm gutted. Could she not have told the
aul' one that she'd do her hair in the morning like
normal people?"

"Oh, no, I forgot to say. The woman is heading off at eight-thirty in the morning for a wedding, God knows where. I think it's her son's wedding. Anyway, it had to be done tonight."

"I don't think Tilda and Joan realise the importance of this. I need them here and now. I need you all. You've no idea what I've been through lately and to cap it all I want to kill my two children."

"You can't do that. You'd miss them too much. Anyway, you'd regret it immediately and then you'd have to live with the guilt thing for ever. It'd be OK for me – I don't suffer from the guilt thing. I could do it for you. What have they done now anyway? Left the kitchen in a mess again? Hardly a crime meriting the death penalty."

"Oh, you can laugh. It wasn't you they did the dirty on."

"Come on, tell me then. What have they done?"

"They only entered me in a bloody competition."

"So what's so bad about that? I think that's nice. Did you win?"

"Yes, yes. That's the whole bloody problem. I did win. First time I ever won anything."

"That's brilliant! Go on then, tell me what you won. A bottle of wine? Box of chocolates?"

"Oh, nothing as nice as that. Sure that would have been a grand bit of indulgence. Wine and chocolates would have meant I might have had to enjoy myself getting pissed or making myself sick. Do you not know by now that I am not allowed to enjoy myself? Have you not copped on yet that I am a woman of toil and suffering with not one bit of enjoyment allowed to come within an ass's roar of me? The prize I won involves more toil and suffering just in case I wasn't toiling and suffering enough. Now I can no longer be happy with a bit of private toil and suffering – I now have to do it covered in sweat and wearing a track suit and in front of a whole room of other sweaty people. They won me a shaggin' year's membership in the gym."

"Wow, what great kids!"

"What?"

"Kelly, that's great. Imagine them doing that for you. I think it's fantastic. I'd love it. Is it transferable?"

"I don't know and I don't care. You're welcome to it if they let you take it because I'm certainly am not going."

"You're mad. It'd be brilliant for you, and free."

"You know I don't do sweat or exertion and I certainly don't do it in a room full of skinny strangers. Anyway I think I'm allergic to sweat, particularly my own. It's true. Every time I get sweaty I get out of breath and at the same time I go all red. No – physical jerks are not my thing and I will not be swayed. My mind is made up."

"Well, I think you're mad and I think you're a

disgrace to be fighting with Becca and Eve over it. Give them a break, will you?"

"I'm pissed off with them and now I'm pissed off with Tilda and Joan. I know at some stage I'll have to stop being pissed off with Becca and Eve. After all, I'm their mother and I'm supposed to love them at all times and never let the sun go down on my anger and turn the other cheek and all that, but goddamit the sun better take a long, long time to go down this evening."

"Calm down, will you? They were only trying to do their best. They thought you'd love it."

"But I don't. Do they not know me well enough to know I'd hate them sending a letter to a bunch of strange fitness freaks saying how much I needed a gym. At least I'll never get to see that masterpiece. They didn't keep a copy, thank God. It's the fact that they don't know me that hurts most."

"Maybe they know you better than you think and you'd just love the gym if you gave it a try."

"No, I'm adamant. I'm not going. I don't think very much of Tilda and Joan either. It'll take a lot longer than a sundown to forgive them for not showing up tonight. I'm gutted. Really gutted. I was all built up to starting my adventure. Well, fuck them anyway. Why is everyone letting me down? I am on the verge of making monumental changes in my life and there they are, indulging themselves in their own lives. The cheek of them. Maybe it's a sign. Maybe I'm supposed to leave things as they are. Not upset the status quo. Live a miserable lonely life all by myself, alone. Maybe I'm not meant to go out and meet someone. Maybe I'm supposed to wither away all on my lonesome, by myself, like a dried-up old prune and just wallow in self-pity for the rest of my life. I'm getting really good at self-pity. I might miss it if I have to stop. I feel really let down to be honest."

"Ah, come on, Kelly. I think you're exaggerating. Everyone's doing their best. You're just in crisis mode. Anyway, you'll never be by yourself. There are too many of us around to make sure you won't be. Anyway, I swear I think the man of your dreams is just around the corner and God help us all if he isn't."

"Right, come on then. Finish off getting ready. Talk to me and try to cheer me up. I'm fierce disappointed and, before you say anything, I know I'm being unreasonable but just indulge me this once, will you? We're all entitled to feel disappointed now and again."

"OK, but only this once."

"Right then, that's it. Get ready and we'll go out and forget about men and children and friends and life and gyms and blood and sweat and tears."

We went upstairs. I felt my humour improve. I was nearly smiling at the thoughts of going out on the tear with Phil, just the two of us. I followed him into the bedroom. I immediately went back into the throes of depression. I wondered was I gone so far into the throes that I might never come back. I might remain in the Valley of Doom and Gloom for the rest of my life. Well, certainly as long as I stayed in Phil's bedroom. To be fair to myself, it was enough to put anyone into the throes of depression. Even a person that didn't know what the throes of depression were would end up in the throes unbeknown to themselves. Phil's bedroom was a pain in the arse it was so neat and clean. We're talking hospital quality clean. It was as neat as a shiny new hospital theatre. You could operate on anyone. It was like one of those rooms you see in magazines and assume no one lives in them.

In fact, the whole house was like a show house. Everything in its place and a place for everything. Everything matched everything. Everything was oozing great taste. The room was minimalist but soft. Maple wardrobes with twisted stainless steel handles. Matching lockers, terracotta walls. A huge window looking out over Dublin Bay. It was a wonderful room. The bed was a massive sleigh-shaped one with a maple headboard. It was covered in a terracotta and navy duvet. You could sink in it. I sat on it and I did. It was as soft as it looked. There was a cream carpet on the floor. Who has cream carpet?

"Is that a new painting?" I called to Phil who was in the en-suite shower doing some sort of ablutions or other.

"Yeah, it's the one I was telling you about. Remember the one I saw at the exhibition I went to. What do you think?" Phil came out of the shower wearing just a huge bath towel. The towel matched the room and was as thick as the quality carpet. Phil walked over towards the painting. He stood looking at it. His back was to me and I could see the shape of his arse through the towel. He had a great arse. I kept staring at it.

"I like it."

"Yeah. I like it myself."

I couldn't take my eyes off it now. The painting not the arse. I had stopped looking at the arse a while ago thinking that it was disgusting. Well, I don't mean that the arse was disgusting. The arse was cute. It was the fact that I was staring at my pal's arse that was disgusting. Bordering on incestuous.

"It's wonderful – very you," I said.

"What's that supposed to mean?"

"I don't know – exciting and vibrant and yet a touch of vulnerability to it."

"I think you're describing yourself, Kelly."

Phil sat down beside me on the bed and we both stared at the massive painting.

It was a very sensual and very compelling

painting. I couldn't help staring at it. Just the same way I couldn't help looking at Phil's arse a few moments before. You know, the way your eyes keep being drawn to things and you can't help staring. Like a pimple on someone's face that you can't help staring at. You know in your heart that the person knows you're looking at it and you're trying so hard not to look at it because you know they feel awful because you're bloody well staring at it. But your eyes just end up looking at it no matter what you do. You're riveted to the pimple. You admire their earrings hoping they'll think that's what you were staring at. I was riveted to the painting. I was riveted to the arse. I couldn't take my eyes off either. It was hypnotic.

I was suddenly aware of Phil's scent. Balmy. I was embarrassed but couldn't move. I couldn't even turn to look Phil in the eye. I felt my face flush. Then I felt my breath quicken and I could hear Phil's keeping time to mine.

I stared at the painting. It was of a naked couple lying on a bed. Barely covered. Just a light, white cotton sheet gathered around their legs. A gentle breeze was blowing the light curtains into the room and the sun was shining in through the gap directly onto the couple. He was up on one elbow looking down longingly at the woman and she was gazing up at him with such wanting. You'd think they were in a secret world. A world where only the two of them existed. The man had his other hand cupped softly around the woman's breast. I wondered if they had just made love.

I swear I saw the woman in the picture breathe. In time to mine and Phil's breathing. The man's hair was grey, as was the woman's. They were not a young couple. Nor were they a perfect couple. They were a tender couple. I'd say they had lived a life together. Grown old together. Knew every movement of each other and every part of each other. Knew each other's very thoughts.

I felt a tear roll down my face. I was surprised and felt foolish, but there was no stopping the tears. Something about the painting stirred everything in me. The tenderness and the love between the couple. Then again maybe it was just the hurt and the waste and the if only's in my own life that were making me cry.

Phil touched my face. Wiped away the tears. More followed to replace them. Phil kissed them away. I nearly died but never moved. I found myself liking it. This shouldn't be happening, I thought, but I said nothing. It was happening and I really didn't think I wanted it to stop. If I did, I still didn't say anything. Instead I turned and looked into the most amazing, caring eyes. Full of love and hope. I put my arms around Phil's neck and we held each other. I needed someone to hold me.

Then it happened. Phil bent forward and kissed me, full on. No friendly peck on the cheek. No wiping away tears. We're talking full-on snog here. I felt Phil's tongue touch the tip of mine and I wanted more. My boobs were heaving to be touched and the all-but-forgotten tingle in my body was back with vengeance. Phil cupped my breasts through my blouse. Then slipped a warm hand down into my blouse and my nipple stood to attention. God, it was so wonderful to be touched again. But, my God, this was Phil touching me! This was so wrong! Was I mad? But all I wanted was more; lots more and it looked like I was going to get it. Were we both mad? We were two adults. We knew exactly what we were doing. Phil was pulling at my clothes and I had the towel off him in seconds. Before I knew where I was, we were in the massive bed. I couldn't get enough. Phil was as bad. He ripped at my clothes and flung them all around the tidy room. Then we clung onto each other tightly, tenderly. Flesh on flesh. Holding on for dear life. I was holding on to a dream.

"I love you, you know," Phil said.

"Phil, it's wrong!" I wanted to cry again.

"Why? What's so wrong with two people wanting to make love to each other? Feck it, Kelly, we're both adults. I want you. I think you want me too."

"Oh, I do!. I really do want you. But are you sure?"

It was too late now. There was no going back. Phil engulfed me and did things to me no man had ever done. Things I'd only read about in books. Loving gentle things I had always wanted but had never felt. Tenderness. Gently touching me and caressing me and wanting me. I tried to hold back. It was useless. I let myself go and started to explore every wonderful part of my wonderful friend.

I wanted this so much and Phil wanted it too. In all the years of being friends I had never even imagined I would ever do this. It was alien to me. I was enjoying it and I felt no shame, only wanting. I could feel Phil's strong legs curled around mine and the loneliness I had felt earlier disappeared. We kissed gently at first, almost afraid of the newness of our feelings for each other. Hesitant, yet wanting. Afraid if we let go one of us would change our minds.

But there is no logic in lust or love and soon we were wrapped tightly around each other flesh on flesh again but this time in a frenzy. The passion was overwhelming and I was dizzy. Feelings I had suppressed and denied for such a long time came to the surface with every touch and every gentle word.

"You're the most beautiful woman I have ever seen." Phil looked at me, not in a smutty way but in a loving way, then held me so tightly I couldn't breathe.

We kissed each other all over and let our tongues run along each other's bodies, exploring every detail. Phil rested his head on my boobs and listened to my heart beating faster and faster then kissed and sucked while my body exploded.

I had never seen Phil naked before and I was stunned by the muscular arms and the broad chest. I had never realised before what a wonderful body he had. His arms and legs were powerful and when he held me I felt so safe and loved. I felt the softness of his clean-shaven face against my skin. Yet there was a roughness to it in places the razor had missed. I revelled in its roughness. Every masculine inch of him in sharp contrast to my own womanliness. I felt beautiful. A real woman. I felt loved. We made love and as our bodies went into mega-delicious spasms I cried out with an overwhelming sense of abandonment and pleasure. He held me and kissed me over and over again. He knew nothing of the quick-bonk-and-then-roll-over-to-go-asleep school of loving I had lived with. He held me close, not wanting to let me go. Held me in his arms for a long long time, saying nothing.

Could this be it, I wondered? Had love been waiting for me under my very nose in the shape of Phil? I did love him. But was it the right kind of love? I was so confused. Was I mixing up sex with love? I know that's the best mix of all but only with the right kind of love. Did I love him the right way?

"Will you stay the night with me? Stay and let me wake you up tomorrow with a kiss. Let your face be the first thing I see in the morning. Will you stay and let your body be the first thing I touch when I wake up?" he asked.

I knew it was his heart's desire.

Everyone should have their heart's desire at least once in their lives, I had always said to him when we were growing up. I never knew what Phil's heart's desire was because he never told me and now he didn't have to. I decided that for once in my life I was going to do exactly what I wanted to do. Not what was the right thing to do or what I thought I should do or what I thought everyone else would want me to do. I looked at this beautiful man beside me and realised I loved him very, very much. Just not in the way he should be loved.

"No, Phil, I want to go home."

He was gutted, but what could I do. "Why?"

"Oh, Phil, this was a huge mistake. I don't know what we've done. What I've done. I'm sorry. I'm sorry most of all because I wish it could work, but I know it won't work." I was crying again. Would I ever stop crying? Jesus, I was becoming a basket case. Snivelling at every given opportunity. "I'm so sorry. Because I know I'm hurting you. I love you more than anyone and it would be so easy to be with you. It would be easy to stay here and love you again in the morning and every morning. But it wouldn't be fair to either of us. We'd plod along fine and it might work. But that's all it would be. Two people who love each other being together for the sake of it. I know it sounds great. It sounds like what I said I wanted, but it's not. Now, I'm all confused about what I do want. The problem is that much as I love you, I'm not in love with you. There is a difference. Can you see?"

I wanted to stop crying because it's very hard to be taken seriously when you're crying your eyeballs out and snivelling all over the place.

"But you could fall in love with me. I know you could. We'd make a great couple. I know we would."

"No, we wouldn't, and you know it. We would have done it years ago if it was meant to be. I want to be in love, Phil. I want all the fireworks and the funny feelings – you deserve that too, Phil. Tonight we were both in lust for a little while and we got carried away on it all. I think we were sex-starved and really fucked up big-time, doing what we did."

"No, Kelly, you're wrong. I wanted to do it. It wasn't just sex for sex sake. Give me more credit will you?"

"We deserve to be head over heels in love with someone and they with us."

"But I do love you to bits, Kelly!"

"You only think you do."

I grabbed up my clothes from around the room and tried to get dressed.

"Don't go, Kelly, you can't go like this. Stay and have a drink at least. We can talk about it. Oh, Kelly, don't go please!"

He was grabbing at his own clothes out of the wardrobe, trying to get a pair of jeans off the hanger. He hopped around the room trying to get his legs in. He did up the button, but left the zip open. Another time I would have laughed at him. This was no time for laughing. This was a time for crying. I might never laugh again. I might never stop crying.

I pulled my blouse across my boobs and barely covered myself as I ran down the stairs. I searched for my keys. I ran out and jumped into my car, the little BMW convertible Phil had helped me pick it out. It was an old one, but I loved it.

Phil followed me. He stood in driveway directing me out. He waved and tapped the car on the boot twice as he always did when I was leaving his house.

Tears streamed down my face as I thought of all the things Phil and I had done together over the years. The years of laughing and crying, always together. The things I had shared with him as a woman and the male secrets he had told me. Things my husband would or could never share. Graham was a man of few words. Not into sharing his thoughts. Real men didn't share their thoughts or

people do it. Like having a row with him about him not returning my favourite CD or book or not turning up when we had arranged to meet. No, that'd be too normal for me. Bonking is the best way to scupper a perfect friendship. Bonking is way up there on the top of the list of stupid things to do with your best friends. Getting them to teach you to drive is second on the list. Why didn't I go for the second thing on the list? Or even the third – borrowing money. I could have borrowed loads of money and taken an age to pay it back. I had made a really bad choice, hadn't I?

Although I really wasn't capable of making any choice at the time. I, not being compos mentis or mentholyptus at the time and all that. I suppose I could always plead insanity. Blame the bloody painting. It was all the bloody painting's fault. That and the towel Phil was wearing. That and the fact that Joan and Tilda had let me down badly. They should have been there. And then there was the Becca and Eve factor. I wasn't sure exactly how it was their fault but I knew somewhere, somehow, they were also to blame. I could figure out the wheres and the hows later. As for Graham, well, he had a part to play in it too. I'm sure he did. The Git. I really had no hand, act or part in the whole thing. I mean, when you think of all the extenuating circumstances that were against me. If the painting hadn't been there. If Phil had been wearing clothes. If he didn't have such a great arse. If Joan and Tilda had found me a date. If Becca and Eve hadn't won me a prize. If Graham hadn't divorced me. There were lots of reasons for the whole thing happening, none of them to do with me. Sure wasn't it inevitable that I would have terrific sex with Phil? When you think about it rationally, what choice did I have? I wondered if Phil would ever speak to me again. Isn't life a bitch sometimes all the same?

Today's List

To do

1. C/fwd. man and cabinet – check measurements – the cabinet not the man – this is getting urgent – the man not the cabinet.
2. Next time I want a bit of sex I'll have it with a complete stranger – it's far less complicated.
3. Keep up the search for the Prince on my own – the others might not be as interested in the whole project as I am.

Not to do

1. Don't ever try to have a new experience again – bonking my best friend was a silly thing to do.

2. Don't ring Phil – wait until he rings me.
3. Don't ever admire a painting again – in fact, keep away from art of all types – it's too sensual for a woman who's sex-starved.

To *ignore*
1. My hormones.

CHAPTER SEVEN

Eve was waiting for me when I got home. She knew something was wrong with me and I knew something was wrong with her too. Apart from the fact that we were mother and daughter and could sense the vibes from each other. There were the usual giveaway signs. All four of our collective eyes were totally bloodshot and we both had designer-type streaks of mascara running down our faces. These small but obvious little clues were a dead giveaway. And the vibes, of course.

"What is it Eve? What's happened?"

"Oh, God, Ma, it's so awful!"

"What is it? For God's sake Eve, just tell me. Are you hurt?"

"No. But I sure as hell am going to be. Becca will kill me. She'll blame me, I know she will. It wasn't

152

my fault. I swear to God I did nothing. You believe me, don't you, Ma?"

"Of course I believe you. Now just tell me what it is, so I can believe you a bit better. Come on, sit down and I'll make us a nice cup of tea."

My stomach was sick. I didn't know if I could hold down a cup of tea. But in every disaster you have to boil water. Her tummy was too flat for me to be using it to deliver a baby, so making tea was the next best thing. I went through the motions.

Dear Jesus, I thought, please let her be all right. Please! I'll owe you big-time. I know I still owe you for the divorce working out all right and for Becca doing OK in her presentation and for Eve getting flowers for Valentine's Day. Just add this to Today's List, will you, and I'll fix up with you during the week. Put it on the slate. I'll do a few good deeds each day for a week. But, please Jesus, make her be OK.

Me and Jesus had a great thing going. We were doing it for years now and it seemed to suit us both fine. He bailed me out of countless troubles whenever I was really desperate. I relied upon him and trusted him totally. It was great to have someone to rely on and someone as dependable as Jesus. But it worked both ways. I wasn't a sponger. I always paid him back. He understood how hard up I was for cash so he accepted good deeds in exchange for his help.

There was one time, just after Graham left, when Jesus had come to my rescue so often that I had so many good deeds to do in a row that I started to frighten myself. I thought I might turn into a very good person indeed. The amount of abuse I got from people I tried to help was chronic. People nowadays don't want to be helped. There are very few helpless old ladies left in this world. They are all fit and capable and probably members of the local gym. Doing good deeds is very difficult nowadays. Most people find good-deed-doing very suspicious. They assume you have some sort of ulterior motive. They keep looking for the catch. The "what's in it for you" angle. It is the pits doing good deeds in our modern cynical world, but I'd have to find a few to do next week though if Jesus came up trumps for me and Eve was OK.

It didn't look good though. I was thinking that poor Jesus had his work cut out for him this time. Eve just sat there in the kitchen like a lump, not looking left or right, just staring at the floor. She was staring at a blob of tomato sauce left there from the previous night. I tore off a piece of kitchen towel and wiped it up. I thought it would stop her staring. It didn't.

"Come on now! Tell me what the matter is. It can't be that bad."

Please, don't let it be that bad!

"Oh, Ma, you look awful. What's the matter with you?"

"I'll tell you if you tell me."

"OK, you first."

So I spilled my guts. I told my poor vulnerable daughter that I had had a wonderful bonking session with Phil. I got carried away with it all and went into too much detail. Told her things she really didn't need or want to know about her mother. Some things are not for sharing with the group. Particularly if the group is someone you have given birth to. I knew I had gone too far by her body language: she crossed her legs and covered her face with her hands. It was a classic case of "don't you dare come near me".

I had read it in one of the self-help books I was so fond of. It gave a list of things to watch out for when you meet a man. Did you know that if they cross their arms or legs they aren't interested and don't want you to invade their space? Men are big into space. They are very fussy who they allow to invade it. I used to think it was just comfortable for guys to sit cross-legged. To tell you the truth I used to think it was odd how they could feel comfortable cross-legged given the fact that they had dangly bits that must've gotten in the way. Now I know they are just being territorial. Men who are interested in you let you know they are interested with their body language. They sit with their legs open. Bit obvious, isn't it?

Men are very obvious all the same. They also hold their palms upwards – not all the time, just if they are interested in chatting you up. I have been searching for a long time for an open-legged, upward-palmed man. They are very difficult to find. As soon as I see one, I'll be in there like a rocket. He won't know what hit him and his space. I will feel it incumbent on me to invade him and his space. In fact, I'll take pleasure in it. It's amazing the number of guys that sit with their arms folded when I come into a room. I've watched them. Sometimes, if you're lucky, you will get either the open legs or the upward palms, but you have to get the two together for it to mean anything. I'm always on the watch out for the open palm and the open leg, together.

I heard a little giggle. Muffled. At first I thought I was hearing things. Then it got louder and louder and it was coming from Eve's direction, but I knew she couldn't be laughing. No one in his or her right mind would laugh at my predicament. Especially not one of the two people in the world who were closest to me. No, I was being silly again; Eve would never be that cruel, I thought, as I looked at her. I wasn't being silly. She was being cruel. She was in knots of laughter. She was shaking. Her whole body was shaking with laughter and she was shaking her head from side to side in disbelief.

"You and Phil in the sack making out! No way! Ah, Ma, you're losing it, big-time!" She could hardly contain herself and had to run up to the loo in the middle of it all, leaving me standing there with egg on my face and a blob of tomato sauce in my hand to go with it.

"Well, thank you very much for the sympathy!" I shouted up the stairs. "Thank you very much for being there for me in my hour of need! I bare my soul to you. Confess all to you and what do I get? A belly laugh, that's what I get. What ever happened to the shoulder to cry on or the let's discuss this more and you'll feel a lot better, eh? What ever happened to all that? Well? Well? Can you hear me? Eve, are you listening to me? OK, I'm coming up there and you better watch out because this is not over yet. Not by a long shot." I stormed up the stairs after her.

I stood outside the bathroom door. I declare to God I could still hear her laughing. She must've had a towel stuffed in her mouth because it was a muffled sound, but I knew she was still laughing. After all, I am her mother and we mothers know everything. That's the wonderful thing about being a mother – your kids think you're some sort of a superhero and for a while it's nice being one. The novelty wears off after a while when they start to ask silly questions like "Where do the puddles go?"

and "Is there ever any food in this house?" and "Can I have some money?".

It's just as well it wears off because as soon as the kids hit their teens they realise that you are not a superhero. You were just pretending to be one and they really don't want a pretend hero whose only claim to fame is that she can wash, cook, iron and sew all at the one time while reciting chapter and verse on the latest methods of studying.

No, kids nowadays want a real action hero, one who can bring their friends for a go in a helicopter or can get free passes into the latest rock concert and throw in a few barrels of beer for good measure. Then, at about thirteen, they get to thinking that they don't need anyone and that the only heroes are themselves and their pals and that together they make an invincible lot. By late teens they have finally copped on that there is no such thing as a hero and life is what you make it. Unless of course, they are teenage girls, in which case they spend a huge percentage of their time talking about and looking for a mere mortal of a man that they will convince themselves is their hero. Maybe women need heroes and men need to feel they are heroes. Maybe I have just solved the battle of the sexes. Maybe that's what was missing from my life. A hero or even a battle or even sex.

"I can still hear you laughing, Eve. That better

not be one of the good towels you have in your mouth – it's full of fluff and you'll only choke and I'm not embarrassing myself by bringing you to casualty with a load of towel-fluff down your neck and you choking to death on it. I'm not having some nurse in a starched white uniform looking at me in disgust and asking, 'Did you not know to wash the new towels first before you use them?' Put the fluffy new towel back, Eve. You know it's only for display. Use one of the old ones, please."

The door opened. Eve came out. I could see she was biting the insides of her cheeks. Trying her best to stop laughing.

"Well, Eve, I'm glad I lifted your spirits for you. Anything else I can do while I'm at it for your entertainment? Slit my wrists maybe?"

"Ah, Ma, sure it's dead funny. You and Phil. Sure me and Becca always thought he was gay. Wait till she hears this."

"Well, I can assure you, young lady, he's far from gay if the performance he put on tonight is anything to go by."

"Please, Ma, spare me the details. I don't know if I can listen to them all over again. Ma's aren't supposed to enjoy that sort of thing. You were only supposed to have had it the twice. Once for Becca and once for me."

"Well, I certainly had it again tonight. With my

best friend. Oh, shit, what am I going to do? I think I just blew it with Phil."

Eve started to giggle again.

"Not literally, I hope."

The hall door swung open. Then it was banged shut.

"Where is she? Where is the conniving little bitch?"

Becca was home and I reckoned she was looking for Eve, although when she heard about me and Phil I supposed she'd have me in the conniving-bitch category too.

"Let me at her! Eve! *Eve! Eeeevvvve!.* Where the fuck are you? There is nowhere you can hide."

We could hear Becca opening all the doors downstairs and then slamming them shut. One by one. She dug her heels deep down into the carpet as she marched up the stairs. We could hear every single step.

I was about to hear what exactly happened with Eve tonight. Suddenly, I didn't want to hear.

"Becca, there is no need for that language," I said.

Well, I was the mother and that's what I was supposed to say.

"Did she tell you? Did she tell you what a bitch she's been? Well? Well? Did she?"

Becca was standing beside me on the landing

now. Eve had just managed to duck back into the bathroom seconds before Becca made it to the top step. Becca was furious; she was fuming and running her hands through her hair. She had the mascara streaks down her face too. Must be a new fashion and, imagine, I was in it. Or maybe it was a family thing. Becca started banging on the bathroom door with her fists.

"Come out of there, you worm, and face the music. I'm going to kill you when you come out. I'm going to tear you limb from limb, do you hear me?"

"Now really, Becca, if you do want Eve to come out that is hardly the right way to coax her, now is it? Leave it to me."

I gently pulled Becca away from the door. I knelt down. I put my face right up to the keyhole. It was freezing cold.

"Eve love," I said gently into the keyhole. "Eve, come on out, pet, and we can all sit down together and discuss it. We can even tell Becca about my total disaster with Phil and maybe it'll cheer her up too. The two of you could have a good laugh at me and we'd all be happy then."

There is no sacrifice too big for a mother. My knees were really killing me. My face was killing me. The handle of the door was pressed hard against my forehead. With my luck I'd have a huge dimple in my forehead for the rest of my life. Jesus, what if the bloody handle of the door had become embedded in my forehead? I leapt up and ran to the mirror on the landing. Thankfully, there was no handle protruding from my face. Thank God, there was only a very, very deep dent in it. It was very red and purple-looking at the edges but at least it wasn't a handle. With relief I returned to the shouting match. Round two.

Becca started banging the door down again.

"I know what you did, Eve, you–you–you bitch, you slut!" She turned to me and tears were running down her face. I felt so sorry for her. She was the one who was always in control and hated losing control and she was losing it now all over the landing. She was pacing and winding her hair around her finger.

"Come here to me, Becca." I put my arms around her and she let go with a damburst of tears.

"What happened? What has you so upset? Eve wouldn't do anything to make you this unhappy. Whatever it was, I'm sure she didn't mean it. Did you, Eve?" I shouted the last bit into the bathroom. "Did you, Eve?" I shouted even louder, giving her the nod to reply quickly. Her timing wasn't great. A bit slow, but at last she spoke.

"No. Becca, I didn't mean it. If you just listen to me I can explain it. Give me a chance to tell you what happened, will you?"

"Explain! Explain my arse! Nothing you can say will explain this."

"What is this all about, girls?"

"Well, if you don't know what she's done I'll tell you, will I? The bitch only snogged Charlie."

I was shocked. I tried my best to hide it, but my hands went immediately up to my mouth and I let out a huge gasp. I shook my head from side to side. I started rocking to and fro. I'm lousy at hiding things.

Becca went on even though she knew that I didn't want her to.

"That's all my innocent little sister did. She kissed my boyfriend. She knew what she was doing and she did it. I'm shagged if I'm going to have her snogging my boyfriend. Next time I see Hugh I'm going to tell him what she's done and then get stuck into smooching him so much he'll think it's his birthday and Christmas all on the one day."

We could hear a loud wailing sound coming from the bathroom. I could hear another loud wailing sound coming from my own throat. Jesus, who'd be a mother?

There should be health warnings down the side of children like they have on cigarette packets. Tattooed at birth from their neck to their feet all along the side. *Children Seriously Damage Parents' Health.* People even considering having a baby would see the warning on all the children walking around and think twice before they fertilised the innocent egg. It would also be a great help later on when the children were teenagers. When they asked their parents could they get a tattoo, their parents would just have to say: "Sure, you already have one." I was feeling very sick now. I could feel a bit of projectile vomiting coming on.

"Eve! Get your ass out of that bathroom pronto! I'm going to be sick."

The door opened and I dashed in and barely made it in time. Becca and Eve stood on the landing having the screaming match. Round three. I was afraid to lift my head away from the toilet in case I puked all over the floor and I hate cleaning up vomit, even my own.

"Why did you do it, Eve?" Becca was crying now. "Were you jealous of me and Charlie or what? I thought you were happy with Hugh. Why go after Charlie?"

"I am happy with Hugh. I love him. I didn't go after Charlie. He came after me. I swear I never even wanted him to kiss me. I'm mad about Hugh and I wouldn't do anything to hurt him. I'm also mad about you, Becca, and believe it or not I wouldn't do anything to hurt you either."

"Well, you've a bloody funny way of showing it!"

"Ah, Becca! Listen to her, will you?" I shouted from the toilet bowl. "She loves Hugh, she loves Hugh." Oh no, she loves Hugh! My voice echoed all around the room. I was debating whether to stick my head all the way down the bowl and flush the loo and be done with it. Drown myself and end the misery. It was a very attractive option, if not a very attractive way to go. 'She loves Hugh' kept ringing around in my head. How many times had I asked them – no, not asked – pleaded with them? How many times had I pleaded with the two of them not to fall in love until they had finished college? Was nobody listening to me any more? Was I being that unreasonable? Finish college. Get a job. Earn money. Fall in love. Move out of here. Buy your own house. Pay your own bills. What was wrong with there being an order to things? Why was the order always being mixed up? I don't think it would have killed either of my two girls to stick to the plan I had for them. Everyone should have a plan – so what if it wasn't their plan?

"Go on then! Give me your lame excuse before I kill you. It better be good. I think I'm going to kill you anyway even if it is. Bitch!"

"Right. Charlie was at the bar getting a drink and so was I. You were in the loo fixing your make-up and Hugh was over talking to some rugby crowd or other that he plays with. Charlie and I were talking and laughing about everything and nothing. It was all innocent stuff. I can't even remember what we were talking about, honestly. Then all of a sudden he lurched forward and kissed me. That's what really happened, I promise you. I pushed him off and he just laughed and said he always wondered if the two sisters kissed the same. "Just curious" is what he said. I told him he was an ignorant pig and that you were too good for him. I said that he didn't know how lucky he was to be with you and that if he didn't tell you what happened, I would. Becca, I'm so sorry. I really am."

"Yeah, well he did tell me, but your story is a bit different to his. How come you didn't tell Hugh if you're so bloody innocent?"

"I did tell him. He told me to tell you immediately, but I guess I just left it too late. I wanted Charlie to tell you. My version is the true version. So now, Becca, it's up to you who you believe. You can kill me and tear me apart, but it still won't change what happened and if he's lying to you to cover it up, well then he's really not worth you being with. I don't want to tell you this, Becca, because you're my sister and I love you, but Charlie has done the dirt on you before now."

I was distraught. I was nearly biting my nails. But I don't bite my nails. I was eating the flesh around my nails instead. I was making great progress and if

I kept it up at the rate I was going, it would be no time at all before I had chewed my fingers down to my knuckles.

Just to make sure I kept up the chewing, Eve went on and on and on.

Round Four.

"Hugh told me that he snogged some French girl who was staying in his house over Christmas. Remember his sister had an exchange student? Well, it was her."

"Shut up, stop making things up!" Becca shouted. "I'm not listening. Do you hear me? Shut up, will you?"

She had her hands over her ears trying to block it all out. I wanted to put my hands over my ears too, but they were stuck in my mouth and I was still chewing them.

"Listen to me, Becca, I'm not making it up. I swear it's true. I think there were more, but I'm not sure. I don't know about anyone else. I only just found out about what he's like and I told Hugh I didn't want to know any more. But I think you should ask Charlie yourself."

I came out of the bathroom and looked at my two morsels. My girls. My lovely girls. I wished I could make it all better for them. I wished I could crucify Charlie. I wished I could inflict lots of pain on him. He'd messed with one of mine and I wanted him to suffer. The slimy, good-for-nothing bastard. I wished and I wished, but this was one they would have to work out on their own. It's hard sometimes standing back and watching.

Eve put her arms around Becca and they both started crying again.

"But I love him," Becca whispered.

Dear God, she loves him. Where had I gone wrong with the two intelligent idiots I had reared? The two of them seemed to be making a hobby of falling in love.

"I know you do," Eve replied and I was superfluous to requirements so I just stood there, eating away at my hands and watched like a big spare part. I had never liked Charlie, I decided.

"Did you really tell him I was too good for him?"

"Yeah. And what's more I meant it. You are too good for that toe-rag, Becca. He treats you badly. Hugh thinks he's a right shit now too. You could have anyone. Why don't you go get yourself one of the nice guys? A real Prince Charming."

Jesus, we'd all be queuing up for Princes at this rate. I'd better make bloody sure to be at the top of the queue. I had strong competition.

"I know. This is the worst thing he has ever done. The bastard. He is a shit. I think I knew it was all over anyway. I was crying a lot more than I was laughing when I was with him. He never wanted to go anywhere I wanted to go. It was always what he wanted and that was mostly to the pub to get smashed. Did he really snog the French girl?"

"Yeah, I only heard about it tonight. I would have told you if I had known. I would have risked life and limb, but I'd have told you. That's the bad bit about being a sister. Sometimes you have to hurt her in order to do the right thing. You have to watch out for each other. Make sure no one hurts the other."

"I know exactly what you mean." They did the group-hug thing again. I joined in this time. It felt good.

"Hey, Becca, guess what? Ma slept with Phil!" Eve giggled.

"Ah, Ma, you didn't, did you?" cried Becca. "That's disgusting! I always thought he was gay."

"Well, he's not. Give over with the gay thing, will you? He's not gay. Christ, I feel crap. Poor Phil. What am I going to do?"

I was pleased to be able to distract them for a while from their own problems and we all sauntered down the stairs wondering how best I could repair things.

"I'm going to finish with Charlie," Becca announced. "It'll be hard, but I know I can do it. I think I've known for a while that he's a bollocks so that's it – consider him dumped."

"Well, fair fecks to you, Becca." I was so proud of her. "You know I don't usually interfere, but I have to tell you that I think what Charlie has done is horrendous. I know it's hard on you finishing with him and all that, but it'll be well worth it."

Yes, yes, finish with the little worm, ASAP.

"Yeah, Becca, I think you're great," Eve chimed in. "I'm proud of you too."

"I'm kind of proud of myself."

I was trying to appear calm, but I was seething with anger. I really wanted to kill Charlie. Slowly and with my bare hands and with as much pain as possible. I wanted to hurt the little louser who'd hurt my daughter. I wanted him to suffer, big-time.

"So listen, Ma, now that I'm doing such a brave thing as finishing with Charlie maybe you could do something to make me and Eve proud of you. You could call it a good deed even."

"Well, of course I will, Becca. You know I'd do anything for you and Eve. Just tell me what it is and I'll do it with pleasure."

I had that all-over warm glow and that lovey-dovey feeling you get when everything turns out grand in the end. I was wallowing in it. Borderline smugness. There was nothing I wouldn't do for these two wonderful women – my darling daughters.

"Will you go down to the gym and see what the story is with the prize? Go on, Ma – you said you'd do anything for us. You even said you'd do it with pleasure."

"Oh, my God! You can't be serious. I know I did say I'd do anything but within limits. I'm not joining a gym."

"Go on, Ma, it'd make us all feel better and it would help you to get over your little faux pas with Phil." She giggled as she said it.

I ignored her. I was getting so good at the ignoring bit, I was proud of myself.

But they ground me down. They wore me out. They appealed to my sense of motherhood. They made me feel guilty. They gave it Dixie and I succumbed as I always succumb. I surrendered. They exchanged smug looks as I hung my head and waved my large white flag at the two of them. Well, not literally. I didn't go around the house with a white flag hanging out of me. Although, I was waving the metaphorical flag so often these days that maybe I should invest in a real one. I could wear it cape-like around my shoulders and be poised at every given moment to do my Caped Crusader routine. I could hop from Superwoman to Wonder Woman and the Bionic Woman in a twirl whenever the need arose. Although I don't think the Bionic Woman was ever given a cape or a flag, which seems a bit unfair. A real flag would make me more authentic when I was juggling everything at frightening speed and, at the same time, being all things to all men, which was proving very difficult due to the lack of men in my life at the moment. I was sure there would be one along soon that I could be all things to. In the meantime I was still being all things to two young woman in particular and that was enough for any Bionic Woman. Anyway, my flag, metaphorical or otherwise, was raised as high as it could go. I was waving it at the aforementioned young women and we all three of us knew I was going to the gym.

Today's List

To do
1. C/fwd – man + cabinet.
2. Finish reading book on finding a hero.
3. Wash the new towels in the bathroom.
4. Make sure to bump into Charlie and kick his ass – big-time.
5. Try on a few outfits for the gym and pick the one that makes me thinnest-looking – no Lycra.

Not to do
1. Don't make a show of myself at the gym.

CHAPTER EIGHT

If you're going to go to a gym, go early in the morning. Becca and Eve had told me that was the best time to go. I listened to them. That was my first mistake. I often make this mistake and no matter how often I tell myself not to listen to them I find myself listening to them time and time again. I even took their advice. This was my second mistake. Of late I find myself making this mistake regularly. To be fair to them, they have advised me very well in the past. There has been the odd mishap or three. One or two mega-blunders, but more often than not that was my own fault for not adjusting their advice to suit my needs. Sometimes they give great advice. Other times they give crap advice. I have to practise sifting the great from the crap.

I was up before myself. I spent hours preening

myself and plucking myself. Making sure my make-up was perfect and my hair equally perfect and all superfluous hair perfectly removed. I sat perfectly still outside the gym for a few minutes watching all the beautiful people going in. Hundreds of them, early in the morning. All of the hundreds of them were in Lycra and they all looked lovely in it. Am I the only person in the world that looks crap in Lycra? I was wearing a magnificent track suit that had cost me two weeks' wages. It was designer and apart from paying for the label I was also paying for the considerable amount of material it had taken to make it so large that it hid all my wobbly bits.

Up to the time the gym was mentioned I didn't worry too much about my wobbly bits nor did I feel I had too many of them. Up to now I was quite happy with my lot. I was able to camouflage very well. Camouflage is an art form in itself. I'm big into art and I was well camouflaged. I braced myself for the obstacle course ahead. I got my sports bag from the boot. It matched my designer track suit and had cost only a half-week's wages – a bargain. I was walking a bit pigeon-toed in my new runners and I thought it made me look very athletic. Well, I had looked very athletic in the mirror last night when I practised. I caught sight of my reflection in the glass door as I went in and I looked ridiculous. I decided to change my walk to the more nonchalant type. I sauntered in, as if I was well used to my surroundings. As if I were at home, only in a tidy home. I went up the stairs to reception.

"Holy Mother of the Divine Crucified Christ!"

There I was in front of myself. A huge big cardboard cut-out of myself stood there staring at me. I was gobsmacked. My jaw hung open like a fish. Not in the photo – in reality. My hair looked shite. Not in reality – in the photo. Someone had gone to the trouble of blowing up my photo to around seven foot tall. Funny, I always thought I'd look great if only I was taller. I was wrong. Whoever blew up my photo should have gone the whole hog and blown it to smithereens. Eve and Becca never told me they'd sent in such a crap photo. One thing pleased me though. At least when I threw the two of them out of the house no one would point the finger and say I was being cruel. They'd say it was self-defence. This was definitely a throw-them-out-of-the-house offence. I might never speak to either of them again. The only saving grace was that the photo was so crap that I felt sure no one would recognise me. I was just about to turn and make the great escape out of the kip when I heard:

"Well, well, well, if it isn't Kelly! Kelly, I'd recognise you anywhere from your picture. Look everyone, it's Kelly! Congratulations! Look everyone – it's our competition winner – it's Kelly!" A young upstart was touching me and beaming from ear to ear with teeth so white I was sure they were false. She looked like a lollipop with teeth. I took an immediate dislike to her and her teeth. She had a stick-like body that her head was far too big for. She had no tits, no stomach, no hips – just one long strip of misery. All arms and legs and action-packed. She started pointing at me and then at my cardboard cut-out. The bloody whippersnapper! The cheek of her, all the same, recognising me and drawing attention to me! I tried to scuttle in behind myself or at least my cardboard self.

"Come out here till we get a good look at you. Come on out now, Kelly!"

The upstart must have been a long-distance relation of Hitler's; she had a way about her that you wouldn't question. Anyway, I reckoned she was probably a black belt in some new-fangled form of self-defence like tai chi or kickboxing or reiki – or maybe that was mental manipulation? Well, either way I know she had a black belt in one or all of them. All of a sudden she started hitting her biro off the wall. I thought she was going to turn and attack me with it. I ducked.

"Listen up! Ladies and gentlemen. Will you give a warm welcome to our competition winner, Kelly Daniels!"

All eyes turned in my direction. I think the eyes in

the cardboard cut-out were even looking at me. The room was full. Five minutes earlier there hadn't been one single person in it. The reception area was buzzing with healthy people. They all stared clapping and cheering.

"Kelly's children entered her in our competition. They sent a very touching letter in about their mother and this lovely photo. Are the two darlings with you, Kelly?"

"No," I said through clenched teeth. "I so wish they were here. In fact, you have no idea how much I wish the two darlings were here with me." Within arm's reach – well, their necks anyway.

"I'm sure Kelly wouldn't mind if we read out the lovely letter her two children sent in. Would you, Kelly?"

"Well, it might not be right on account of them not being here," I tried. God help me, I tried.

"I'm sure they'd be delighted for you, Kelly, to have a bit of limelight and your letter read out."

Cringe-factor of a million. I blushed. At least I pretended I was blushing – I was really seething, raging, bulling. I searched for a hole in the ground. I was sure one would open up for me and I could fling myself into it. What with the track suit and runners, I could do a great fling. But in this high-tech, top-of-the-range building there was not a hole to be found.

177

The sweat was pouring off me. I thought I was going to faint. Maybe I should faint, but then all the healthy people would do all sorts of things to revive me. They'd pull the clothes off me and see that the new white sports bra I had bought was squashing my tits and it didn't match my new boxer knickers with the tummy control which were black and digging into my waist. If they pulled at my underwear all my flesh would burst forth like yeast rising. Fainting was totally out of the question. I mustn't faint, I repeated to myself over and over again. The more I said it the more I wanted to faint. My track suit was smothering me. If it succeded I'd sue. There was no warning on the designer label about smothering. Maybe it was in the small print. I'd have to check that out later, if I survived.

I pulled at my track suit top, trying to take it off. I pulled so hard at the neck, trying to breathe properly, that I put a hole in the bloody high-tech, top-of-the-range suit. I wanted to cry. Two weeks' bloody wages. I pulled the top over my head and upset my hair. I hate upsetting my hair. It reacts very badly and goes into a right huff and does nothing I want it to do.

The lollipop with teeth cleared her throat and stood up on the nearest chair, preparatory to reading the letter. I didn't know what was in it. Becca and Eve hadn't wanted me to know what they had

178

written. All of a sudden I felt like a Christian being flung to the lions. I knew deep down in my deepest cushion-soled shoes that I was going to be made a right eejit of. I knew I was not going to like what was about to be read out to the masses. I knew I was out on a limb and Becca and Eve were the ones sawing the branch off. Aided and abetted by the toothy wonder.

"Come on up here, Kelly, and stand beside me while I read it out."

I turned, looking for any means of escape. I looked at the crowd and they had all turned into lollipops with teeth. I was looking at a whole room of them. It was like some horrible science-fiction film. The world was being taken over by lollipops, fit and healthy ones at that. I was terrified. I had visions of myself being taken over by one of the toothy lollipops. I didn't like what I saw. People would be licking me and sucking up to me all the time. I turned to run. I caught myself on my hip. Literally. The arm of my cardboard cut-out had a vice-grip on my hip. I couldn't get it off. It was pinching me. The pain was bringing tears to my eyes. I pulled at myself to get myself off myself. I fell over – well, the cardboard me fell over. I went flying onto the ground still holding my hip. Unfortunately, it was not my cardboard hip. I flung my arms up in the air and opened my mouth wide and screamed in pain for all I was worth.

"My hip, my hip!"

The crowd erupted and in one voice they shouted back at me:

"*Hooray!*"

They waved their arms and clapped and whistled. With the fright of the whole thing, I finally let go of myself. The cardboard me lay forlorn on the ground and I wondered if I swapped places with it would the crowd even notice. I picked myself up and stuck myself in a corner where I was happiest. Even a cardboard me deserves a little happiness. The crowd pushed me up to join their leader. My feet didn't touch the ground. They all stood to attention staring at me.

I wondered if I shouted '*Fire!*' would everyone run from the building? Then I could steal the letter and burn it, thereby starting a small fire. I opened my mouth to shout, '*Fire! Fire!*'.

But my voice wouldn't work. My mouth was moving all right but nothing was coming out. I know the fire thing would have worked if only my voice had worked. I knew it; I knew I was being taken over. The voice was probably the first thing to go when the toothy lollipops took over.

The leader took to the podium again – well, the chair, but it may as well have been a podium – and poured forth with such a load of crap that I am nearly too embarrassed to share it with you.

180

*Ladies and kind gentlemen, and whoever else it
may concern,
Our weak-willed ma needs your help – she's got
calories to burn!*

*She always puffs and moans and creaks when
going up the stair,
She really is a challenge – take her on if you dare!*

*We need to help her quickly – the situation's
getting dire,
Get her started on a work-out before she grows
another spare tyre.*

*She's quite oblivious to the danger of her middle-
aged spread,
But we, her two doting daughters, are afraid
she'll drop down dead!*

*So put her through her paces – ski-machines,
bikes, treadmills,
And do it all for free, please – she can't afford
more bills.*

*Our ma just got divorced and needs the spring
put in her step,
Try the sauna and Jacuzzi and aerobics too might
help.*

*But for God's sake please don't tell her that we
think she's so unfit,
She'll only throw a wobbly and not get over it.*

*Please, please, judges, won't you listen to our
deepest heartfelt plea?
Kelly Daniels is in crisis and needs help from you
and me.*

*We've tried our best to convince you to make our
ma the winner,
See the enclosed "before" photo – make the
"after" one be thinner.*

*Our mam would be the most enthusiastic winner
we believe,
So please give Ma her rightful prize, with love
from Becca and from Eve!*

I will never forgive my children for it. They will
never forgive the lollipop leader for reading it out.
They were going to sue her because they had been
given to understand that all correspondence to the
competition was private and confidential. I stopped
them suing her because I knew the letter would have
to be read again and again and again and again in
court and in the paper and on the television and at
Mass on Sunday and from the highest mountain in

Tibet and all over the world and universe. I knew my humiliation would be worldwide.

I knew the gym was only the start of my humiliation. Today's humiliation was only in front of a small throng of keep-fit fanatics, who didn't seem to have a job to go to and had nothing better to do at sparrow-fart in the morning only watch the likes of me being humiliated. Why stop there when there was a huge audience countrywide who could enjoy my humiliation? I knew it was only just beginning. Today the gym, tomorrow the world.

"Isn't it wonderful? We have several nationwide newspapers that want to print the letter and the photo. Kelly, I think you're going to become a household name."

Or a laughing-stock. What did I tell you? Nationwide humiliation.

I was trying to think what I would do with the spare rooms that would become available in my house tomorrow. I would give them till tomorrow to move out. I thought I was being much fairer to them than they had been to me. I thought about turning one of the rooms into an office. I was thinking of writing a book and what with all the ideas I had, I'd need a whole room to do it in. The plot would be something along the lines of a middle-aged woman impaling herself on a lollipop in desperation and killing herself. It would be a tale of betrayal and desperation.

Then again, I could always get in two paying lodgers and go on a bloody good holiday every year. The rent and the thousands I'd save not having Becca and Eve sponging off me for the rest of their selfish lives would allow me to live in a very comfortable manner or even manor for the rest of my natural. I have to admit that I did have a small twinge of guilt (only small, mind you) when I thought about throwing the two of them out on the street. After all, I am their mother and they are still young – well relatively. Compared to me, they are young. I do love them dearly. But look what they had done to me! This was all-out war. Then I saw the toothy lollipop making a beeline for me again with her arms flying in all directions and she ready to whip me into submission. I raised my two hands and the fucking white surrender flag again. I'm good at surrendering. All guilt feelings regarding Becca and Eve quickly disappeared into a more seething, bubbling, rage type of feeling.

"Now, Kelly. What about a bit of a snack before we show you around the place? You're probably dying for something to drink too. Good, eh?"

Oh, wasn't she a lovely woman all the same? I could murder a cup of tea and a creamy bun. Boost the energy levels. Maybe the place wasn't as bad as I thought if it had a restaurant. I could use it for my lunch at the weekends and spoil myself. Maybe the whole thing could turn into one of those places where they pamper you. Maybe some bloke would give me a massage and an all-over rub. I quickened my pace to catch up with the speed-walking lollipop. I smiled at her and nodded as she spoke to me. I laughed a little too loudly at her jokes so she'd know I was making the effort to be friendly. After all, she was going to feed me and not a lot of people did that.

"Bit of something to eat. Then a look around the gym and a bit of a try-out of our equipment and finally a swim. If you're very lucky you'll just make my aqua-aerobics class. Won't that be fun? What do you think? Good plan, eh? Eh? Great, isn't it? Good, eh? Oh and my name is Lolita by the way – most people call me Lolly for short."

I stopped dead in my tracks and track suit. She was that blatant. Admitted straight out that she was really a lollipop. I had been trying to convince myself that the lollipop story was a bit silly until now. Now I knew she meant business.

On the way to the restaurant she kept on talking.

"Now, Kelly, there you are. Your membership card for the next twelve months. Great, isn't it? Good, eh? "

She handed me a card like a credit card only this one had a hideous picture of me on it. Obviously taken from the picture Becca and Eve had sent. Also

I was sure this one wouldn't allow me to go berserk in the shops which was another minus against the gym.

"We want to watch your progress every month so we were thinking we'd take a photo of you every month and blow it up to life-size and hang it here in reception with the original one for everyone to see the improvement as time goes by. What do you think? Good plan, eh? I think it's a brilliant idea."

"Well, I'm not so sure it's that brilliant, Lolly," I managed to say at last. "Are you sure you have enough room to hang up all my photos?"

"Of course it's brilliant, it was *my* idea! We'll make room. What do you think? Good, eh? What are you thinking? Go on, tell me. Come on. Dead exciting, isn't it?"

I realised that Lolly didn't need much breath. She could talk for Ireland in the Olympics while running across the world with the Olympic torch up her ass giving off this warm "I love everyone" vibe and shouting "Good, eh?" to the four corners of it. I love enthusiastic people. I strive to be one myself. I love people who love everyone. I also strive to love everyone. But this in-your-face, jolly-hockey-sticks, happy-go-lucky lollipop was driving me crazy. If she said "Good, eh?" once again I was going to explode with annoyance right into her face.

There was a good crowd in the restaurant. It was

one of those ultra-modern type restaurants. Everything was stainless steel and red. All the cooking appliances were hidden. I couldn't see them. All the smells of the cooking were absorbed or at least they must have been because I couldn't get even a hint of a smell of the sausages or rashers not to mention the eggs. I was thinking I'd have the full Irish breakfast and it would do me for my lunch.

"Let me pick something tasty out for you, Kelly. On the house."

"Thanks a million, but I wouldn't dream of it. I'll pick it out myself. I wouldn't want to put you to any bother and anyway I'm a very picky eater." I lied. I just knew that Lolly would pick something healthy for me to eat like a banana and if I was very lucky a plain yoghurt. I was really hungry now.

My mouth was watering and my stomach was churning. It thought someone had cut my throat and that it would never be fed again. I hadn't eaten since last night because I was so worried about going to the gym in the first place.

"Well, if you like, just help yourself. What would you like? It's all so deeeeelicious. Go on, help yourself. Enjoy. Go on, get stuck in, and don't be polite. Good, eh?"

No way was I being polite. I was starving. Polite and starving don't go together. I was just about to say, "I'll have the full Irish and a creamy bun, thanks" when I caught sight of the fare on offer. Rabbit-fodder. Lettuce. Tomatoes. Rocket. Watercress. Grated carrot. Bowls of grapefruit and prunes mixed. Grapefruit on its own. Prunes on their own. It was a total disaster. No fry. No cup of tea or coffee even. Just grapefruit juice or vegetable or fruit smoothies.

What sort of miserable existence do these people have? Whatever planet they came from I didn't like it.

"Deeeeeeeeelicious!" Lolly gestured towards the food. "Good, eh?"

I started to giggle. It started off in my throat and then came out my mouth like a high-pitched hysterical wail. It lasted for ages and I had no control over it. I thought I might go straight into a cry as well, just to make a total show of myself, but I managed to hold off. I stopped.

"What?" Lolly said.

"What? What?" I said.

"What's wrong?" she said.

"Nothing," I said.

"I thought you were wailing or crying or something," she said.

"No. No. I'm fine. Ab-sol-ute-ly fi-ne," I replied.

"Good, eh?" she said.

"Good," I said and hung my head in compliance.

"Don't worry about not being fit. If that's what's

worrying you. You'll be brilliant. We'll get you into the exercise gradually. I'm having a strawberry smoothie and a serving of carrot. What are you having?"

"Apart from a nervous breakdown, I think I'll have a banana." It was the nearest thing to a sausage that I could see. Well, the shape was similar anyway. The cheek of your woman all the same saying I wasn't fit.

"Nervous breakdown? Is that what you said? Do you suffer from your nerves? Have you had problems? You should have told us. There was no mention of this before now."

"No, I didn't say nervous breakdown – you must have misunderstood me. I said I'll have a banana, thanks."

The girl dishing out the food looked like she was about to make scrambled eggs. I was elated. She was cracking the eggs open for all she was worth.

"I'll have some of those, please!" I nearly shouted at her.

"Good for you!" Lolly was delighted. "I'm thrilled you're going for them."

I thought she was going on a bit. A bit OTT if you ask me. I just wanted a bit of scrambled egg.

Plop!

Plop!

The girl plopped two raw eggs into a glass and

handed them to me. No pot. No butter. No milk. No whisk. What good were raw eggs to me?

"Down the hatch!" said Lolly.

Plop!

Plop!

She got two raw eggs too.

She opened her jaw and let the eggs pour down her mouth. They must have tasted awful because she didn't speak for at least three minutes.

"Deeeeeeelicious!" she said at last and smiled a big toothy smile. "Come on, Kelly! Down the hatch!"

I slipped the two eggs down my throat and tried not to retch. It felt as though I were swallowing some living thing. It was slimy and squiggy and deeeeeeegusting! I shoved the banana into my mouth and nearly choked on it. It covered up the taste of the eggs. I grabbed at the yoghurt and swallowed it down because it was edible.

"Right, now that we're all full up, you can have a bit of a tour and then we'll just show you the equipment."

"Thanks," I said grudgingly. I was sulking now, having had nothing proper to eat.

We walked back along the corridor. Lolly talked non-stop all the way. I sulked non-stop all the way. She kept talking as she dragged me through two swing doors directly into the Chamber of Horrors. There were excruciating machines everywhere with blokes sitting on them sweating profusely. Painful-looking steel weights being lifted and other even heavier weights being squeezed into very well-toned chests. Blokes everywhere were pumping iron. Very nice blokes if I'm to be honest. Very nice men indeed. I mean really nice. Maybe Becca and Eve were right about my meeting my Prince here? Meeting any one of these blokes would do me. Who cared if he was my Prince or not? He'd have the body of a Prince. I could close my eyes and pretend he was my Prince. It would be easy to pretend if he had a body like any of these. I had never seen such perfect bodies before. Well, maybe once, on holiday, never on my own turf. Never so many in one place. I was staring. My mouth was hanging open. I was holding my tongue back from hanging out. There was one guy on a thing that looked as if he was mountain-climbing. The muscles in his arms were really big and like concrete. His calf-muscles were huge. I was afraid to look at his Lycra shorts. It might have been too much for me. He might see me peeping. He took up his snow-white hand-towel and wiped his face in it. I did what any red-blooded woman would do in similar circumstances. I snuck a look at his Lycra. Very nice. Very nice indeed.

The lot of them were probably posers, I was thinking.

"Hi! I haven't seen you here before. Are you new?" The Lycra-clad, well-built poser asked very nicely.

"Just started today. Getting to know the ropes. You know how it is. I'll be a dab hand at it in no time."

"Ah, you'll enjoy it! It's great fun if you don't take it too seriously."

I found myself liking this poser. Even if he had overdone the fake tan a bit too much. Who has a tan like that in February?

"You should join one of the team events. They arrange trips away for all the teams. My wife and I are on the swimming team and we're just back from Puerto Rico – bit of a heat wave but hey, who's complaining?"

"Thanks for the advice. I was just thinking you had a lovely colour. I was thinking you must've been away all right."

"Kelly! Kelly!" Lolly was all excited. "Come on, Kelly, and I'll show you the changing rooms and you can get ready for the aqua-aerobics. I assume you brought your swimming togs? If not, I can sell you a pair."

"Oh, I have my own, thanks very much."

I knew I'd never even fit one of my legs into a pair of hers. I wondered if the powers that be knew she was selling second-hand bathing suits.

I stood there like a woman about to be shot from a cannon. Rubber skullcap hat on my head and a tight black bathing-suit stuck like a skin to my body. I had heard about verrucas and didn't want one so I had a big pair of flip-flops on. As I had none of my own I had borrowed Becca's, which were bright yellow and covered in flowers. I waddled out the door and tried to get into the pool as quickly as possible without drawing any attention to myself.

"Well, there you are, Kelly, our competition winner! I thought you were never coming out. Good, eh?" Lolly drew lots of attention to me. "OK, now we'll start with a few warming-up exercises. Lift those legs. Left! Right! March! March! Come on, march it out! March it out! Come on! You're useless. Are you here to do this or just splash around in the pool for an hour?"

Jesus, Mary and Joseph – an hour.

"No time for wimps in this class. Come on now! March it out! March it out! To the left! Right! Front! Back! Centre! Forward! Come on now! Arms in the air this time! Push yourself into the floor down under the water. Don't drown on me, will you?"

I was splashing around going hell for leather. Giving it Dixie and I have to admit I was enjoying it. I was really into it, but I knew I wouldn't last the hour. I was trying to think of an excuse to get out.

"Right then, down under the water, then arms outstretched, propel yourself right out of the water as high as you can go! After three! One, two, three!"

Down, down I went. Right down. Then held my arms up over my head. I pushed off the floor of the pool with my feet. I shot up out of the water. My tit shot out from my bathing-suit. It just about missed hitting a man in the face. He too was one of the skullcap brigade.

He ducked just in time, and then bobbed up again.

"Well, well, if it isn't young Kelly Daniels! It is you, isn't it? I'd recognise that boob anywhere." He was laughing as he resurfaced.

It was James.

I popped my very ample bosom back into my less ample bathing-suit.

Now, it's not as if my boob is so great that those who have seen it once never forget it. It's more likely to be the fact that I have a birthmark on my boob that helps guys remember. I have a birthmark exactly like the symbol of a Mercedes Benz on my right tit. I kid you not: it's like a circle and three triangles inside it. It's exactly the same as the car symbol.

Not a lot of people have seen my birthmark. James was one of the lucky few who had. The first time he saw it he nearly lost his life and a lot more with the shock of it. You see, James owned a garage and was the sole agent for Mercedes on the northside of Dublin. Everyone thought that getting the Northside was a bit of a bum deal for James and that no one on the Northside would know what to do with a Merc, except steal it. But James and his big house up in Howth knew different.

I was delighted to see good aul' James again,

looking bigger and better than I remembered him. He had always wanted me to have my photo taken topless on one of the cars outside his garage. He said my birthmark was a great advertising weapon. I told him my tits were not weapons and that everyone would assume I had painted the symbol on. He said we were made for each other and that I had solid proof of that on my chest. What more did I need, he said. But then he also said the timing was all wrong, way back then. I had messed up big-time snivelling about Graham all the time. But now I had to show him how I had moved on. I had to let him see I was completely over my break-up with Graham.

"How's the car business?" I asked

"Brilliant. Never better. Howerye doing these days, Kelly?"

"I'm doing great these days. I never think about Graham at all." OK maybe that was just that little bit too obvious.

"Well, that's good. Do you have anyone else you think about?"

"Well, funny thing is . . . I can't believe bumping into you like this because I was only thinking about you the other day."

"That sounds good. Really good that you were thinking about me, but what exactly were you thinking?"

"Nothing in particular. You just popped into my

head, that's all." You and your tightly fitting condom.

"Well, that's nice. I'm glad I popped into your head. I often think about you, you know."

"You do? How often?" I know I was flirting; my eyelids were hurting I was blinking them so much.

"Well, I guess I think about you a lot, Kelly."

"Me too – about you," I said.

James splashed me in a friendly way. I splashed him back.

"Kelly! Kelly! James! You're disrupting the class. Come on, stop talking, march it out! March it out!"

So me and James did what we did best and marched it right out of the pool. It was cold and we ran for the changing-rooms.

"See you outside in fifteen minutes," he said as he went into the men's dressing-room.

"Great." I was shaking, not with the cold but with the excitement. I hadn't been this excited about anything in years.

Today's List

To do

1. *Man and cabinet.*
2. *Stay away from Lolly – we have nothing in common.*
3. *Buy bigger bathing-suit.*

4. *Get one of the lovely, sexy bodies to show me the ropes.*

Not to do
1. *Don't ever eat raw eggs again.*
2. *Don't listen to Becca and Eve again. I know I've said this before – this time do it.*

To ignore
1. *My photos plastered all over the gym wall.*

CHAPTER NINE

He was true to his word. He was waiting outside for me.

"Well, well, there you are. Come on, let's go somewhere where they have coffee and some sort of a sugary bun. I'm starving."

"I can't go anywhere looking like this."

My track suit was stuck to me because I hadn't dried myself properly. My hair was dripping wet and the little bit of make-up I had on this morning was gone.

"You look great."

"Look. I'd love to go home and change my clothes before we go anywhere. Leave your car here. My house is only up the road and I can change and we'll go for coffee and then I'll drop you back to your car."

"OK, you're on. It's great meeting you again after all this time. Lead the way."

Ooooh, I was so elated! I knew the house was clean because Becca and Eve had been keeping it spotless since I threw the wobbly about them entering me in the competition. I might have to thank them yet for entering me in the competition. I'd never have met James again if I hadn't been in the gym. I loved the gym. I decided not to tell the girls too soon about my loving the gym. I could drag it out for another few weeks and they'd continue to keep the place clean.

"Here we are. Make yourself at home. Actually there's a bottle of white wine in the fridge and I know it's a bit early but I'd love a drink. What do you think?"

"OK, I'll open it. You go on up and change."

"I won't be a minute." My bedroom was a bit of a mess, but what the hell, he wouldn't see it. I pulled off my track suit and peeled my sporty underwear off. I stood staring at my open wardrobe, praying for inspiration. I got none. I got out some underwear and put it on. I sprayed some *Obsession* all over me.

"Hi. I thought you might like some wine while you're getting ready."

Jesus, there was James. Standing in the doorway. Bottle of wine in one hand. Two glasses in the other. I spread my hands out over any part of my body bits

I could cover which to be honest wasn't much. I have small hands and big bits.

"Oh. Yeah. Right. Thanks. Well. Grand, eh?" Jesus, I was starting to sound like Lolly. Then I spotted it. The shiny gold band on his fourth finger. Left hand. I was gutted.

"I'll just put these down here." He put the bottle and glasses down on the bedside table and poured out two glasses. I stood cross-legged, arms folded.

"I see you got married since I last saw you." I was direct.

"Yeah, about two years ago. She's lovely. A bit younger than me. We have a little girl. She's the cutest thing you ever saw. Takes after her mother. She's just great. I love being a dad."

It's the husband bit you have a problem with I thought. If it's all so wonderful, what are you doing here with me in my shaggin bedroom? Jesus, were even the good guys gits? I swear he used to be a good guy.

"Here you go. Bottoms up!" He handed me a glass.

My bottom isn't going anywhere and certainly not with a married man, I thought as I took the glass. How the hell was I going to get him out of the bedroom? I sipped a bit of the wine. It went straight to my head and to my kidneys.

"Sorry, I have to go to the loo." I ran into the

bathroom. How the hell would I get him out? Right. Be direct. Just say 'James, you've got this all wrong. Nice and all as you are I didn't ask you here to sleep with you. I genuinely wanted to change my clothes and go out for coffee and catch up on old times. Reminisce a bit.'

I braced myself and marched back into the bedroom. I flung the door open. Thank God. He must've gone downstairs again while I was in the bathroom. He was probably just interested in having a chat too. He was probably just being nice, bringing me up a glass of my own wine. Boy, I nearly made an ass of myself assuming he wanted more. See? He was one of the good guys after all. My faith in human nature was restored, I closed the door tight all the same.

And nearly jumped out of my skin. Someone was lying in my bed. Flat out on their back and it wasn't Goldilocks. Oh, how I wished it was Goldilocks! She'd have been happy with a bowl of porridge and a bit of a kip. Unfortunately, it was James. In total *flagrante delicto*. I mean he was totally and utterly without any doubt, bollock-naked. Lying there on my bed. I was flabbergasted. He didn't even have the duvet pulled up to cover his dignity. Not that he had much of that either. To tell you the truth, age had done very little for James. How had he got it so wrong?

"Come on in here beside me, Kelly. Come on and givvus a cuddle!"

He put out his hand, grabbed my arm and pulled me onto the bed. There was no way I was getting in beside him. Time to nip it in the bud. Before his bud got any bigger.

"James. You're married and I'm –"

"Ma, Ma, we're home! Where are you?" Becca shouted up the stairs.

"Ma, wait till we tell you what happened!" Eve was with her.

I heard their footsteps on the stairs. They were heading this way. With one huge, for-all-I-was-worth push, I pushed James off the bed. He fell with a soft thud on the floor. The floor was covered in towels that were making their way to the hot press, so at least he had a soft landing. He was lying on the window side of the room. Furthest away from the door. There was room for very little on that side of the room anyway. Now that James was there, there was no room at all. I threw the duvet on top of him. Then I lay down in my underwear on the bed.

"Kelly, What the hell . . .?" I could hear James protesting from under the mountain of clothes.

"Shut up, you randy bastard – my two daughters are coming in. If they so much as hear you breathe, I'll kill you. Stay down there until they leave."

"Oh fuck! OK!"

"Hi, Ma! What are you doing in bed at this hour of the day?"

"Are you all right? Are you sick?"

Yes, I'm sick. Very sick. Sick to the stomach that you might find my potential lover on the floor.

"Ah, I'm fine. I just decided to have a lie-down because I was worn out after my work-out at the gym," I whispered.

"How did it go? Was it brilliant? Are they letting me and Eve join?" Becca whispered back.

"I don't know if I'd call it brilliant. They read out the letter!" I whispered even lower.

"Oh! Are we in big trouble? We made it all up just so you'd win." Eve was whispering now.

"It worked, didn't it? We're really sorry, Ma," said Becca. "Why are we whispering?"

"Because I'm tired. Keep whispering. We won't talk about the gym now if you don't mind." I didn't want James to hear all the gory details. "To be honest, girls, I'm really knackered. Will you give me about an hour to have a bit of a snooze and I'll be down then and we'll have a good chat about everything. Go on now, the pair of you."

"Well, was there some awesome talent there like we told you? Did you meet the man of your dreams?"

"Will you whisper, for God sakes! Anyway, I don't know what you're talking about. Will you both get out and let me sleep! Please!" I was hoping the duvet was blocking all the sound and that James couldn't hear Eve making a show of me.

"Can I just tell you one thing?" Eve was bursting with some news or other. I knew she wouldn't leave me alone until I listened. I was hoping James wouldn't smother by the time she got it all out.

"Go on then, but make it snappy."

"We're all invited to Hugh's mother's party tomorrow night. Isn't that brilliant."

"Yeah, brilliant. Now, go on, get out."

"She seems so nice to have asked us. I told Hugh that you'd probably be giving me and Becca a lift and he told his mam and she said you should come too as you'd be dropping us off anyway. She told him it would be a pity for you to have to drop us and collect us and that you should stay and enjoy yourself. Doesn't she sound really nice?" Eve was all starry-eyed.

"We can all go together," said Becca. "Will you come, Ma? It'll be great fun and you might even meet some really nice man!"

I started coughing hoping it would cover up Becca's "nice man" bit. She was really letting me down badly.

"Right, that's enough! Come on and let me get a bit of a sleep, will you?"

"Ah Ma, say you'll come! You could provide the moral support to me when I meet Hugh's mother and her boyfriend, or should that be man-friend.

I'm dying to meet them, but I'm terrified at the same time. I keep thinking I'm going to say the wrong thing and let Hugh down. It'd be great if you were there. Come on, Ma, if you're worried about being on your own, don't – me and Becca will look after you, won't we, Becca?"

"Yeah, we'll look after you big-time. You'd never let anyone down, Eve. Hugh should be glad you're going out with him. He's probably dying to show you off to everyone." Becca was being the loving sister.

"Let me think about it. Now get out of here, the two of you."

"Ah, Ma, come on, it'll be good fun. Just the three of us and Hugh of course. Oh yeah, Eve, Hugh will have to dance with me and Ma. You'll have to share him with the group." There was a twinkle in Becca's eye. I thought I heard a grunt and I could swear I saw my duvet moving. I was hoping I was the only one who heard or saw it. I braced myself. Eve and Becca seemed oblivious. Oh, I wished they'd just leave.

"OK, OK, I'll go and dance with Hugh. Whatever you want, just get the hell out of here, will you?"

"Touchy or what, Ma – we're going. Who rattled your cage anyway? I can't believe one trip to the gym and you're wrecked. You're even more unfit than we thought. You better get yourself into shape before you meet your Prince!"

She laughed. I laughed too with a tinge of hysteria.

Becca laughed but with a little tinge of sadness. I wondered was she thinking of Charlie. I was hoping she wasn't. I was hoping she'd forgotten all about that toe-rag.

"Do you want the duvet on you? Where is it?" Eve went around to pull the duvet off the floor. I leapt up.

"Stop! Stop!" I shouted. She froze and looked at me as though she thought I had finally lost the plot. "I'm too hot. Can't you just leave me alone?"

"Right." She stormed out.

"If that's the way you want it!" Becca followed her.

"I'll be down soon," I whispered loudly to the two of them as they left the room. I knew I was being unfair, but all's fair in love and war as they say and this was, well, this was neither but it sure was a mess anyway. I lay star-positioned on the bed. I couldn't believe my luck. That I hadn't been caught with a bare-arsed married man was miraculous. Speaking of bare asses, I jumped out and round the other side of the bed. I pulled the duvet off James. The bastard was lying there naked and asleep. I remembered now what used to drive me crazy about him. It used to drive me spare the way he could sleep anywhere at any time and he snored loudly. He'd fall asleep mid-sentence at the drop of a hat. In the cinema. At the theatre. In the car. Standing in a queue. James slept. The only time he had difficulty sleeping was after sex; at first the latter compensated

for the former, but it wore off pretty quickly. The nerve
of him all the same. I gave him a shove. A bit harder
than was necessary, but at least I didn't give him a
thump which was what I wanted to do.

"For God sake, James, will you get up and get
out of here quick!"

"What? What? What the hell is going on, Kelly?"

"My children are downstairs. Get out, will you?"
I flung his clothes at him. He pulled on his boxers
and his trousers and went to go out the door
carrying his shirt and shoes.

"No, wait. You can't go out that way. Let me
think."

"Are you mad? I have to go out this way unless
of course there is a hidden door and escape route for
all the blokes you bring up here. You might not like
it, but as far as I can see there are only two escape
routes out of this room: the door and the window.
We are on the first floor so the window is out. I have
to go out the door. You go down and distract them
and I'll make my escape."

"No, wait, wait, the window – that's a great idea."

"Feck off! There is no way I'm going out that
window." He stood staring out the window. I joined
him. It didn't look that far down to me. Then again
I was the one who was going to be staying on terra
firma. It must have looked very far down for James.

"Oh well, if you're such a coward! Wait here for

a minute. If anyone comes, get under the duvet again or into the wardrobe. I'll be back in a tick."

I ran down the stairs and shouted in to the girls who I knew would be in the kitchen making tea and talking about me being so mean or engrossed in chatting about the party.

"I'm just running out to get something off the line that I want to wear tonight. Back in a sec." I was sure they wouldn't follow me. They'd be afraid I'd ask them to take in all the washing and that would be just a bit too much for them. I dashed into the shed and dragged out the ladder. I pulled it out into the front garden. Then, with the strength of Samson before Delilah got at him, I pushed the ladder up against my bedroom window and ran back into the house. I was a woman possessed. I had super-human powers.

"Be back down in a sec!" I shouted to the girls again.

I dashed up the stairs at breakneck speed into my bedroom. James was standing there like a big idiot.

"Well, open the window, will you? You big idiot!"

I felt a pain in my chest. So this is what a heart attack feels like I thought. Acting superhuman really doesn't agree with me.

"I am not going out the window."

"You are. I have a ladder on the other side. You'll be fine." I flung the window wide open.

James handed me his shoes and jumper. He climbed up on the windowsill and flung one leg out onto the ladder.

"Are you sure it's safe?" He whinged as he looked down a bit doubtfully.

"Of course it's safe. Go on, will you! You big idiot!"

He put his second leg out the window.

"Ma?" Eve shouted.

"Ma?" Becca shouted.

"Ma, what's going on?" They both shouted together.

"Who's that? What's he doing?"

"This is not what it looks like," I said and I flung James's clothes out the window. He stood there on the ladder frozen to the spot. The big idiot didn't move.

"Oh, this is so sick, Ma!"

"This is base. I can't believe you. Oh my God, has he been here all morning? Oh shit, was he in the room when we were here?"

Becca was standing with a cup of tea obviously meant for me in her hand and Eve was holding a plate of cake.

James got sense and courage all at once, said "Sorry!" and scarpered down the ladder.

I sat on the bed. Becca and Eve sat on the bed too. They were shaking their heads from side to side in disbelief. I was trying to form a sentence that would make sense of the whole thing.

"So where's the party tomorrow night then?" was all that came out of my mouth.

"You're pathetic, Ma. Did you just pick someone up off the street or do you at least know him? First Phil, now some big half-naked idiot. You're pathetic."

"Of course I know him. Don't be so judgemental. We weren't doing anything, much as your dirty minds would like to think we were. Me and James go back a long way. I met him in the gym and we were going for coffee."

"But you decided to have desert first. It's sick."

"No. I didn't do anything with him."

"Not for the want of trying, it looks like. Only that we came home and interrupted your bit of fun you'd still be at it hammer and tongs. I think there's a word for that."

"Coitus interruptus," I supplied. "Not that I was coitusing anything and you didn't interruptus any coitusing because there was no coitusing going on in the first place."

"The word I was looking for was 'nymphomaniac'."

"Oh, stop at me! I've had a nightmare day. The only good thing that happened was that you two came home in the nick of time."

I poured forth and told them all the gory details and they believed me. Or at least they pretended to believe me. One way or the other, I felt a lot better. We decided to get a Chinese for the dinner and just veg out for the night in front of the telly in preparation for the party tomorrow night.

Very ordinary things were happening in the soaps. One character was about to sleep with a married man. Another was sleeping with her best friend. Some sad git had just split up from her husband. Sometimes life is more exciting and confusing than any soap.

Today's List

To do
  1. *Usual.*
  2. *Check out fourth finger left hand on guys in future.*
  3. *Lock bedroom door at all times.*
  4. *Clean out one of my wardrobes in case I need to hide anyone/thing again.*

Not to do
  1. *Don't ever let a man into my bedroom again.*
  2. *Don't ever let a man into my bedroom again.*
  3. *Don't ever let a man into my bedroom again.*

To ignore
  1. *James.*

211

Chapter Ten

CHAPTER TEN

I was determined to enjoy myself. I was determined to look my very best. I was determined not to meet James again. I was determined about everything these days. James was only after one thing and while I liked that one thing, I didn't want it to be with a married man. I lit a few candles, not in the church, although if I had had time I would have run down there and lit the lot of them, in thanksgiving that the Eve and Becca episode was resolved. I lit the candles in the bathroom and poured nearly a full bottle of some mixture or other Tilda had given me into the bath. It was supposed to get rid of cellulite.

"Pour a capful into your bath and watch that nasty cellulite disappear", it promised. I reckoned that if a capful got rid of the average amount of cellulite then a half bottle might make some sort of

a dent in mine. I was lucky in the cellulite stakes though – I had the all-over type. Poor Joan, the bad beautician, had it in patches. She had tried every product known to man, or woman should I say, but to no avail. I had tried nothing until now. If everyone had it then what's the big deal, was my thinking on it. Should we not consider cellulite to be normal and just get on with it? Be done, once and for all, with the great cellulite debate? Could we not start remarking on people without cellulite, saying how awful it must be for them to be abnormal and to be without it?

But lately I'd been thinking that if I was going to find my Prince it would be a shame for him to be turned off by my orange-peel arse. He might be prepared to chop down thick hedges and climb towers to give me the kiss of life, but he might do it with more gusto if he thought I was a firm cellulite-free zone. The stuff in the bath had a bit of a funny smell, but I lowered myself in and waited for the miracle to happen.

I was trying to think what to wear. What does one wear nowadays for a Prince? The full ball-gown with glass slippers was definitely out. Glass slippers are very hard to get these days and since I had slept with the nearest thing I had to a Fairy Godmother, I didn't think he was going to come up with the goods.

I still hadn't heard from Phil, but then again I hadn't rung him either. I wondered if he was missing me as much as I was missing him. I hoped so. We were all meant to be meeting up tomorrow in Joan's house and I couldn't help thinking that Phil wouldn't show. The Sad and Lonely Tribe was becoming sadder and lonelier, what with the Tilda and Dan situation and the Me and Phil situation and poor aul' Joan trying to keep it all together.

Joan had been married to the most boring man in Ireland for endless years. They seemed to date for a lifetime and we heard every boring detail about their very boring romance. They had no children and had agreed before they got married that they would have none. He went and had a vasectomy before they got married, the way other blokes have a stag party. He told us all every boring detail about his vasectomy. We were all sorry he didn't just have a normal stag; it might have been less boring – then again maybe not.

Joan and The Bore's relationship and marriage seemed clinical to say the least. Everything they did was planned with military precision. They never did one impulsive act. Well, none that they shared with the group anyway. For all I knew they could have been swinging from chandeliers and sporting the latest PVC outfits at every opportunity, but I couldn't imagine it. Come to think of it, they did have a very unusual light-fitting in the bedroom. Sort of trapeze-like thing hanging over the bed with two lights and a steel bar.

Joan would have been a good mother had she

been given the chance. She loved children. Anyone's but her own, she said. Kids liked her. She just accepted them as they were and never told them they were as big as a house or the image of their auntie somebody or other. She was comfortable knowing that she'd never have any.

Joan was always singing. She is a brilliant singer. She could sing anywhere and she should have been a professional singer, but according to Joan's boring husband, singing wasn't a profession. She was also a brilliant accountant, which he thought was a great profession. Funnily enough, he was an accountant too so that would account for why he thought it was so brilliant a profession.

Then all of a sudden, about eight years ago, Joan made a major life change. She announced that she was sick of minding other people's money and was going to start minding other people's bodies instead. She was going to be a beautician. Full marks to her: she got all her bits of paper and opened up a thriving little business. Her saving grace was that she hired a terrific fella to work for her.

Christopher was a godsend. He just walked into the beauty parlour one day and asked for a job. Joan, being the kind soul she is, felt sorry for him and gave him one. She sent him off to get training and she paid for it. He came back a new man with a magic pair of hands. His hands were like shovels, only they were spotlessly clean. Women queued up for weeks to let the bold Christopher and his shiny shovels massage them into shape. Christopher the Godsend was worth his fabulous weight in gold. He was a big burly handsome man with iron six-packs and steel biceps. He had short blonde hair and a designer beard. No one went to Christopher for a waxing. He waxed lyrical on every topic in a hypnotic way. He rubbed and pummelled and stroked and oiled, and that was only himself, as he psyched himself up for a full body-rub on some willing client. Maybe there'd be a Christopher for me at the party tonight. Joan's Christopher was completely out of bounds to the rest of us.

Then about seven years ago Joan made another life decision. She left the boring man that was her husband and moved in with Christopher. She had a permanent smile on her face ever since. She hadn't forgotten her initial training; in true accountant style she secured her best asset. The business and the marriage were thriving ever since.

Funnily enough, after Joan and The Bore split up, he met a lovely girl who taught in the local school. They fell madly in love. Ran off to the nearest registry office and got married. The Bore had his operation reversed and was now the father of six really boring children. Three sets of twins. All of them like peas in a pod. Joan and the Reformed Bore see each other all the time and they get on great now.

His kids call her Auntie Joan. She says he's the life and soul of the party and that being a bore must've been a phase he was going through. All he needed was the right woman to snap him out of it. Joan says she and the Bore are a great advertisement for how important it is to marry the right person. I think it's very magnanimous of Joan to admit this, but that's Joan for you. She is so matter of fact that sometimes you have to wonder is she human at all. I mean she's just so bloody nice. Mind you, if I had a Christopher on my arm morning, noon and night, especially night, I guess I'd be very nice too.

I wondered was my cellulite gone yet. I pulled one of my legs out of the water and wondered would I get away without shaving. There was a crop of hair around my shin. Like a little line of freshly sown grass. Not long enough to be lying flat, but there all the same. I did a quick razor job on them and did the same under my oxter. I'd be a hair-free zone tonight.

"Ma, are you ever coming out of there?"

"Yeah, I'm all done now. Be out in a minute."

"Well, hurry up, will ye?"

I dried myself off and rubbed lots of nice-smelling body lotion all over my bits. I noticed no change in the orange peel. I made a mental note to tell Tilda the stuff was totally useless. She did say something about having to use it for a few weeks before you'd notice a difference, but if it ain't instant I don't want

217

it. I was always trying new things. I had all the latest products. I had bottles of different types of stuff for everything you could imagine. You had to use each of them over a course of weeks. All of them had a capful missing from each of the bright coloured bottles. Every time I treated myself to some really expensive treatment or other I swore that I would pamper myself every night for the rest of my life with all the potions and lotions. But then I'd forget my promise to myself.

I never forgot to put the bin out or make the dinner. I never forgot to get up in the morning and shower. I never forgot to iron and wash the clothes that are constantly housed in the huge linen basket, clothes vomiting out at me every time I go to do the washing. We have a bottomless linen basket that Eve and Becca attend to the filling of, and I attend to the never-ending job of emptying. I never forget to try to empty it. It was now one of my greatest ambitions to finally empty it and have it empty for even one day. I never forgot my ambition. I always forgot my promises to pamper myself.

I tried on everything in my wardrobe. The green skirt with the matching top was too frumpy. The red dress was too racy. The black suit too sombre. The blue sexy short skirt and strappy top was perfect. The matching strappy sandals were even more perfect. Blue was Graham's favourite colour on me. As I did a quick twirl in front of the mirror I thought that maybe he was right. It was the only thing he was ever right about.

I spiked up my hair and did the full make-up routine on my face. Jesus, I looked great. Becca and Eve came into the bedroom. All young and fresh and fabulous. Jesus, I looked old.

"Right, remember," I said, "no drinking too much. We don't want to make a bloody show of ourselves meeting these people. So how do I look for an aul' one?"

"You look great."

"Terrific, Ma. Oh, I feel sick at the thought of meeting Hugh's mam. Do I look OK? I don't look like a tart in this skirt, do I?"

"You look brill."

"You both look stunning. Now come on. Our carriage awaits and my Prince will wonder where I am if I'm late. I have a good feeling about tonight, girls. This might be the night."

"Oh, no!" Eve shouted.

"Well, thanks a bunch! I think this might be the night and that's all that matters."

I couldn't believe that anyone in his or her right mind could think tonight would not be my night, considering the effort I had put in and how well I was looking. I knew I was dressed to kill because my feet were killing me already in the strappy sandals. One strap too many across the toes and a strap too little around the ankle, I was thinking. When a woman dresses to kill it's always her feet that start killing her first.

"No, Ma, it probably is your night. It sure won't be mine. I've just remembered that I never got Hugh's mother a present. What am I going to do? I can't go to a party with one hand as long as the other. The three of us can't march in there like begging asses. We'll have to stop and get her something en route."

"We can't stop now – there'll be nowhere open." Becca looked at her watch.

"Well, then, I'm not going." Eve was determined.

"Well, if you don't go, we can't go. We can hardly go in and say we came without you and without a gift." Becca started giggling. Giggling at this point was a mistake.

"Go on – have a good laugh at my expense, why don't you?" Eve was getting in a right bake. She'd have a face on her as long as a pelican's beak if I didn't do something.

I ran up the stairs and searched in my drawer. It's my miscellaneous drawer. Every drawer in my house houses miscellaneous items. I threw out the nail files, nail varnish, notebooks, biros, photographs, and bills. I pulled out a couple of boxes of tights and a small little book called *The Wonders of Good Sex*. I put that on the bed promising to myself to have a good read of it later on. I had bought it in a book sale and

I wasn't sure if it was second-hand or not. I hoped whoever had it before I bought it got rid of it because it had become superfluous to their requirements, rather than because they would never have a need for it. One of the wonders was to get to know every inch of your lover and let him get to know every inch of you. Some of this was easy; I could do the getting to know his inches and let's hope it was a good bit more than one inch I'd have to get to know. I was finding the bit where the lover gets to know every inch of me, inch by inch, a big stumbling-block. There were a lot of inches to me and I always pretended to have less inches than I actually have, so I really didn't want him getting to know exactly how many inches I had at all. I was betting a man wrote the *The Wonders*.

At last I found what I was searching for. No, not the lover. That would have been too easy and nothing in my life is easy. There was no lover lurking in my drawers, wooden or cotton – drawers not lover. I ran down the stairs. Becca and Eve were sitting in silence in the front room. Becca was lounging on the leather sofa with her feet and her sharp little stiletto heels dangerously flung over the arm of the soft leather. I stopped dead in my tracks. Any sudden movement and the couch was a goner. Open couch surgery. Eve was sitting on a matching chair. At least her feet were where they should be, on the floor. She had her head in her hands. The good news was that it was still attached to her body and she hadn't done herself any mortal damage, but she was in a right mood I could see.

"Becca, get your feet off the bloody couch! I worked hard to get it. Blood, sweat and tears went into it."

"I knew it smelt funny," she said as she swung her long legs around onto the floor. "Well, are we going? Or are we just going to sit here bolt upright and watch Eve as she gets further and further into a Right Royal Puss-face."

"Ta – da!" I said as I produced a candle in a lovely holder from behind my back. There was a small card attached to it that looked like a little flag announcing that I was surrendering.

Eve jumped up. She was delighted with the gift. I even thought I saw a glimmer of a smile.

"Oh, I remember this." The glimmer disappeared.

"Jesus, isn't that the candle The Git sent you last year?" Becca said in disbelief.

"Yeah. It is. Look, I hate it. It's been lying in the drawer upstairs for ages. We could wrap it up nicely and give it to Hugh's mom. What do you think, Eve?"

"Well, I suppose."

"It's perfect." Becca was on my side. She badly wanted to go to this party. She wanted to see if Charlie was at the party and, if he was, she wanted him to see what he was missing. How he had the chance to be with her for the rest of his life and he had blown it. She had spent ages getting ready and she really looked stunning and, if he was a man at all, he'd be kicking himself at what he had let go. I was hoping he'd be kicking himself right between the legs. Save me the bother of doing it. But I had to admit I was hoping to bump into him accidentally on purpose tonight and give him Dixie. So I was hoping he'd be there too. I was nearly looking forward to the confrontation. I hadn't had a confrontation with anyone for ages.

Eve found some wrapping-paper left over from Christmas. It was silver so it looked all right and if you didn't look very closely you couldn't see the little bunches of holly all over it.

Becca entertained herself by reading out loud the little card we had taken off and thrown on the coffee table.

Happy Birthday, Kelly.
I'm sorry I forgot your birthday for
all the other years.
I hope this makes up for it.
Have a lovely birthday.
Regards, Graham.

Ps. I've met a woman and we were wondering
how you'd feel about agreeing to a divorce.
Think about it and let me know, will you?

"The feckin' cheek of him all the same." Becca threw the card away again as if it was burning her hand. "Imagine him sending you a present out of the blue like that on your birthday. He's got some balls all the same. He never bothered his arse with Eve's or my birthday. When I think of him my blood boils."

"Yeah, but *we* couldn't give him a divorce, now could we?" said Eve. "He only sent that to Ma to soften her up. As if it would. Anyway, it doesn't bother me any more. I don't want anything off him."

"It'd take more than a lousy candle to soften me up. But there was no point in not agreeing to the divorce. I wanted it sorted out properly too. I'm glad I did agree. But he should acknowledge your birthdays. It's wrong of him not to. He should be more of a man. Imagine it all the same, the nerve of the man, bringing me a birthday present and asking for a divorce on the same day. Cut my head and give me a bandage, why don't you? I should have flung the bloody thing back at him. At least it'll come in handy tonight. I hope she likes candles. She'll never know where we got it."

"OK then, are we ready now?" Becca looked at her watch again. "I don't want to miss anything." Like Charlie. I was hoping she wouldn't succumb to his charms and go back with him. He'd been upset when she had finished with him and he had rung back several times begging her to go back with him again. But fair play to her, she stuck to her guns.

"Yeah, we're right now. Just let me find my keys and we're off."

"Ah, Ma. Don't tell me you've lost the keys again."

"No, I didn't lose them, I just misplaced them. I'll find them in a minute."

I had made a hobby out of losing my keys. I had had a car for about ten years and still couldn't cope with the keys and where to put them.

"Here they are." Becca came down the stairs. "You left them on your bed." She had a wide grin on her face and was holding my keys high above her head, waving them from side to side.

"Just beside this." She held up the sex book I had left on the bed for later above her head and started flicking through it.

"Givvus a look!" Eve was grabbing it from her.

"How come you never gave us this to read? So this is what your little reading group gets up to, is it? Well, now we know why you're all so enthusiastic about it."

"Give me that book, Becca. I have no idea where it came from. I put it on the bed to throw out." I grabbed it from her and opened the hall door in a sweeping gesture. I stamped over to the bin and threw the book in, making a mental note to get it later. When I turned around I could see from the look on my two daughters' faces that they were making the same mental note. It would be a matter of whoever was quick enough and desperate enough to get there first later on. I knew it would be me.

Today's List

To do

1. *c/fwd man/cabinet.*
2. *Ring Phil.*
3. *Get book out of bin, read it, learn it off by heart and hide it.*
4. *Have a good time at the party.*
5. *Tell Tilda the cellulite stuff is useless.*
6. *Find permanent home for keys.*

Not to do

1. *Don't make a show of myself at the party.*
2. *Don't leave sex books lying around the place.*

CHAPTER ELEVEN

The house was magnificent. There was a wide curved driveway up to the door and the garden was a pleasure of colour and smells. It made you wish they'd take their time to open the heavy timber door with stained-glass panels that were works of art and kaleidoscopes of colour. But they didn't take long at all to answer. At least Hugh didn't. He was dying to see Eve and had obviously been watching out for her. He was smiling from ear to ear.

"Does he never stop grinning?" Becca whispered at Eve who was grinning so much herself that her ears must've popped or else she was just ignoring her sister.

Hugh led the way through the spacious hall. I kept my bag close to my body, not for fear of pickpockets but for fear I would knock over one of the delicate antiques that were precariously balanced on tiny tables.

My head was on a swivel trying to take it all in. A set of glass double doors opened up into a bright cheerful sitting-room. Dripping in good taste. The walls were painted white and were covered in exquisite paintings. Now my jaw was wide open and I couldn't close it. My head was still swivelling. I had never seen so many magnificent things all together under the one roof in my life. My feet sank into the carpet and it was an effort for me to walk as the heels of my stiletto sandals were stabbing into the carpet with every step I took. Anchoring me to the last spot.

Hugh led us through another set of doors out into a big conservatory. It was a real treat. It sat like a huge birdcage attached onto the house. All rounded edges and ornate ironwork. Along one stretch of the glass wall there were a variety of little glass nooks and crannies. Parts of the glass jutted out in little V shapes. It left little indents in the glass just deep enough to hold beautiful pieces of cut coloured glass. A vase. A bowl. Glasses of every shape and form for every drink imaginable. There was a light shining up from the floor, which caught the coloured glass and created a rainbow-like effect all over the room. I bent a bit as I moved along the wall to see where exactly the light was coming from. There were three of them. Three lights fitted into three large glass balls. Big bright balls that rested on the floor. I was gobsmacked at them.

"Look, Becca!" I whispered. "The balls, the balls!" I was pointing, like a lunatic at the lights.

"For God's sake, Ma, you're making a show of us. Stop swivelling your head, close your mouth and stand up straight. You can do your Quasimodo impersonation later on when everyone has had a few drinks. It's far too early in the night for it now."

"But I –"

"Will you stop? Here, have a drink."

Waiters and waitresses were walking around in uniforms offering me free drink. Forcing it upon me. It would have been rude to refuse. There was a punch that was particularly nice.

"Be careful with that punch, Ma, it's lethal," Becca warned me and added under her breath, "This place gives me the creeps. Nothing is worn out. It's all so clean. I'm afraid to breathe out without wearing a mask in case I damage anything. Bet you won't see Eve light up a cigarette in this place." She disappeared off to mingle and suss the place out. I think she was looking around the place for Charlie. I was keeping an eye out for him myself. I straightened up and tried to look as though this type of surrounding was the norm for me.

Someone opened the double doors out onto the patio area. Masses of tubs filled with masses of colourful flowers filled the timber decking. I imagined they were fake – after all, this was February. It was cold. The breeze blew a wonderful perfume into the room from the flowers, proving that they were real. It also blew at the glass wind-chimes that were hanging from the ceiling in the conservatory. They moved and glistened and twirled and made a gentle sound. I wondered were we all being hypnotised. Maybe I was at some weird party where we'd all end up handing over all our worldly possessions. They wouldn't be so lucky with me on the possessions side as they'd be with some of the other guests. They were all dripping in diamonds. One or two of them had chandeliers around their necks. I was a bit disappointed to see that there were very few men on their own. Most of them were with one or other of the chandelier-bearers.

The breeze was getting a bit nippy and I wished they'd shut the doors over, but it was hardly my place to shout out remarks about the draught nearly giving me frostbite. Not to mention the danger to male brass monkeys. I was aware that my nipples were starting to show through my top. Then to my complete mortification I nearly took some poor innocent man's eye out. Not with my nipples, I hasten to add, but with the arm of my cardigan as I flung it around over my shoulders. The poor man put his hand up to his eye immediately, but not before I saw the tears ooze out if it.

"I'm so sorry," I said. "Here, let me take a look at it."

"No. No. I'm fine, thanks. I'll be all right in a minute." He was a real gentleman. He took out a spotlessly clean handkerchief from his pocket and I nearly got sick when I saw the colour of his eye. He had the most amazing bluey-green eyes I had ever seen. Aquamarine. I'd say that when the red bloodshot bit wasn't there they were even nicer. He was gorgeous. He wasn't a bit aware he was gorgeous which made him even more gorgeous. He had dark black hair with streaks of white, which made him very distinguished. But the bit that really captured my heart, the bit that always gets to me was the boyish look. Lovely laughter lines around his eyes. Tom Cruise, Sean Connery, Brad Pitt all have it. It's the boyish charm. Well, this guy had it in bucket-loads. All in all, he fitted my idea of my Prince perfectly – well, not exactly perfectly, but who wants a stereotypical Prince anyway?

"Let me hold that for you," I said and I put my hand to the hankie. I was wondering should I tell him that I thought it was destiny that we met. Should I tell him I'd been looking for him all my life? I held the hankie gently to the sore eye and tried to look lovingly and longingly into the one that wasn't bloodshot. He was pulling at the hankie. He moved it just that little bit too quickly and my nail poked him in the good eye. He moaned a bit, but at least had the good manners not to start ranting and raving the way another man would have done. I was really getting to like this guy.

Just then I noticed that my nail was missing. It was a false nail so I wasn't bleeding all over the place, which was something to be very grateful for. I wasn't used to wearing false nails, but I had broken a nail and the girls said it looked ugly and to put on a false one. So I took their advice (have I learned nothing?) and wore one. However, I was very upset because we had run out of the usual nail glue and I had used super-glue. It had promised to stick anything to anything and indeed I knew it worked because the cup of tea I was drinking when I was doing the nail job was now stuck fast to my bedside locker. I had been wondering whether I should smash the cup or just wash the dregs out and use it as a pencil-holder. Then again what need would I have for a cupful of pencils beside my bed? So how come the super-glue didn't work on my nails?

And now there was another problem. The other problem was that I couldn't see the nail anywhere.

"Excuse me. I wonder . . . do you think . . . might my nail still be stuck in your eyeball?"

Well, it was very important to establish it now. If his eye had been nailed and the offending nail was still protruding from his ball, eyeball that is, then he'd never be able to sleep again. It would be essential to get him to a hospital. We would have to go off together in a car to the hospital, just the two of us. It would be up to me to give him lots of tender, loving, care while he made a full recovery.

"My eye is fine. In fact, both my eyes are fine. Just leave me and my eyes alone. I can manage, thank you. Excuse me but I am going now. I am going to the very furthest end of the room."

He was looking at me, but I could see he wasn't focusing. Both his eyes were really red now and tears were streaming from both of them. It was a mark of how handsome he was that the tears didn't put me off. I got the hint. If you could call it a hint. It was too blunt to be a hint. It was obvious he wanted me to join him at the furthest end of the room. Why else would he have mentioned it? He was being such a gentleman about his sore eyes too. Pretending he could manage on his own. I'd give him just a minute and then I'd follow him. I watched his bum all the way up the room. He had a great bum. I was glad he was going to the furthest end of the room. He put his hands out gently against the wall and felt his way along it. He was a bit unbalanced.

"Hi." A stunning-looking woman put her hand out to shake mine. She was so familiar to me. Her hair was very, very short and very, very black.

"I think I've seen you around the village," I said. "Isn't this the most amazing house you've ever seen?

"Do you like it?"

"Well, I don't know if I like it exactly. I'm not sure if 'like' is the exact word I'd use. I'm still trying to decide if I like any of it or if I think the whole lot of it is just that little bit too showy-off for me, if you know what I mean. They must be loaded. I think she's filthy rich – well, so I hear anyway. I never saw the like of it. It should be opened to the public. Mind you, there's a breeze coming in off the patio that would skin a rhino, but I suppose they want to leave the doors open to show off the patio. Not to miss the opportunity for showing everything off. Don't you agree? Isn't it a bit OTT all the same? A touch of the nouveau riche, if you ask me."

"What? Are you joking me?"

"Well, I mean look at the bloody lights stuck in balls over there." I took a fit of laughing as I continued. "All the same, I could stay here all night just looking. I'd love to see the upstairs, wouldn't you? I'm going to try to sneak up in a while when nobody's watching."

"I – I – !"

"Sorry, sorry, I know I'm going on a bit, but you don't see museums like this every day of the week, do you? Do you know the birthday girl then? I don't know her at all. I'm dying to meet her. If she's anything like her house I should be able to spot her easily enough. She'll be strutting her stuff up and down the room, dressed up like an elaborate turkey no doubt. Do you know I really do know your face

234

from somewhere? We've probably bumped into each other at the supermarket."

"I don't think so. I think I'd remember you," she answered. "Well, dear, I hope my strutting doesn't disappoint you. I never thought of myself as a turkey before, never mind an elaborate one. And actually now that you ask, I get to see this museum every day. It's my home! As for knowing the birthday girl – well, I know her very well indeed! She is me or I or whatever the case may be. She and I are one and the same! Did you get a drink or two or three? I'm sure you did! Now what is it you're drinking? Bloody Mary or what?"

Oh my God! I was desperately looking for a hole to bury myself in. Any hole would have done. But in this birdcage there was none. Not even a small one. Is everywhere being built perfectly these days?

"I eh, well eh, so eh, eh eh." I really didn't know what to say to retrieve the situation. This would have been the best time for my Prince to come charging down the room, with his bleedin' aquamarine eyes, mounted on his white steed (not just his eyes all of him) and whisk me up into the saddle and carry me off into the sunset or anywhere for that matter – even back to my house would do. Whatever else I can say about my Prince his timing was really lousy; there was no sign of him.

"Hi again, Gwen!" It was Eve. "I see you've met my mother. Mam, Gwen is Hugh's mother."

Where was my bleedin' Prince?

Eve was beaming from ear to ear. She didn't know that the smile was about to be wiped off her beautiful beaming face.

"Your mother!" Gwen was flummoxed.

"Yes," beamed Eve.

"Yes. Gwen and I have met, so to speak."

"Yes. Your mother and I have met, so to speak."

Gwen and I spoke in unison. But I spoke in a whisper in unison. Gwen was shouting in unison.

I was hoping Gwen wouldn't tell Eve that I had made a complete ass of myself. If she told Eve the full story Eve would never, ever speak to me again. I know it was a bit silly of me to expect this woman to take sides with me and come to my assistance. But we mothers stick together at times like this and I knew Gwen wouldn't bury me. It was an unwritten rule we mothers had, worldwide, to back each other up in all these sticky situations. Gwen had class and she could see I was in a very, very sticky situation. She'd do the decent thing and say nothing. I straightened up and smiled confidently.

"Yes, Eve. She wants a tour of this turkey's museum even if it is a bit OTT, so if yourself and Hugh aren't doing much later on perhaps you could give her the guided tour bit and let her open a few drawers and presses along the way."

So Gwen betrayed me. She betrayed mothers

everywhere. She let me and her breed down badly and with not a second thought. She was no friend of mine. Now that I looked around I could see the place for what it really was. Now that I knew she wasn't a nice person, I could see that the place was a bit tacky. Very tacky, to be honest.

"What the hell did you say to her?" Eve scowled as Gwen went off to attend to some of the 'lovely' people who were coming in.

"I said nothing. To be honest, Eve, she's a bit uppity, don't you think? I think she fancies herself as one of the young and beautiful set, only she has lost all two of the qualifications necessary for entry into the set. She's not young and beauty is something she has tried to buy." I was a bit chuffed with myself for summing this woman up so quickly.

I glanced around the room and still saw no sign of my Prince coming back to me. I was hoping he wasn't getting fed up waiting for me.

"I have to give her the present. It's still in my bag." Eve was worried Gwen would think that we only came armed with insults and no gifts. I felt like getting the candle and shoving it. It would keep the poker up her ass company.

"Give it to her in a while. Where's Becca?"

"She's over there giving it loads to Hugh's brother. He's nice actually. I hope they get on well."

"At least one of us is doing well." I was very

despondent. The night was turning into a complete mess and I wanted to go home and ring Phil and tell him all about it. I couldn't even do that.

Gwen passed by again in her designer dress. All sequins and no back. Black, of course. The dress and her back. Fake tan I'd say. She was enjoying being the birthday girl.

"Gwen!" Eve called out to her.

Gwen turned and came over. No doubt expecting an apology or something of the sort.

"Your tan is terrific. The weather in the Bahamas must've been wonderful. Here's a little gift we got you. Happy birthday." Eve leaned over and gave the woman a kiss on the cheek. Judas. I was disgusted with her. She was lick-arsing big-time. And what was with the tan? Was no one wearing fake tan these days only me?

Gwen took the gift and looked a bit funnily at the wrapping paper. I think she knew it was re-cycled Christmas stuff – but what the hell difference did it make? It was going in a bin anyway. Talk about picky! She took out the candle and holder and for a minute I thought her face dropped. In fact, I thought it dropped so much it would hit the floor. Then she made a great recovery.

"It's beautiful. Thank you very much, Eve and eh – ?" She glared at me.

"Kelly, Kelly, my name is Kelly," I said.

"Kelly, Kelly, your name is Kelly?" Gwen said as if she didn't believe me. Then I noticed it. The vein.

"Kelly? Kelly?" a man said.

I looked up.

"Graham? Graham?" I said.

"The Git? I mean Dad?" Eve said.

"Eve, this is Lover Boy – eh sorry, I mean Graham." Hugh, who had just arrived on the scene, started doing introductions.

"Graham, my father?" gasped Becca who was standing behind him.

"Your father?" gasped Hugh's brother, who was holding Becca's hand.

"Kelly? Rebecca? Evelyn?" gasped Graham The Git.

I felt like fainting or at the very least going into my Quasimodo routine again and being carted away to the nearest bell-tower for a quiet cup of tea with Esmerelda. My bloody Prince will have a lot to answer for when I get my hands on him, I thought. He should be here now to save me again. That was twice that night he'd let me down badly. I know I had only just met him, but it was still a little bit too early in the relationship for him to be letting me down so much.

"Well, isn't this very nice? Very nice indeed," I said through clenched teeth.

No one else spoke. As usual, it was left to me to

fill the void. I am a great void-filler. I can always be relied upon to think of something wonderful and witty to fill any void. The bigger the void, the better I fill it. But sometimes I use crap to fill the void.

"I should have known this tacky kip was yours, Git," was all the crap I could think of to fill the void. It didn't work.

Still no one spoke. There was just a very sharp intake of breath. In fact, I think it only made the void bigger. Everyone was standing around looking at everyone else. I looked at Graham and The Floozy. Their veins were throbbing at a terrific rate. The Floozy looked directly at me. She looked different to when I'd seen her outside the court. She was obviously going to a different hairdresser. Her hair was completely different. I hate to admit it, but it was beautiful. I made a mental note that when everything calmed down I'd ask her where she got it done.

Then I heard whispering as everyone tried to fill the void by explaining to everyone who everyone was.

"He's my mum's lover."

"He's my dad."

"She's my mother."

"She's my dad's floozy."

"My dad will be your stepdad when they get married."

"Jesus, it's like that song – 'I am my own grandpa'."

"Are we related?"

"Jesus Christ." Eve shouted and all heads turned and stared at her. She was oblivious to her audience. "I slept with a bloke who's going to be my stepbrother!"

Everyone froze. There was a stunned silence. A void. I filled it.

You what?" I said. "You slept with this tart's son? Have you no dignity? Letting me down like that! Have you not got the brains you were born with?"

"It's OK, Eve," Becca interjected. "Even if he ends up being your stepbrother he won't be a blood relation. It's fine. You can sleep with him whenever you want."

Becca was still holding tight to Hugh's brother's hand and she was making sure everyone knew it was OK. She looked like she enjoyed holding his hand. I wondered what his name was?

"Hi, I'm Kelly, what's your name?" I asked. He was completely distracting me from tackling Becca on the 'sleep whenever' remark.

"I'm Raymond. Ray for short."

"A little ray of sunshine," Becca added with a sickly smile on her face. She was recovering very nicely from the Charlie heartache.

"I think I'm going to be sick," Eve said. So she was. She got sick all over the perfect Persian rug. I was delighted. It gave us a great excuse to leave.

241

"I'd better get her home," I said pushing her as hard as I could towards the door.

"No, I won't hear of it!" said Gwen. "Let her have a lie-down upstairs. We can't have her going home like this. I'll get her a drink of water and a cool cloth for her head. Don't worry about the floor – it's only a carpet, it can be cleaned. It's Evelyn we have to think about now." Gwen appeared to be human after all.

"Thanks. She prefers to be called Eve," I said, grudgingly acknowledging her kindness.

"Graham, are you ever going to speak again?" Gwen asked a bit sharply. "I didn't invite them. Hugh did. I hadn't a clue," she added. Then went on: "Here, put that candle down. Why are you holding on to it?"

"Isn't this the one we . . ."

"Well done! You are capable of speaking. Yes, dear, it's the same one. Isn't it lovely? I told you when we bought it to sweeten Kelly up that it was lovely. They gave it to me for my birthday tonight."

She whisked past me. She and Eve were arm in arm. The Floozy was bringing Eve off somewhere. No doubt to ask her a lot of questions about me. I tried to run out after them, but the heels of my shoes were a terrible handicap.

"This is a nightmare." I spoke out loud even though I thought I was only thinking it.

"Another one?" My Prince with the bloodshot eyes was at my side again. See, I knew he fancied the knickers off me.

"Hi again," he said and stood back a little. "It'll all be all right, don't worry."

Ah, such kindness!

"I hear your daughter got sick."

Ah, such a wonderful man!

"Hardly worth calling it a nightmare." He rubbed his eyes. "Worse things have happened!"

Ah, my Prince, my Prince!

"Well, come on, I'd better take a look at her. My name is David by the way. I'm a doctor. Gwen asked me to look in on Eve."

He held his hand out. I took it and held it. He had the good manners to try to pull it away again. I had the good grace to keep holding onto it. I knew that was what he really wanted me to do.

"Oh, thank you. She got a bit of a shock. She usually vomits when she gets a shock or excited. I'm the same myself." I noticed him jump backwards when I said this, but I think he was just being nice and letting me go up the stairs first. I kept a tight grip of his hand.

"Nervous tummy, I suppose. I have a touch of one myself. So do you have a name then?"

"Kelly – Kelly is my name."

"OK, Kelly, let's go and take a look at your

daughter." Again being the gentleman he tried to pull his hand away. I smiled at him, knowingly, gave it a little squeeze and held on tight.

And we went up the stairs hand in hand. We found the bedroom Gwen had put Eve in. It was all frills and flounces. More frills on the flounces and flounces on the frills. Yellow. Everything in the room was yellow. Except the plush carpet. That was midnight blue. I looked at poor Eve lying on the yellow bed. She would never recover in a room like this. It was too clean. She'd only feel more and more sick. David walked over to the window, pulled open the flouncy curtains and opened the window. A gentle breeze wafted in. We were still hand in hand.

He turned and looked at me and he paused and sighed a very deep sigh. He looked straight at me. Honest, in the middle of all the puff-white and lemon see-through material draped around the room, I heard a little *"Ting!"* at my heart strings. I knew he was feeling the same.

"I need my hand back if I'm to attend to your daughter."

I understood. I let go and he shook his hand and spread the fingers open and then closed a few times.

I could tell he really wanted me because he started to take off his jacket and roll up his spotless white shirt-sleeves. Now why else would he do that unless he was going to make a wonderfully exciting pass at me? *"Some day my Prince will come!"* rang out through the whole house or maybe that was just in my head. It was all so confusing and David the Prince kept looking straight at me which was only making matters worse. Much worse.

I moved across the room and put my cardigan over a chair. He started to walk towards me. I saw him and I stood perfectly still. I closed my eyes and waited for him to engulf me in his arms and take me for all I was worth. So what if Eve was lying on the bed not able to make her mind up between vomiting and fainting? She'd understand. I had to carpe diem and if I didn't carpe it now the diem would be gone forever. Carpe diem, seize the day. I had drilled it into my two girls often enough. I was certain Eve would want me to carpe the man.

I kept my eyes closed. Opened my mouth slightly and held my arms out towards him. I felt something brush against my arm. I opened my eyes a tiny squinty bit. I could see him sitting on the edge of the big yellow four-poster bed. I sat beside him. I was sure that's what he wanted. He started talking to Eve. Asking her how she felt and if she still felt like vomiting. Eve was fine now and kept saying she wanted to leave. She pushed him away as he tried to put his hand on her forehead. She didn't know he was my Prince.

"Ma, get me the hell out of here, will you? It's the worst night of my life! Where the fuck is Hugh?"

She sat up bolt upright and glared at my Prince. "Who the hell are you and why have you got tomatoes stuck in your eyes?" she shouted.

"There is no need to talk to my Prin – David like that. He hurt his eyes and he is trying to make sure you are all right."

"Well, get him off me, will you? Ma, come on, we're going."

With that she leapt up out of the bed and was off down the stairs, leaving me and David sitting open-mouthed on the bed. I turned to him.

"Well you seem to have done the trick," I said smiling. "Thank you so much, Prince or eh – should I say David?" I leant forward to thank him. Had it not been for the punch I would have shook his hand and said a gentle thankyou. But there was the punch factor so I leaned over and gave him a full-on snog. Well, I was very, very grateful to him. It was wonderful, but I think he was surprised by it. Maybe it was too soon for a full-on snog. Maybe a peck would have been more appropriate for a thankyou, but time was of the essence and I was having a great time and time and tide and all that waiting for no man. I was glad I did what I did when I did. If he was too much of a wimp not to throw me down on the bed and have his wicked way with me then that was his problem, not mine. He was enjoying the snog though, I could tell.

"*Jesus, Kelly, what are you doing with Gwen's brother? For God's sake, put the man down!*" Graham The Git was bellowing in the doorway. He was a great bellower, was Graham.

"Get off me, who are you? Are you mad?" My Prince betrayed me.

"Oh, I'm so sorry," I said to him. "I thought you were someone else. For a moment I thought you had a backbone. I see now I was only mistaken. I see now you're only another frog. Thanks all the same. Bye, Graham, and say bye to Gwen for me will you? Talk to those two stepsons-to-be of yours, will you, and tell them to leave my daughters alone."

I high-tailed it out of the house and was relieved to see Eve and Becca standing at the door of the car. I was less relieved to see that they were being kissed goodnight by Hugh and Ray. Sometimes there is nothing a mother can do but get into the car and blow the horn, loudly. So, that's exactly what I did. Eve drove. She was the only one who wasn't punchdrunk.

Today's List

To do
1. *Cabinet.*
2. *Be careful who I snog no matter how desperate I am for a snog.*

3. Find out in future exactly whose party I'm going to before I go – less stressful.
4. Write to superglue and complain.
5. Buy proper nailglue.
6. Buy a couple of glass balls and see can I make lights out of them.

Not to do

1. Don't stick nail with superglue ever again.
2. Don't wear pointy heels on good carpet.
3. Don't poke anyone in the eye ever again.
4. Don't ever not admire anyone's house until you know whose house it is.
5. Never speak to The Floozy again – no matter how nice I think she was to Eve – there is a danger I might like her.
6. Don't ever wear sandles that are too tight for me again – my poor toes are red raw.

To ignore

1. The Floozy.
2. The fact that I am a prat.
3. The row of cherry tomatoes that are now what were once my toes.

CHAPTER TWELVE

No one spoke. No one even grunted or moaned. We were all deep in our own thoughts. Some of our thoughts were more sobering than others. Becca was in love again. Eve was still feeling a little bit sick, but in love. I was beginning to feel very sick and very unloved. Eve's driving was making me feel sick. Everyone was making me feel unloved. Becca smashed the silence.

"I can't believe the show of us the two of you made of us tonight."

Eve and I sat in silence trying to work out what she had just said. "Eve, you walked us right into it. How in the name of God did you not know The Git lived with Hugh? Even someone as slow as you should have copped on to it. Then you pull your getting-sick stunt and leave me stuck with The Git and The Floozy. It was a nightmare. Only for Ray I'd have been fecked altogether. He came to my rescue like a true Prince on a white steed. The poor bastard! He talked about everything and anything except of course the touchy subject that you can't talk about in front of my family. The sensitive issues. Not sex. Not drugs. Not violence – oh, no – he steered away from the real sensitive issues like families, fathers, floozies and gits. But The Git wasn't happy with that. He kept interrupting him and asking me foolish questions: 'Rebecca, do you think your mother stabbed Gwen's brother in the eyes on purpose? Do you think Eve puked all over the good quality carpet on purpose? Did you all think it was a great joke coming to the party? Did you think there would be a huge big cake that all three of you could jump out of and shout 'surprise' or what? Has your mother lost her marbles? Is she mad? What posessed her?' Only for meeting Ray I'd say it was the worst night of my whole entire life. I hope the two of you had a great time having your little lie-down and leaving me to deal with all the mess."

Eve and I hung our heads in shame.

Then Eve spoke up. "Do you think for one minute that if I'd known Graham would be there that I'd have gone myself, let alone bring Ma?" she pleaded. "Hugh only ever called him Lover Boy so I didn't know my father and Lover Boy were one and the same and he only ever called his mother 'Ma' or 'Mum' or something like that. He never called her The Floozy so I didn't know his ma was The Floozy. I'm sorry. It's all my fault."

"Don't be ridiculous," I snapped. "It happened. Shit happens. We'll just have to try to forget about it. The three of us will make a pact. Right here. This very night. We will promise each other that we will keep well away from that whole family. We won't have anything to do with them ever again. Are we all agreed?"

"Agreed my ass!" said Becca. "I like Ray and I owe him big-time. He asked me to go out with him tomorrow night and I said yes."

"But, Ma, I love Hugh! I have to see him."

"Well, I can tell you this. I won't be seeing any of that lot again. The turkey's welcome to Graham. Graham is welcome to the turkey. As for the brother, the doctor chap, if I never see him again it'll be too soon."

"What about Hugh?"

"And Ray?"

"Well, I'll give them a chance and we'll see what they're like. I can't say fairer than that."

We all went back to the comfort of silence. My mind started to wander. Deep into a horrible place. It started to wonder what would happen if Graham did marry Gwen. He would be Ray and Hugh's stepdad. Then I started to wonder what would happen if either of my lovely daughters decided to marry one of The Git's stepsons. Or worse still if the two of them decided to marry both of The Git's stepsons. I was sure my girls would never do that to me. It would be just that little bit too cruel, even for them.

There had to be a law against it. I could sue them. I made a mental note to look it up. It was the one area of child-rearing that I wasn't au fait with. The legal aspect. I never before felt the need to sue my children for mental cruelty. But there was always a first time for everything. I mean there must be at least one law to help me in my hour of need. This was parent abuse. Plain and simple. If there was a law against parent abuse I must try to find out if there is a Statute of Limitations on it. My children had certainly abused me on more than one occasion. But this abuse would be a mega-infringement.

I would go so far as to say that this even beat the time when the neighbour from a few doors up brought my two lovely girls home. Pie-eyed drunk. My girls, not the neighbour. Steam coming out of every orifice. My neighbour, not my girls. He had found them in his garden. Crotch-deep in his pond trying to catch his fish at three in the morning. When the neighbour asked them exactly what they were doing they said:

252

"We're just catching a nice fish for our mam's dinner tomorrow. She hasn't a penny to her name and she'd love a nice bit of your tasty smoked cod. You have so many of them swimming around, one less won't make any difference to you."

With that, Eve held up her skirt and tried to catch a fish in it while Becca pushed her boot down as far into the water as it would go hoping the fish were thick and would surrender no problem at all. As luck would have it, she caught one.

"Wheeeee! I got one!" She was charmed.

"Look, look, me too! I got a smoked cod too!" There, lying flat on his side in Eve's skirt was a huge fish.

"Smoked cod? Are the pair of you mad? They're coi carp. They're Japanese. Put them back this minute, do you hear me? You get out of there now! They cost a fortune and you can't eat them. Get the hell out of there! Hey, I know you – you're the two lassies from a few doors up. Here, come on out! I better bring you home. You don't look as if you're capable of getting there under your own steam."

So the three of them trundled up the road to me. Becca was debilitated by the fact that she was only wearing one boot. Eve was debilitated by the fact that her skirt was wet and rubbing between her legs. The neighbour was just plain debilitated. He shook his head and tut-tutted as I opened the door. He wouldn't come in, he said. He felt safer out walking the streets in the middle of the night than sitting in our house having a cup of tea. I looked out past him into the street. There was a gang of kids with cans shouting and roaring and staggering along the road. Cars were skidding around corners. A police car was flashing its blue light and sounding its siren. He looked at it all and again he repeated that he felt safer on the street than in our house. Someone had been talking. Where else would he have got that idea from?

The latest humiliation in my life, the going out with The Floozy's sons, would far outweigh the fish or indeed any other previous humiliations. This time they were really rubbing my nose in it. It was a case of rubbing my nose in it to end all rubbings of noses in anything. They probably wouldn't even have the good grace to have a double wedding and have just one miserable day. I was probably going to have to suffer two miserable weddings where The Git as the Father of the Groom would sit beside me, the Mother of the Bride, and try to make polite conversation. Admiring my hat and the like. Imagine it. The little Git. My mind wouldn't even go there. Sometimes I am very proud of my own mind.

I had always imagined my girls would get married to wonderful, handsome, kind, thoughtful, rich men. I pictured flowers and lace and white veils and trimmings. I imagined myself looking like a twenty-year-old in a wonderful couture suit, size ten of course, and a terrific-looking designer hat perched on my head and a terrific-looking designer man perched on my arm. Well, not perched exactly, but arm in arm. Looked like another little dream was over.

We got home in no time and just grunted goodnight to each other and went into our separate rooms. I wanted to ring Phil. I didn't.

I slept late the next morning and then headed over to Joan's house where we were all supposed to meet for lunch. Phil was there. He was just getting out of his car. I parked mine beside his and he came over and opened the door to talk to me. I was delighted to see him. He had a huge bunch of freesias, which I assumed were for Joan. I was wrong. They were for me.

"How's it going, Kel?" he said as he handed them to me and put his arms around me. He only called me Kel when he was nervous. God love him, my heart went out to him.

"Shite," I replied and gave him a huge hug. "Thanks for the flowers. They're beautiful. I've missed you."

"Me too."

"Do you think we can go back to the way it was?" I asked.

"As if nothing happened? Sure we can."

I was hoping it would be exactly the way it was before sex got in the way. Much and all as I love sex, it does complicate everything, doesn't it? I mean a relationship has only two stages as far as I'm concerned: pre-sex where he does everything to get your knickers off and post-sex where he does nothing only get your knickers off. He forgets the niceties post-sex.

"Tell you what," Phil said. "Let's make a pact that if the two of us are still on our own when we get to be fifty-five that we'll shack up together while we're still young enough to enjoy each other. What do you think?"

"Wow, Phil, are you proposing to me?" I giggled. "If you are I think it's the best proposal I've had all evening. Not that they're beating down the doors to propose to me, you understand. Thanks, Phil. I think it's a great idea." I hugged him again with real affection. He was a man in a million and I wished I was in love with him. Isn't it a bugger all the same that here was this wonderful available man and I wasn't in love with him? I just loved him. Knowing my luck, I'd probably fall in love with a right bastard who'd treat me like shit. Someone who'd never think about me and send me flowers just for the hell of it like Phil did. Or buy me some little thing just because he knew I'd like it. Knowing my luck, I'd get some mediocre guy who'd buy me two presents a year – birthday and Christmas – and think he was doing great. But it was lovely to know that Phil was proof positive that there are some great men out there and all I had to do was find one. Easy. Right!

"Come on then and let's see what happening with the other two," he said.

Phil and I crunched our way up the gravel driveway and let ourselves in. Joan and Tilda and Gary were sitting down drinking. Joan was on the wine. Tilda was on the water and Gary was on the tit. He seemed to be enjoying his drink the best.

"Hi, everyone!"

"Hi. Any news?"

"Howerye?"

"Come on in. Sit down. Clotilda's filling me in on the latest Dan story."

"Has he not been in touch then?"

"Go on, girl, tell us."

"Well, he rang last night and said that he wasn't coming back for a while because he thought that was what I wanted. He asked if Gary and me were doing OK. Apparently, he's been offered a big contract and he thinks he's going to take it but he'll have to go to England for a few weeks if he takes it. I told him that he hadn't a clue what I wanted and to let me know what he decides. To be honest I hope he doesn't take it. I still love him. But he kept on saying he was trying to be the man I wanted him to be and he was letting me down. I haven't a clue what he's talking about, but do you think he could be having an affair?"

"Dan? Affair? No way. *No way!* The cheek of him! What is he up to?" I was horrified and annoyed with Dan.

"Funnily enough, I'm not sure how I feel. Numb, I suppose. Dan and me will have to talk about it face to face I think. I'm afraid to, though. I'm afraid in case I don't want to hear what he has to tell me about some bimbo or other. Now come on, let's stop talking about me. It's giving me the creeps. That's me sorted, now what about the rest of you?"

"Listen, whenever you want to talk, we'll all be here for you," I said.

"Well, I have a bit of news," Joan said. "Christopher and I are going on holiday. We booked a little villa in Spain. We're going for a month so if any of you want to come over to see us you'd be really welcome. We're going to look at buying a villa of our own over there."

"That's great, Joan," said Phil. "Things must be doing well in the beauty business. You can count me in for a week of sun any time." Phil was always enthusiastic about everything.

"If I can manage it, of course I'll come over too – even for a week," I said. "So come on then, all of you. Did you come up with any suggestions for me to meet the man of my dreams? Or have you just been dreaming of sunny climes with the man of your own dreams, Joan?"

"I'm sorry, Kelly. I had a mad day today. I had this lunatic of a client in for the full works today. She wanted a massage and anything else I could do for her. Seems it was her birthday yesterday and she had a party and her partner's ex turned up and made a holy show of herself. Even tried to get my client's brother into bed. She said it was like a circus. She was in an awful state altogether. I felt really sorry for her; she was at the end of her tether. Apparently, the ex called my client a turkey. Can you imagine it all the same? Would you let yourself down like that? I have to say I'd never do anything like that to the Bore and his new wife."

"I never called her a turkey. She took it up wrong."

"Don't tell me it was you!" Joan was horrified.

"Good enough for her, I say!" Phil was one terrific man.

"Well, was she a turkey?" Tilda asked.

"And how!"

We all laughed and I gave them the low-down on my night out.

"Well, Kelly, you'll have to meet someone new now. Even if for no other reason than to save yourself the humiliation of Graham walking up the aisle with you on one arm and Gwen on the other. All the same it's one way of cutting down on the number of invites."

Clotilda had tears in her eyes, which was either because Gary was sucking that little bit too hard or the fact that she was laughing at the thoughts of the potential fiasco that she could see was ahead of me.

"Now listen," she added when she stopped laughing. "I've got a great idea. I found a great way for you to meet someone and if you don't like it you can just tell me to butt out of it, but on the other hand you might think it's a brilliant idea. I think it's great. I love it when I get a good idea and this really is one. You might not think so, but then again . . ."

Clotilda was repeating herself. She always repeated herself when she was nervous or excited. She was all excited and wound up.

"Oh, please Clotilda, tell us! Will you go on, for pity sake! I'm listening."

"Well, you know the way I always keep in touch with my parents in France by e-mail? Well, when I go into the site there are loads of chat-rooms and loads of people talking to each other and they seem nice. I only ever went in once or twice out of curiosity, but you could give it a try. What do you think?"

"I never thought about it," I said. "I don't know if I'd like it. Isn't that where you're supposed to meet axe-murderers and the like? It'd be just my luck to have my Prince beating me over the head with the self same axe he used to cut his way through the overgrown weeds and brambles that surrounds me."

"Don't be ridiculous, Kelly – your garden is only a little bit out of condition. A quick mow of the grass would be enough to get it back to normal, no need for an axe. Anyway, they can't all be axe-murderers, now can they? I think it's a great idea." Joan was getting all businesslike. There is a danger when Joan gets too businesslike that she will re-arrange everything that is absolutely none of her business and all of yours.

"Well, there is no time like the present. Come on." She led us like lambs to the slaughter into her little office and her big computer. She clicked on the Internet symbol and then connect. Her password was verified and we were in. She clicked chat and lists and lists of rooms came up for us to go into. She scrolled down. I think Joan had done this before.

"OK so what do you fancy? Laughter Room. Music Room. Romance Room and hey look at this!" She tapped her very long, very well-polished bright-red nail at the screen right under the words 'The Intimate Room'.

"No way. Gimme a break, will you!" I laughed, but made a mental note to go in and have a look at it later in the privacy of my own home. I noticed the others were concentrating on it very hard too. I guessed there would be a lot of visitors into said room later on. Just then I spotted a room called 'No messin' just chattin'.

"Here, go in there!"

Joan clicked and a message came up for us to log on or register.

"We can't go in until we register." Joan scrolled and filled in all the boxes as she saw fit. Name, address and all the usual stuff.

"Here, you need a nickname. Come on, think of something."

"Madforit!" Phil laughed.

"Manmad," Clotilda offered.

"Thanks a lot. You're no help at all. I want a name that describes me. What about 'Dote'. I am an aul' dote after all."

"No – too ordinary," said Phil.

"Yeah, you want something that'll make them wonder what it means," said Tilda.

"'Sunny'."

"No, too boyish," said Phil.

"OK, let me make a list. Who's got a pen and paper?"

"God, Kelly!" said Joan, laughing. "There are some things you don't have to make a list for!"

Everyone laughed. I was a bit hurt. I made a mental note to make a list of all the things I don't need to make a list for.

"Just call out a few names and we'll pick the best."

"Right," I said a bit sharply. This was my life and if I wanted to make a list of names I bloody well would. After all, it was supposed to be my new name. If anyone was picking it, it was going to be me.

"OK then, if it's a Prince I want then I want to be treated like a Princess. So my new name will be Princess."

"It's not a new name – it's just a name you'll be known as in the site, silly."

I was hurt again.

"Well, I want Princess." I was getting a bit thick and I knew it. "What's wrong with Princess?"

"Well it's a bit prissy and childish, even a bit silly." Clotilda, with the very silly name, said.

"Well, we'll put in 'Princess' and see does it accept it or are there other Princesses in the site."

We all held our breath. The computer, bless its little microchips, accepted my name.

"Now a password." Joan was really into it now.

"Prince," I said emphatically. No one argued with me this time.

Joan hit another few buttons and we were in.

There were only five people in the room.

– Hi – someone called Beefy Boy said.

Joan typed quickly.

– Hi Beefy Boy. I'm new in here. What's happening? –

– Nothing much, Princess, where you from? –

– Ireland. Dublin to be exact. –

– No kiddin' me too. I'm from Ireland, Lough Carrig. Ever hear of it? Not many have. The others in here are from all over the world. I think they're chatting to each other in private rooms so it looks as if it's just you and me, baby. –

– Private rooms? –

– Yeah. If you click on a name you can go into private chat with that person. Want to try it? –

– Yeah. Let's give it a whirl. –

At the corner of the screen we saw Beefy Boy's name come up and when Joan clicked on it we got to talk to him and no one else could read what we were saying.

– So how old are you, Princess? –

– Late thirties – Joan lied – What about you? –

– Early forties –

–You come in here all the time then? –

– No. Only sometimes for a chat when I'm a bit fed up. You meet all sorts of different people in here. Some people think it's full of axe-murderers. – We all giggled.

– Imagine that. – Joan typed. Then she added. – Are you married or single? –

– Single. I was married, but we split up two months ago. I found her in bed with my best friend. –

– Wow! That's awful. What did you do? –

– I did what any decent man would do. I walked in the door and saw them at it hammer and tongs, closed the door quietly and went down and slashed the tyres of his brand new convertible Saab and then I cut a few holes in the roof for good measure. Nice proper circles, mind you. Made a nice pattern. Then I went back upstairs and told him to get the fuck out of my house. I told her to pack her bags and get the hell out after him. If I lay me hands on either of them –

At this point we were all glued to the screen. Joan had stopped typing.

– You still there, Princess? –

– Yeah, Beefy, I'm still here. That's just so terrible.

We didn't know if Joan thought that what the wife did was terrible or if what Beefy did was terrible. I was thinking they were both terrible.

– All water under the bridge now. So listen, Princess, what size are you anyway? –

– I'm about five seven. What size are you? –

– I'm a big boy. I meant what cup size do you take? –

We all looked at each other a bit perplexed.

"Tell him I like mugs not cups. Nobody uses cups nowadays, do they?"

– I like mugs myself – Joan typed.

– You that big then? Go on! –

"Oh, oh, girls, I think I know where he's going with this." Phil, being a man, was first to spot it.

"What?"

"What's he on about?"

– Is it DD? – Beefy Boy wanted to know.

"Oh, yeah, now I get it!" I said.

It finally dawned on all of us at the same time: Beefy Boy was into boobs and God knows what else.

"Do we want to continue with Beefy Boy?" Joan said

"No," we all said together.

"Beefy has one or two things to sort out methinks and I don't think he's Prince material."

– Hi, anyone in here? –

We all stared at the screen. A new bloke had come into the main chat-room. We couldn't believe our eyes. His name was Prince Charming!

– Princess? You in here or are you in a private chat? –

– Hey, Prince Charming. I was chatting to Beefy, but we've finished. Haven't we, Beefy? –

– Yeah, Princess. I have to go. Chat to you later maybe. –

– Well, Princess, how's it going? I never saw you in here before. You new? –

– Yeah. First time in here tonight. –

– You'll get the hang of it soon enough. I'm from Ireland, Dublin. I'm forty-one and at the moment I appear to be single. What about you? –

– Late thirties, single and Dublin. –

– So we could be neighbours then? –

– Yeah. –

– What you do when you're not in here, Princess? –

– Oh, I like to go walking and do all the usual stuff. I love reading and cooking and my favourite hobby is painting, landscapes mostly. –

"Christ, Joan, I don't love cooking and I don't know one end of a paintbrush from another except that one can poke the eye out of you. What are you saying?"

"Well, I can't tell Prince-bloody-Charming that your only hobbies at the moment are looking for a man and shopping, now can I?"

I could see Joan was getting carried away with the whole thing. She was inventing a new me. Phil and Clotilda were enjoying every minute of it. Clotilda was pouring Joan another glass of wine. This was all going to get out of hand and I knew it and could do nothing about it.

"Stop fussing, Kelly. It's perfectly normal to lie. We have to make you sound interesting."

– You paint? I'd love to be able to paint. I wouldn't know one end of a paintbrush from the other except that one end can give you a good poke in the eye. lol. –

– What's lol stand for? –

– Well, it can mean 'laugh out loud' as I meant it or it can mean 'lots of love'. Depends on who you're talking to. I don't do the love bit on the net though. –

– So, listen, when do we meet? lol lol lol lol –

"Jesus, Joan!" I was getting a bit nervous now. I couldn't believe what she was saying. This was all getting out of hand.

– Sorry. I don't usually agree to meet women I've only spoken to for five minutes. –

– Well then, I'll keep talking and when I've talked enough for you to agree to meet me, you just let me know. Right? –

– Lol. OK, OK. I surrender. I'll meet you. Anyway we seem destined to meet, don't we, given our nicknames? So if you fancy meeting in a very busy pub I'd really love to meet you. What do you think? I'd be as nervous as you by the way. I should confess here that you'd be the first woman I ever met from the net. I am not in the habit of coming in here and chatting up women like this. I hope you believe me. We could meet as friends to have a chat and a drink. If you like you could bring a friend if you felt it would be safer. –

"Just say thanks but no thanks, Joan," I pleaded.

– Thanks, Prince, that would be great. I'm not sure about the friend though. There are three of them and if I can't bring them all then I can't bring any of them. lol. –

– OK, Princess. Bring them all. So will we say tomorrow night? Eight o'clock in Reilly's Bar. Do you know it? It's in the new hotel on Font Street. Everyone knows it. –

– Yeah, I know it. Now how will I know you? –

– Yeah, that's a tricky one, isn't it? Well, I'll tell you what – I'll bring you a bunch of roses. I bet I'm the only man carrying a bunch of red roses. –

– Way to go, Prince. I like your style. I'll bring you a book. I'd say a painting only it'd be too big. lol. So you'll have to make do with a book. –

– It's a date then, Princess. I should tell you that I'm dying to see what a real live Princess looks like. –

– And you better be charming. Do you hear me, Prince? I have to go now. See you tomorrow night then. –

– C U then. Bye –

Joan hit the little x in the corner of the screen and he was gone.

"Joan, Joan, what have you done?" I was distraught. "That poor bastard will be walking around with a bloody bunch of red roses searching for the lady with the book all night. You're some bitch to do that to him. What did he do to you? That's the meanest thing I have ever seen."

I was aware that everyone was staring at me.

"Are you not going to go to meet him?" Clotilda said. "Because if you're not going, I bloody well am. He sounds like a really nice guy."

"Are you mad?"

"I think he sounds great too. In fact if I wasn't so happy with Christopher I'd give it a whirl myself," Joan agreed wholeheartedly with Clotilda.

We all turned and looked at Phil.

"Don't even look at me. I'm not the slightest bit interested in him, but if he has a sister, you could let me know."

"Well, I'm not going. Have you all lost the plot completely? Are you all prepared to stand by and lead me like a lamb to the slaughter to this guy? Do you want to get rid of me or what?"

"Ah, it's only a bit of fun. Sure we'll come with you and we'll all have mobile phones if anything happens. You'll be fine – sure it's a busy place, as he said himself."

"You will not all come with me! If I go at all, and, at this particular moment in time, I can tell you there is no way I am going to go, I will go alone."

"Great! I knew you'd go! Now what will you wear? Come in to me at about six and I'll do your make-up for you. I think your eyebrows could do with a pluck. Remember I did them lovely for you before? Have you ever considered wearing a darker foundation?" Joan was charmed with herself. Not alone had she set me up with a date but now she was going to pluck me, plume me, paint me and send me out to be hung, drawn and quartered. At least I'd be going in disguise.

Today's List

To do
1. *Man/unit*
2. *Check law on parent abuse.*
3. *Man must like bringing me little things like flowers and tapes etc.*
4. *Give the guy I'm meeting tonight every chance – go for it.*

Not to do
1. *Don't make a holy show of myself.*
2. *Don't let Joan organise my love life.*

CHAPTER THIRTEEN

Town was buzzing. The pubs were full. Everyone was having a good time. Couples were walking along hand in hand looking all lovey-dovey. Gazing into each other's eyes. Planning wonderful futures together. Other couples were marching along one in front of the other, their body language shouting volumes. A lover's tiff or in some cases the end of a wonderful affair. The place was humming.

The town was alive with the sound of music. It was a bit different to the sound of music that kept Julie Andrews and her hills alive, but good stuff all the same. Some pubs had loud popular music to get all the young ones geared up for the clubs. Most of the young ones had hardly any clothes on, but they were young and that's what the young do, and sure aren't they right to do it before the bloody cellulite takes over? Then there were the traditional pubs with the typical Irish stuff aimed at the many tourists who were hungry for a taste of Guinness and a bit of the blarney.

There were people of all ages and creeds everywhere. All having fun. A gang of fellas enjoying one of their pal's last night of freedom. They were wearing tee shirts with the groom-to-be's picture printed on the back and a caption below saying: *The Condemned Man*. The man himself was standing in the middle of the floor with a weird-looking grin on his face. He had a plastic ball and chain tied around his right ankle. Not that there is a right ankle for a ball and chain. He was trying his best to focus and keep his balance, all at the one time. His pals kept clapping him on the back and lining up the pints and the shots. They were cheering and clapping as they counted out how long it took him to down each one.

One, two, three, four! They stamped their feet and watched as he raised the umpteenth pint and tried to get it in the direction of his mouth. Five, six, seven, eight! They stamped their feet harder and louder as half the pint poured out from the side of his mouth and all over him. Leaving the poor stinking bastard toppling over in a big slop of beer that had spilt on the floor. Nine, ten! He threw the shot down his throat. He made a horrific face of disgust as the liquor burnt the gullet off him.

He wobbled and swayed from one foot to the other. He had the stupid grin back on his face and was lurching forward, hand curled open, ready to clasp his next pint like a man that would never be allowed to drink again and therefore had to drink a lifetime of the stuff in the one night. The lads were egging him on. He had to be held up and supported by the only two men in the group that were sober. One was the best man which only proved what a good choice he had been for a best man. The other was the bride's father who couldn't believe what a silly choice his daughter had made for a husband. He was hoping his daughter would run off with the best man. But sure it was all great fun, wasn't it?

I toddled along the cobblestones up to Reilly's Bar. I was hoping to be early. I wanted to take off some of the make-up Joan had covered me in. I should never have let her give me the full body tan. It was streaky and orange. I looked a bit sunburnt in the face and she had outlined my lips in red and given me the bee-stung look. My lips were enormous. I looked remarkably like a parrot. She had spiked my hair that little bit too much. Green eye shadow does nothing for me. I was wearing green eye shadow and plenty of it. Parrot-like.

It had taken me all I knew to get Phil, Joan and Clotilda not to come with me. I had to agree to the face-painting and body-tanning bit in order to get my way and go it alone. My phone was in my pocket at the ready to send an SOS if I got into any difficulty. Three people were waiting beside their phones.

I was sick as a parrot at the thoughts of meeting the guy. He could have been anyone. I was nervous and felt like a teenager. Suppose he was a really horrible person, what then? Well, all I will have to do in that case is get up and walk out. What if he follows me? Well, all I will have to do in that case is to go to reception and say there is a man following me. There is nothing I cannot cope with. Supposing I fall madly in love with him? What in the name of God will I do? I don't think I'd be able to cope with that. He could be gorgeous. God's gift to the female population and he could be all mine. What would he want with me if he were God's gift? I'd be a bit suspicious if he was God's gift and he wanted me. Well, best foot forward and go for it.

I was wearing my blue tailored trouser suit and my frilly blue and yellow halter-neck top. I had a strapless bra on that belonged to Eve and was far too small for me. I had to keep pulling it up over my boobs. It kept rolling down under them. Next time it rolled down I was going to leave it there. I had a book under my oxter. It was a book on computers and the Internet. Clotilda had given it to me. She said all men loved it. She said it was the best book she had ever seen on computers. Her Dan had written it with some other computer anorak. Tilda had loads of them around the house, books not anoraks. At least it saved me going out to look for a suitable book to bring along with me.

The lobby of the hotel was lovely. Rich terracotta walls and carpet. Cream curtains and black leather seating. Large ornate vases with even larger, more ornate jungle flowers were dotted around, everywhere. I expected a parrot to appear any minute and make a play for me. Land on my shoulder. Peck me on my bright red lips and squeal in a loud squawk, *"Who's a pretty Kelly then?"* I decided to sit as far away from the imitation jungle as possible. I sat in a quiet little alcove in the corner. I had to stand up every few minutes to see if there was anyone in the room with a bunch of roses. Every time I stood up the waiter came over and asked: "Would madam like anything?"

A quick escape route, I was tempted to say.

"A Pina Colada," I said.

I downed the creamy drink in one gulp and felt a bit better. I stood up again to see if I could spot my date.

"Would madam like another drink?"

"Yes."

I downed the second one as quick as the first.

I bet the bugger wouldn't show. I risked standing

again and looked around for any sign of a man with flowers. He wasn't there. He had probably got cold feet and who could blame him?

"Would madam —"

"No, madam would not. Can madam not stand up without you coming over to see if madam wants a drink? I think it's a disgrace the way you are shoving the drink into me. Madam will have one more Pina Colada and then, if madam's date hasn't shown, madam will sit here and cry her eyes out silently. Then madam will be a little less quiet and go into a full cry and leave. Now is that all right with you?"

"Whatever madam says."

He scurried off with a flea in his ear. I swear he had a flea in it. That's what comes from working in a place with tropical plants and the like. It was very unhealthy and very dark.

Then I spotted a man. He had just come in. I nearly missed him. He was fidgeting and kept looking around. He looked like he was looking for someone, anyone. Someone or anyone was obviously late. He had no flowers, but then again maybe there was nowhere open for him to get the flowers. Maybe he had decided not to bring any.

God, he was gorgeous. Rugged and handsome in a rugged sort of way. You could play ball against his chest. He was wearing a brown leather jacket and denim jeans. His skin was tanned and his eyes were darkest brown. But he had no flowers. He was supposed to have flowers. He promised. But I could forgive this man for not bringing flowers. I could forgive this man anything. I really liked the look of him. So the chemistry was right. In test-tube loads. And my Bunsen burner was hotting up quiet nicely, thank you.

I kept staring at him, hoping he'd notice me. I waved the book around a bit. I stared again, closely this time. Then I noticed it. I couldn't help but notice it. His hair. I thought it might be a wig. At first I wasn't sure, but the more he moved the more it moved. It was like a living thing on his head, but it was very, very dead and well past its best-before date. It was very smooth and very dark brown. It moved. I swear it moved. Then it moved again, but only when the guy moved. It seemed to move in the opposite direction to his face. When the guy lifted his eyebrows his hair moved forward. When he frowned the hair moved back.

It was fascinating. I wondered how it was stuck on. Where, when and how long? Where had it been before it had been stuck onto this guy's head? I felt sorry for the guy. He must've been all alone in the world. No family or friends at all. If he had any family or friends they would have pleaded with him to lose the wig. They would have crept into his room in the dead of night armed with a knife and a scalpel and with the skill of a surgeon removed the offending piece. He smiled over at me. I lifted the book and waved it at him. He looked away, quickly. A woman came from the direction of the ladies'. She walked straight over to him, gave him a kiss, and sat down. He took her hand and held it very tightly. Then he looked over in my direction again. I ignored him. If he wasn't interested in me, I wasn't going to let him see I had been interested in him.

The door swung open again and I could see someone with a huge bunch of flowers trying to negotiate the five little steps that led to the bar and coffee area. I couldn't see his face. I stood up and put the book under my arm.

"Coooey! Hellooo! Pisst, pisst!"

I waved my arms as best I could in the direction of the roses. I kept flaying my arms over at him, but he still couldn't see me. I leaned forward and waved at him again. I turned slightly and my worst nightmare became a reality. I saw this big, huge, enormous parrot coming for me. Flapping its big huge wings. I jumped up and ran straight past the guy with the wig. The corner of the book I was waving caught the guy's hairpiece and we all stopped dead in our tracks and watched as his hair took to the air in slow motion. It landed 'plop' right in a bloke's lap. He looked like he was wearing a sporran. He jumped up and shooed it off his knee. It landed on the ground and he stamped on it. The poor bald guy that belonged to the wig went over and took it up off the floor. Dusted it off and put it in his pocket. He looked really gorgeous without the wig. He sat down and the girl he was with started rubbing his bald head and smiling. She kissed him right on the top of his head. I guessed he would be losing the wig, big-time.

I turned again and bumped straight into the guy with the big bunch of roses. I stopped dead in my tracks. I turned again and stood face to face with a five-foot-seven parrot with big boobs bobbing all over the place. It was staring at me. Just standing, staring back at me. I moved forward, it moved forward. I shooed it away with my arms. It flapped its wings again. I turned to run. The shaggin' parrot did the same. I looked to the man beside me to help me, but he was staring at the floor. Staring at all the roses he had dropped in all the confusion. They were lying at his feet. He was standing with his head bent in disbelief looking at the carpet they were forming around his feet.

Then it all went into the slowest of slow motion. I looked again and saw the parrot had a book under its oxter. The very same book I had under mine. I looked at the guy who was now on his hands and knees on the floor. There were two of him. His mirror image was also on all fours on the floor. They were both picking up the roses. His mirror image . . . Slowly, very slowly it dawned on me . . . I started to giggle. I looked at the parrot and vowed never, ever to let Joan do me up again. Time seemed to stop altogether. The man and his mirror image looked up at me. We were staring at each other. Face to face.

I was staring into a very familiar face.

"Dan?"

"Kelly?"

"Dan, what the fuck are you doing here with all those roses?"

"What the fuck are you doing here with a book under your oxter?"

"You can't be my Prince. I won't allow it. There has to be a mistake."

"Well, you most certainly can't be my Princess. Here, you can't cook and you sure as hell can't paint. Why are you done up like a parrot? You nearly killed me."

"Well, at least I'm not married to one of my best friends." I knew that last bit came out wrong, but I let it go. He looked guilty so he knew what I meant.

"Oh, bugger it, Kelly. Can we sit down and talk? I'm sorry. I had no idea it was you I was talking to in the chat-room last night."

"Well, actually it wasn't me – it was Joan doing all the talking for me. Anyway, you shouldn't be in there in the first place. What about Clotilda?"

"Joan? Well, who'd have thought Joan would be in the chat-rooms. Is she not happy with Christopher then? I thought they were like Love's Young Dream – that's what Tilda says anyway."

"She is and they are. She was in there for me. I'm sick of being on my own and I'm on a mission to find my Prince. Tilda thought he might be lurking in some chat-room. How am I going to tell her it was you all along? She even gave me this book to give you. She said it was the best book you could get on computers and the net."

I handed him over the copy of the book he had written.

"She said that?"

"Yeah, she was waxing poetic about how brilliant it was."

"She was?"

"Yeah."

"I always thought she hated that part of my life. I thought she wanted me to save the world and it takes me all my time to save myself and her and Gary and now she's pregnant again. I know, I know before you say it – I'll say it for you. If I didn't dip my wick, it wouldn't have happened. But I don't mind having another baby. I really don't. I'd love it in fact. It's just that I can't stand the whole Mother Earth bit and me having to do little stories to make her feel good about Eggy and Spermy. It's driving me potty."

I couldn't believe what I was hearing. He wanted the exact same thing Clotilda wanted, only each of them thought the other wanted something else.

"It was great in the beginning. There was a balance. I did what I love doing. Computers. But at the same time I wanted to be a good husband and father and I really want to make the world a better place for my children. But I don't want to do it ad infinitum and to the detriment of everything else. I want the balance back."

"Don't you know that Clotilda wants the same thing? She says it's driving her insane that you have turned into some sort of a save-everything weirdo. She thinks you've lost the balance and she wants it back."

"I don't believe you! Are you sure? Oh, Kelly, I love her! If I thought she would have me back, I'd go back tonight. I'm so lonely without her and Gary. That's why I went into that chat-room last night. Then I stupidly arranged to meet someone. How thick is that? I was sorry immediately after I made the arrangement. I had decided earlier on not to turn up here at all, you know. Then I felt so guilty thinking of some poor idiot sitting here waiting for me with a book under her arm. Little did I know that idiot would be you. I decided to come along and I was all set to tell whoever it was that I was madly in love with my wife. But why didn't she ring me and tell me what you're telling me now?"

"I don't know. All I know is I asked her to ring one night and she pretended to ring. I think she was afraid to ring you in case you told her you didn't love her any more. I think she loves you too much to risk you telling her that and she was afraid you'd say you were never coming back. That's something she doesn't want to hear."

"I was talking to her the other night and told her I might be going on contract to London and that I would have to go away there for a few weeks. She seemed pleased I was going away. I was gutted. I had been hoping she'd ask me not to go. How can she be pleased about that and love me at the same time? It doesn't make sense, does it?"

"Of course it does. She wanted you to do what you love doing and if that meant she had to miss you while you were in England, well, so be it. She wants the old Dan back. The one that was the IT wizard *and* the Save the Whale fanatic. She wants the Dan that is the real Dan, not the one that can't be himself with her. That's what a perfect relationship is, Dan – being able to be yourself with someone you love. It's a rare thing and it'd be a shame for you to walk away from it."

"Oh, Kelly, I've been such a fool, haven't I?"

"No, Dan, just a bit of a toad."

"Will you tell her about tonight?"

"I have a feeling I won't have to, will I?"

"No. I'll tell her myself. Do you think it's too late? I mean too late to call in there now? I really need to talk to her."

"No. I don't think it's too late. I think she'd be delighted to see you. If we can salvage some of those roses she might like them as well. When you tell her what happened here, I'd like you to tell her that I will never, ever breathe a word of it. Phil or Joan will never know who I met here tonight. I'll keep it to myself. I'll never even talk about it to you and Clotilda."

"Thanks, Kelly, you're one in a million. Some man will be very lucky to get you. What will you tell the others? Who will you say you met?"

I leaned over and gave Dan a friendly kiss on the cheek.

"Ah, Dan, that's easy. I'll just say I kissed another frog!"

We stood up and the waiter appeared.

"Would madam like another –"

"No, thanks – madam is going home where she belongs."

Dan and I walked along together through the busy streets. People were coming out of the clubs. All in couples. I wondered if any of the passers-by thought Dan and I made a lovely couple.

Jacinta McDevitt

Today's List

To do
1. *Man/unit.*

Not to do
1. *Never wear Eve's top again.*
2. *Never let Joan near my face or body.*
3. *Never date a man with a wig.*
4. *Make sure you know who you are meeting in future before you meet them.*
5. *Never tell Joan or Phil that Dan was the guy from the Internet.*

CHAPTER FOURTEEN

Eve and Becca were up in arms and I have to say I didn't blame them. They were getting on like magic with Hugh and Ray. That is not the reason they were up in arms. In fact, it was a very good reason not to be up in arms. They were having a great time with the two lads. The four of them had become a right little clique. They went everywhere together and were inseparable. Ray was good for Becca and he knew how to tame her impulsive spirit. Charlie had rung several times to ask Becca to come back to him, but she told him he was the wrong fella for her. I was proud of her.

Hugh was steady too and nearly old-fashioned in the way he treated Eve, which was just what she loved. Against everything I had thought, against every bad thought I had about these two lads they were, in fact, lovely young-fellas. Loath though I am to admit it, Graham's Floozy had done a good job on the two of them. I kept these thoughts entirely to myself. It doesn't do to admit you were wrong too often. I know it takes a big woman and all the rest, but, big as I am, it can become a bit tedious admitting all the times that you are wrong.

Anyway, the reason Eve and Becca were up in arms is that they were sick and tired of listening to the two lads waxing poetic about Lover Boy, their soon-to-be step-dad – Eve and Becca's real Dad. It was a bit confusing for all concerned.

"Our Git is taking Hugh and Ray fishing tonight," Becca told me.

"Sure he wouldn't know one end of a fishing-rod from the other," I laughed.

"Well, Hugh and Ray can teach him. They have always gone fishing with their uncle – remember, the doctor at the party."

Why did she have to mention the bloody party? I was doing all right forgetting about it until then. Now I was cringing at the thoughts of everything at the party. There was not one thing I was proud of about that night, except of course that I looked so well. So now, it looked like Graham wanted to play happy families, but with the wrong family.

"It'd make you sick, Ma, if you saw the goings-on up in that house. Only that we have to call in for

Hugh and Ray's sake I wouldn't go near the place. Gwen is lovely though. She's no turkey. She's genuinely nice. You'd wonder what she's doing with The Git. He's like someone going for the Father of the Year Award."

"Yeah, you ought to see it," Eve said. "I have to stop myself from laughing. He hasn't a clue. Poor Git. You have to hand it to him though – at least he's making the effort with the lads. He never bothered his arse with Becca or me."

"Do you think it was because we were girls?" said Becca.

"Don't be ridiculous. It had nothing to do with either of you. It was all to do with him and me. No matter what you were he wouldn't have stayed. I thought you understood it wasn't your fault."

"Yeah, we know the leaving part was nothing to do with us," said Becca. But the fact that he never bothered his arse with us when we were growing up is a bit odd when you see him now doing Super Dad."

"He probably feels guilty about what he did with you and doesn't want the same thing to happen again. That's all."

"Well whatever it is, it's making me puke and really annoying me."

"Yeah, it's pissing me off big-time. I wouldn't mind going on this fishing trip with Ray, but I can't because of Graham. Graham has become a regular Popeye. He's been using the lads' tackle, but now he's decided he needs his own stuff. He's buying himself a rod and a reel and any other gear he needs. They're all going into the tackle shop today to tog him out." Eve was gutted.

"Hugh and Ray can tie flies and everything. They wanted us to go on a fishing trip in a couple of weeks with the family, but we said it'd be too awkward, what with Graham and all."

"Yeah," Becca added. "We wouldn't even know what to call him. Git might be a bit too much in front of his bird, the turkey."

"Will you give over with the turkey bit? I've suffered enough for that little faux pas."

"OK," said Eve. "No more turkey references, we promise."

I looked at the two of them and I felt so sorry for them. Graham had been cruel to them when they were young. He didn't even know it was cruel which made it worse because he never said sorry. He forgot birthdays and Christmas as if he didn't live in this world. It's one thing forgetting a birthday or anniversary but, let's face it, everyone knows when it's Christmas. People buy presents for people they barely know at Christmas. He never bought anything for these two lovely young women. They were easy to buy for too. They'd have been delighted with a bit of make-up or a book token or music token. They weren't fussy. It was the thought that counted, or in this case the lack of thought that counted, and built up and left them angry and entitled to the anger.

Now it must have been so hard on them to watch him spoil another woman's children and it wasn't as if the other children he was spoiling were babes in arms that needed spoiling. No, he was doing the worst thing possible. He was choosing one set of young adults over another set. All in and around the same age. Turning his back yet again on his own. Even the animals in the forest had more respect for their young. Tears flowed down my face at the thoughts of it.

I could forgive Graham for all the injustices he had done to me. For all the times he hurt me. For all the things he did and for the thousand he didn't do. I was a big adult and big adults can weather the storm and move on. Big adults have a way of coping and throwing themselves into something else. I threw myself into the rearing of my two girls. But I would never be able to forgive Graham for what he did to our girls. No matter what went on between him and me he should have been beating a path to our door to get a glimpse of them. He never bothered. I would never understand it. I would never condone it. I would always loathe him for it. I would always blame him for it.

I was a bitter woman where he is concerned. I was bitter and twisted for what he did to his own children. They needed him time and time again and he wasn't there. They never had a daddy at the school concert or at the Deb's dance. They never had a daddy to teach them how to drive or suss out their latest boyfriends. They only had a mother and I hoped to God that I was enough for them. I climbed mountains and wired plugs. I plastered walls and built them dolls' houses. I hoped I was enough. There was no joy in feeling bitter.

There is no funny side to a father walking out on his children. There is a strong bond created between the people he leaves by the very fact of his leaving. The bond had started on the day he left and now we three were safe in the knowledge that no man or beast could separate us and our thoughts. We were linked stronger than before and no matter what corner of the universe we three were scattered to, we would still be linked. Linked by a sadness that we recovered from together.

We were no longer sad. We were happy. It was a wonderful luxury to be able to say that we were happy. Wasn't that what the whole world was striving for and how lucky we were that we didn't have to wait until we were too old to finally discover the secret. I would always be grateful to Graham for leaving. Had he stayed he would have changed our lives for the worse. We wouldn't have discovered at a very early stage that happiness is in people and the way they think about us and the way we, in turn, think about them. It's in knowing that those special people whose life you touch are happy you did and you, in turn, are happy to have had them in yours. Even if it's only for a fleeting moment in time. A glance along the street or a nod in passing by. There are wonderful people everywhere and there are thousands of gits everywhere too. The secret is to weed out the gits and move on.

It was time. The time had come. There was one thing I had to do to make it all right for everyone. I picked up the phone and dialled.

"Helloo."

"Hello, is that Gwen?"

"This is she – who's that?"

"It's Kelly. Listen, I'm sorry about the other night, calling you a turkey and all that. It was one of those times when your foot gets so badly caught in your mouth you just decide it would be better to swallow it whole. You know what I mean. I think I had too much of your delicious punch."

"It's nice of you to say sorry, Kelly, but to be honest I have no idea what you're talking about. I have never put my foot in my mouth nor do I intend to."

Sometimes it's very hard work being nice to people.

"OK, Gwen. Well, for what it's worth I am sorry about it all and about hurting your brother's eyes. I hope he recovered all right and has his perfect vision back by now. Anyway, sorry and all as I am, that's not the reason I'm ringing. Is Graham there? I think I need to talk to him."

"Certainly, Kelly, I'll get him. He's just looking at some fishing stuff with the boys."

Oh boy, this was going to be harder than I thought. Much harder. Maybe he had changed. He was certainly treating his new family well. Maybe it was just me. Maybe it was like Joan said and that when he was with the right person he could act like a caring human being. That still didn't explain why he never wanted to see Becca and Eve.

"Kelly? Everything OK?"

"No, Graham. I need to see you. Will you call around? I'd prefer it if you came alone, but if Gwen wants to come she can. I will be here on my own. Becca and Eve are going out for a walk with Hugh and Ray. They'll be leaving here at about eight so if you could call anytime after that it'd be great."

"Is there a point to all this, Kelly?"

"Yes, I think there is."

"OK. I'll be there at eight thirty."

"Thanks." It was the first time I had occasion to thank him for anything in years.

Every bone in my body told me not to do what I

was about to do. But every time I thought of Becca and Eve I knew what I was about to do was the best thing I would ever do. I would never tell them I did it.

I gave the floor a cat's lick and had a quick cat's lick myself and put on a lovely blue print dress and plain blue cardigan. Well, I didn't have to look like a frump, did I?

Hugh and Ray called.

"How's it going, Kelly?" Ray said with a big smile on his face.

"Hiya, Kelly!" Hugh lent over and gave me a little peck on the cheek. It was as if he sensed the impending danger and was wishing me luck. They all went out hand in hand. Well, one boy holding one girl's hand and it was the right boy with the right girl so that was all right.

I opened a bottle of wine. White. I loved white wine. Graham loved red. I got out two glasses. I poured myself one and drank it back and waited. The sharp pang of dread disappeared in a soft black haze just for a moment. Maybe, just maybe, I was dreaming. Maybe, if I was very lucky, I only dreamt what I was about to do and I hadn't really asked Graham over.

The doorbell rang and I nearly dropped the glass with the fright of it. Graham was standing there, looking puzzled to say the least. He was alone. The turkey had stayed at home.

"What's this about, Kelly? Why do you want to see me? Look, I know you saw the house and all the stuff at the party and I know you think I'm loaded, but it's all Gwen's. She holds the purse-strings. I have nothing. Her parents are very wealthy and they give Gwen money all the time. Her husband was filthy rich and he died and left her loaded too. She has the Midas touch. She also has some sort of a trust; it's a huge amount of money. It doesn't mean I'm well-off. I'm not, so I can't give you any more money."

I looked at this sad, sorry man. A man I had once held and told I loved. A man I had shared everything with, not least a bed, and yet he didn't know me at all. It gave me a wonderful sense of satisfaction to think that I was now a stranger to him.

"I don't want your money. It was never about money. It was always about doing the right thing. Most fathers give up everything they have for their children. You were too miserable even to give your own flesh and blood anything. You begrudged them everything, smug and safe in the knowledge that I would give them all I could."

"If this is just going to be you getting at me, Kelly, you can forget it. I'm out of here."

I poured the wine, handed him a glass and we both sipped away.

He was wearing tight Levi's, 501s, and a paler

blue denim shirt. He had brown boots on and a matching belt. He was trying to look young. It wasn't working. He was trying too hard. I felt nothing for him – sitting there looking around at my home that was completely different to when he had lived in it with me. I had changed every stick of furniture. The first thing to go had been the bed. I felt an urge to tell him I had torn it up into smithereens and dumped it. I knew he was looking for quality items. Trying to put a value on me. He was comfortable sitting in this room that was about half the size of his hall. I knew by the way he was sitting now that he was perfectly at ease. He uncrossed his legs and rested his arms on them, palm upwards. You can't help but be at ease in a proper home.

"So what's this all about then? You look well by the way. You looked well the other night too. I nearly died when I saw you – and what do you make of the two girls dating the two lads? Isn't it gas?"

"Well, that's exactly what I wanted to talk to you about. Becca and Eve have been seeing Hugh and Ray a lot and they're up at your house and down here all the time. I noticed though that they are uncomfortable going up there when they know you are going to be there. They have told me about some of the activities you do with Ray and Hugh. They are upset that you never asked them to do anything with you or go anywhere all the time they were growing up. Can you see how hurtful it is for them to watch? It's like the whole thing happening all over again. All the old familiar feelings of rejection are coming back to them and I don't like it. You have to do something."

"What can I do?"

"Well!" And here's where the real test of a mother came in. "I think you should include Becca and Eve in some of your family trips and weekends away." I had said it. I think I passed the test with flying colours.

"But Hugh said the girls won't come away with us because they'd feel awkward."

"Well, maybe it's not Hugh that should be asking. Maybe it's you. They might be able to take it better if you asked. I will back you up here and tell them it'd be great for them to go." I could nearly hear the violins in the background. This was martyr-for-the-cause stuff. I really didn't want my girls anywhere near him and his floozy.

"OK, I'll give it a try." And there it was again: Graham being nice.

"Thanks, it might be hard work at the beginning. They might give you a rough time, but it'll be worth it in the end to have a good relationship with them. Even if they all break up you would still have a relationship with Becca and Eve which could continue."

"Yeah, I might even ask them to the wedding. I'm sure Hugh and Ray will want them there. You really did a terrific job rearing them, you know." He leant over and rubbed his hand in my hair, the way he used to do. If he had hit me a smack across the face I couldn't have been more shocked. Maybe I was just imagining it.

"So, I hear there's a fishing trip coming up in the next couple of weeks. Will you ask the girls to go with you?"

"Well, eh, that might be a bit awkward this time."

"Why."

"Well, Gwen wants me and the boys to have . . . well, it's a kinda . . . sorta . . . bonding session before the wedding. She thought this trip would be a good place to do it."

"You're going to bond with these lads that have no blood-tie to you and leave your own children out of it? Whatever happened to bonding with your own kids?"

"Ah, give it a rest, Kelly! You never give up, do you? You always want to make everything all right for everyone. Little Miss Fix-It. Well, you can't fix this one."

"What do you mean? I never try to fix everything. I'm only trying to do my best for everyone. Do you think it's easy for me to ask you to do this? Do you think I want you near the girls after all this time?

I'm only doing this for two reasons: Becca and Eve."

"There you go again! Putting the kids first. It's so annoying. You did it all our married life and it pissed me off. The nights I asked you to leave them alone to let them cry. It's only normal for babies to cry at night. No one does what you did. Leave my bed to rock and sing them back to sleep. All the times I wanted you and you were always looking after them!"

"My God, I don't believe this! You cannot be jealous of your own children, can you?"

"I'm not jealous of them, but they did take you away from me."

"No, they didn't! You excluded yourself from them and me. You were always on the sidelines waiting for one of the three of us to balls things up so that you could say 'I told you so' and have a good laugh at us!"

"Shut up, Kelly! You made your choice a long time ago. You were a better mother than you were a wife!"

"The two go hand in hand, Graham. I loved you and I loved the girls. From time to time they needed an adult to help them and I did that. I make no apologies for it. I loved it. Perhaps if you had done your share of parenting, things would have been different. You opted out of it, Graham. You weren't even there when either of them were born. You always wanted to be a single man. Out entertaining the lads. Enjoying your pints and missing out on a wonderful life you could have had here with me and the girls. Be honest with yourself now, Graham – you hadn't the balls to be a good father. You didn't even bother trying. You have a chance to make up for it now. Have you got the balls now, Graham?"

"Oh, shut the fuck up! You haven't a clue what you're talking about!"

I could see the vein throbbing in his forehead.

"Well, you're bloody good at playing Happy Families now, aren't you? Bonding sessions and the like. You make me sick!"

"Oh, you're such a bloody know-it-all, aren't you. I don't particularly want to bond with anyone's fucking kids. Not with Becca and Eve and certainly not with Hugh and Ray. I'm being forced into it, if you must know. You know me too well, Kelly. You're right – I don't have the balls. You know exactly how I tick. You disappoint me though. I was hoping you would be congratulating me on my good fortune. Finding a rich woman who loves me. She's not that bad-looking either. I don't have to put a bag over her head in the sack. She's an easy shag if not the best shag I ever had. She has one weakness though. The very same one you had. Her two wonderful children. Did you know the sun sets and shines all day from their arses? I hear it often enough, so I know it's true. She says if a man doesn't love her children then she wouldn't be interested in him. I have to be sweet to the two fucking lads until the wedding. After that, life's a piece of cake. I'll be a rich man and never have to work for the rest of my life."

I couldn't believe it and then again I could. A leopard never changes his spots. He was using Gwen and her family. He wasn't in love with her. He was madly in love with her money.

I was staring at him. He got up and went to leave. I stood up and then he turned around and looked at me. Really looked at me.

"You're the only woman I ever loved." He put his arms around me and went to kiss my lips. I turned. He missed. He got my cheek.

He saw them first. Over my shoulder standing at the doorway. I was oblivious. I was in full flight.

"Forget it, Graham! Forget everything I said and everything that I asked. I don't want you getting close to my girls. You're a dangerous man. I hope Hugh and Ray are the men I think they are and beat the shit out of you when they find out what you're up to. I don't think they'll stand by and watch you hurt that poor woman you're going to marry."

"Ah, you all make me sick, Kelly!" he said. "You're so sanctimonious. Get down off the soapbox!"

"Graham!"

"Gwen!"

"Graham!"

"Gwen!"

"Git!"

"Fuck!"

"Oh! I didn't realise you were all there. I'm sorry. I seem to be saying sorry to you all the time, don't I?" I was mortified.

"Graham? What's going on?" asked Gwen. "What do you mean the sun shines out of their arses? And 'after that, life's a piece of cake'? What's happening here? Why were you kissing her? She obviously didn't want to be kissed."

Graham turned to Gwen. "Gwen, honey, what are you doing here? Kelly's just doing her usual ranting and raving and making things up. Don't believe a word you heard. She's just stirring it – it's her speciality. She's a basket case. But what are you doing here?"

Gwen ignored him and addressed herself to me. "The girls came back to the house with the lads and I offered them a lift home and Becca asked me in for a coffee to get to know you properly. She said we'd got off to the worst possible start."

"That's because she's so high and mighty!" Graham butted in. "Living in her ivory tower with life passing her by." He was being cruel. He was brilliant at being cruel. He turned to me. "No wonder

303

you don't have a man in your life. You expect too much. You'll never find one that comes up to the expectations you have of him. No one has your standards. You're going to be a sad and lonely old woman." The vein in his forehead was throbbing big-time now.

"You git! I'd rather be on my own than treat people the way you do. I'm not one of those people who cannot be alone, cannot function alone. If I have to settle for second best then I don't want it. I don't have to go through life with any partner just for the sake of having a partner. But I'll tell you one thing. If I want to find a partner I certainly won't be checking out his bank balance first. You sad git! I lived with you for so many years of drudgery that I have a very long list of things I most certainly don't want in a partner. A man with a backbone is one thing I'd like this time around. Now if you don't mind, Graham, I want you to leave. Have a miserable life!"

"Ah, please yourself, Kelly, I'm going home," he snarled. He turned to Gwen. "Coming, dear?"

"Are you mad?" Ray was furious. "You creep! You only wanted our mother for her money. You don't even care about us. Mom, you're not going to let this creep back into our house, are you? If you do, I'm moving out!"

"Graham, you're a scumbag!" Hugh was obviously holding himself back. "Keep away from us."

Gwen was in tears.

"Ah, come on, Gwen!" pleaded Graham. "Let me explain. I only said all that shit to stop Kelly interfering with us and the boys. She wants me to become involved in her life again."

"Don't you dare show your face near my home again! I'll have your bags in the driveway tomorrow and good riddance to you!"

Graham opened his mouth as if to argue further, but then thought better of it. He stormed out.

How could I have been so stupid as to think that he had changed? To think I nearly blamed myself for him being a complete shit to Becca and Eve.

Poor Gwen. She was just standing, staring, hunched and crying. Her mouth was wide open and she was shaking her head from side to side. She reminded me of someone. She reminded me of me.

Today's List

To do

1. All in my power to forget about Graham The Git.

CHAPTER FIFTEEN

The phone didn't stop ringing. I was in great demand. I didn't want to be in great demand. I wanted to sit down and veg out. I wanted to be a slob. I was dying for a cup of tea and a bar of chocolate. There was a bar of chocolate in the fridge waiting for me. It looked all forlorn among the lettuce leaves and the tomatoes. I knew it wasn't comfortable in its healthy surroundings. I was going to have to put it out of its misery and eat it. Tonight. I had a brilliant book to read too. I was hoping to get stuck into it tonight and take notes. Plenty of detailed notes. I had my notebook and pencil at the ready. I could make list upon list to my heart's content. The book was all about relationships. Compulsive reading. It gave advice on what to wear and what to say and how to act. It went through all the different stages of a relationship in great detail. From the first puckering of your lips together right up to the "I do" bit and let's have a rousing chorus of 'Here Comes the Bride'.

I had flicked through the book at least three times hoping to hit on the chapter on how to meet this person you were to have this relationship with, but I couldn't find it. A more detailed search was obviously called for. Unless of course the person writing the book was fool enough to think that anyone who spent their hard-earned cash on the book already had a person. Sure, what would be the point of buying the book then? It would be too late. The first few chapters would be useless as you would have already worn the wrong thing, done the wrong thing and said the wrong thing. Reading the book then would only let you see how exactly you had bugged up the relationship. So, as the book wasn't entitled *What You Did To Bugger Up Your Relationship*, I felt confident it would have detailed instructions on how I would meet a man who would handle me with care.

The bloody phone rang again.

"Hiya, Kelly."

"Hiya, Tilda. What's the story?"

"Well, I think you know what the story is. Dan's back and I believe I owe it all to you."

"No, you don't. I did nothing, only told him

307

what you had told me. He's mad about you, Tilda, really mad about you."

"I know. He told me. But there is one doubt niggling at me. I think it was peculiar him being in that chat-room. I mean he shouldn't have been there at all and he certainly shouldn't have arranged to meet anyone. What do you think? It's driving me mad thinking about it. You're the only one I can talk to about this."

"No, I certainly don't think it's peculiar – not where Dan is concerned. He was lonely and he wanted to talk to someone that's all. It all got out of hand. Let's be honest – it was us that forced him to meet me. He feels at home with computers so it's only natural he'd turn to his computer when he was at his lowest. He honestly only turned up last night because he's a nice man and didn't want to let down the woman he had arranged to meet. I think that's lovely."

"I was hoping you'd say that. I really want this to work. He says he's sorry and I believe him. I said I was sorry too. The whole thing was silly. I should have talked to him about it. I guess I was too scared to. Thanks for doing it for me."

"Isn't that what friends are for?"

"So listen, I'm doing a nice romantic meal for Dan tonight. I have candles and all the trimmings. We're going to talk it all out and see what we both want. It'll be like it used to be before everything else got in the way."

"That's great, Clotilda – I hope it goes well for you. I never saw a couple that were more perfect together. Remember that, when the two of you are together tonight."

"OK, I'd better go and organise the meal. I'm making all his favourites."

I had visions of Clotilda surrounded by lobster and prawns and mussels. If he was lucky he'd get a few snails thrown in for good measure. I wondered would she go the whole hog and do her famous frogs' legs dish. I hoped not. The last time she did it there was a little pile of the tiniest bones on everyone's plate when they'd finished. It was like a little cemetery on each plate. I only kiss frogs, I never eat them. Maybe that was where I was going wrong.

"Enjoy it, Clotilda."

"Thanks again. Talk to you tomorrow.

I knew everything would be all right with her and Dan. I knew they'd end up tonight locked in each other's arms making mad passionate love on every flat surface in the house. I knew she'd fill me in on all the details. It was enough to bring a tear to my eye and a longing to my groin. A gentle sigh was called for. I sighed a lonely gentle sigh.

I only had the phone down when it rang again. This time it was Joan.

"Hi, Kelly. I hear you're still kissing frogs!" She laughed. "Was Prince Charming really awful? Phil said you said you were never going to meet anyone off the Internet again. Don't be put off by one bad experience. Lots of people meet their one true love that way. It's the modern-day Ballroom of Romance you know."

"I know, and I might do it again, but next time I think I'll do it properly. I'd like to talk to the guy for a while before I'd agree to meet him. Build up a bit of a dossier on him. I think it was all just a little bit too quick. My nerves were gone at meeting him so quickly after just one chatting session, good and all as it was. Anyway he was a very, very, nice guy. He just wasn't the right guy. So what's up with you then? All set for the holiers?"

"Yep. Our bags are packed and we're all set. I'm expecting you to come over sooner rather than later to see us and get a bit of a tan."

"Well, I'll see how it's going here and I'll try to get over with Phil's when he's going. You know, Joan, I have a feeling you and Christopher will end up living over there."

"Well, you never know. I'm thinking along those lines. Wouldn't it be terrific? Sunshine all year round."

"It'd be perfect, but I'd miss you. Listen, if I don't see you before you go, have a great time and good luck with finding the perfect villa."

"Thanks, Kelly. I'd miss you too, but you'd be over all the time and I'd be back a lot too. Anyway, I'll be talking to you before I go, I hope. Good luck with finding the perfect man."

"Well, take care of yourself."

"God bless, mind yourself, bye."

Joan was in the lucky position to be able to take off anywhere she had a fancy to. She had seen every corner of the world. She just packed her bags and booked a flight. I didn't have that luxury. Not yet. I was in no position to take off to foreign climes and leave Becca and Eve to look after themselves. Although, as time went on I was becoming more and more redundant. I didn't envy Joan, all the same. I was a home bird. I'd miss everything here including the lousy weather.

The doorbell rang. There was no end to it tonight. I hadn't even had time to change out of my trouser suit. My track suit was up at the end of my bed waiting for me. It was the only thing that waited on my bed for me these days.

"Oh, good, you look decent." Phil barged in. "Come on, we're going out. There's a big hooley on in the school hall. They're taking enrolments for evening classes tonight and they're doing it like a social thing. Some genius came up with the idea. It's the social event of the year. You can have a few nibbly bits and a glass of wine and at the same time try out all the classes." Phil was a man on a mission.

"All the classes? Are you joking?"

"No – come on or we'll miss it. All the classes are going on and you can dip in and out of them for a few minutes and get a feel for them. Just for tonight. Like an open night kind of thing. Then you choose which one of the classes you'd like and enrol for the ten-week course. Or even just have a piss up. Come on, shift yourself."

I put on a bit of lipstick and ran my fingers through my hair. A quick squirt of my favourite perfume, *Take Me*, and I was ready for the taking. We went in Phil's car. The carpark was full. Jam-packed. Phil managed to find the only empty spot. The hall was even more packed. People were standing around chatting and drinking. There were big notices showing which room everything was on in. I looked down the list of classes.

"Here, Phil, let's try this one."

"Oh, yeah, what a good place to start!"

We found the room and as we went in I did a quick recce to see were there any eligible bachelors. I found myself doing this everywhere now. Was it a sign of desperation or just me being sensible? There was not one bachelor in the room. Not one. Plenty of men all right. About ten of them all standing around in a circle with the teacher (well, I assume it was the teacher) standing in the middle of them all dressed up in his pale blue trousers and polo-neck. He was wearing a white cap. He had to be the teacher. He was the only one who looked as if he knew what he was doing and he was dressed for the occasion.

He was wearing a wedding ring. Every one of the men was wearing a shiny wedding ring. All of them were standing on the balls of their feet. All of them had their knees bent. Each one of them looked as if he was the last man left standing in a game of musical chairs. Only there was no music. They each had their arms held straight down, hands clasped together between their legs. Each one was sterner-looking than the next. This was serious stuff. Each one was in dreaded competition with his neighbour, every last one of them looking anxiously from side to side making sure he got it right. It all hinged on the stance, according to the teacher.

"Come in, come in and join us," the teacher said. "Come on now, make a bit of room!"

"Is this the ballet-dancing class?" Phil was foolish enough to make a little joke. It didn't go down well. This was serious stuff.

"It's golf!" the all-male chorus chorused and all ten heads turned and glared at my pal Phil. Phil just smiled. If looks could kill I'd have been weeping and mourning the demise of my friend.

We had to push and prod a little to get into the

circle. It was harder to get into the circle than it was to get into a bloody golf club and you know how hard that is. You have to be a friend of the corpse and be able to write a very large cheque. We persisted and pushed and shoved our way into the circle. We both assumed the position.

"Well done. That's it. You're naturals. Look, everyone! Our latest arrivals have it to perfection. Wait till we give the pair of you a set of clubs." The teacher was charmed. I was charmed. Phil was charmed. The rest of them were disgusted. I would dread to be playing a real game of golf with any of them. You'd end up with a club wrapped around your neck and, by the looks of these fellas, they'd be too cute to use their own club – it'd be one of your own.

We were cruel, we knew, but it was a bit of fun. We really should have mentioned to all and sundry that myself and Phil had been playing golf for years and though I say it myself we were very much up to par. There is no point in joining a golf club to meet a man. All golfers are only interested in one thing on the golf course. No matter how sexy or stunning you're looking, the only thing with dimples that golfers are concerned about is the little white ball. Eagles, birdies and hole in ones are of prime importance. Golf is too serious a sport to mix with pleasure.

We excused ourselves, much to the disappointment of the coach and the delight of the others.

"Now here's something I've never done before," I said to Phil. "Let's try it."

"Oh, I don't think it's me, Kelly."

"Ah, come on. It'll be fun."

We opened the door quietly.

"And now I want you to close your eyes and let your mind go blank. Think of nothing at all. Think of your inner light shining from you."

The coach gestured to us to come into the room and join in.

"Leave everything at the door. Leave it all behind you as you enter!" she said. Myself and Phil emptied our pockets and made two little piles at the door. Keys, money, receipts, and in my case lists.

"No, no. Don't leave everything at the door. They'll be stolen. I mean leave all your worries and cares at the door. It's just an image I want you to create. I want you to feel you have parted with all your worries. It's metaphorical speak."

Phil and I stuffed all the stuff back into our pockets.

I spent a few moments longer than Phil ditching all my worries at the door. This was because I had a few more worries than Phil. I made a mental note to forget to pick up all my worries on the way out.

There were candles burning and sleeping bags all

around the room. Waves were beating against one wall. Thanks be to God, they were only on a tape and it wasn't the swimming class we were in. Phil is like a lead lump in water.

We both lay down on the floor.

"Now we will do some gentle exercises. If you come for the ten weeks we will add a new position every week."

Phil and I looked at each other with glee.

"Did you hear that, Phil? We're definitely in the right class! New positions!"

"Maybe we should enrol for the full ten-week course."

We were always interested in new positions!

"Now I want you to lie on your back and slowly and gently breathe in and raise your right leg slowly, slowly, lift."

"Ahhhh, ahhhh, Oh, Jesus! Christ!" Phil was rolling around the floor.

"Phil, will you stop! You're making a show of us. They're all looking at us."

"Ahhh, ahhh!" Phil kept it up. I was mortified.

"I'm ignoring you, Phil. Do you hear me? Stop. I'm not even looking at you now." I turned my back.

A beautiful-looking girl got up from where she was lying. She had a face like a porcelain doll only softer. Her hair was blond and silky. She was, tall, willowy and leggy. Very leggy, in tight black Lycra leggings. Bloody Lycra again. She had a snow-white crop-top on. She was beautifully tanned and had a wonderful smile.

"Are you all right?"

"No, my leg is killing me. I have a cramp."

"OK, it will be all right in a minute. Now just try to straighten it out slowly. It will be fine." She started to rub Phil's leg. Phil was enjoying it. I'd say the cramp was long gone and Phil was just lapping it up. I knew by the starry-eyed look. I'd seen it before.

"I'm sorry to be interrupting your enjoyment of the class. I guess yoga just isn't for me. Maybe my legs are too long. What do you think?"

"I think they are very long and very strong."

"Do you think you could help me to get outside? I don't like the way the teacher is glaring at me and the rest of the class appear to have gone into a coma."

"No problem. Your girlfriend can help us." She smiled over at me.

I got up and between the two of us we got Phil up off the floor.

He put his arm around both our shoulders but looked directly into her face when he said: "She's not my girlfriend. She's just a friend. I have no girlfriend."

We dragged Phil along and out the door. I ignored

all my worries and then had second thoughts and went back for them. I couldn't abandon them when they were unsolved. I made very sure not to take anyone else's worries. That would have been a real bummer altogether. To come home with a pile of strange worries. Well, stranger than the ones you had in the first place would have been very foolish. It was better to have familiar worries. I was sure a few undesirable people would try to shove a few of their worries into other people's piles. There is always a cute whore. I was cuter and came away with the ones I had arrived with. Becca, Eve, Tilda, Dan and myself were just some of my worries and now Gwen – I had the added worry of Gwen. I didn't remember having that worry earlier. Although maybe I had and didn't notice. I decided to give the worry the benefit of the doubt and take it. Poor Gwen was in a terrible state when I saw her last and was maybe worth a bit of worrying. I was nearly going to ask her to join the Sad and Lonely Tribe, but I didn't know what way she'd take the invite and anyway, I wasn't sure if I wanted her there. That was my thing.

"What's your name?" Phil was really interested.

"It's Laura. What's yours?"

"Philip. Everyone calls me Phil. My dad is called Philip too so they call me Phil to differentiate between the two of us. Ahhh, ahhh! My leg!" Phil was overdoing it.

318

"Come on, let's get you on to a seat," she said.

The two of them were completely ignoring me.

"Hi," I said. "I'm Kelly, in case you were wondering."

"Hi, Kelly. I'm sorry. I am interested. I'm just worried about Philip's leg. I think we should find him a chair."

So another woman had added to her worries at the door as she left.

"Look, there's one, over there." We dragged Phil all the way over.

Just as we arrived a snotty-nosed kid sat down on the chair. He had a bottle of Coke he had just got out of the vending machine and was pouring it down into his mouth with great gusto.

"Excuse me, but would you mind giving us that chair?" the lovely Laura, asked. She had a very gentle voice.

"Naa, I got it first."

"But can you not see that my friend has a cramp in his leg and we can't hold him up much longer."

"Yeah. But that's his problem. Not mine."

"Ah, would you not give him your chair?" Laura asked again gently. "Come on, he's in agony. Look at him."

"Here, just get up and give us the bloody chair." I was losing it big-time.

"Get the fuck off the chair now!" Phil finally spoke up.

The young fella withered. He jumped up off the chair and went wailing down the corridor to his parents.

"The parents will be up here like two bulls in a minute. Eating the face off us for shouting at their little Johnny," I said knowledgeably.

"Well, we'll just deny everything. Tell them we don't know what the brat is talking about – OK!"

I noticed Phil was a lot better. I, on the other hand, had really wrecked my shoulders, dragging him all over the place.

Laura was back on her knees. She was rubbing Phil's leg again. He was loving it.

"That's lovely, Laura. You're a lovely person. Thanks a million. I don't know what we'd have done if you hadn't helped us. Isn't that right, Kelly?"

Well, I for one would have left him where he was on the bloody sleeping bag. I was really getting into the yoga class before we had to leave.

"Oh, we'd have been lost without you," I said, smiling.

"It was a pleasure. I'm very good at massage and if you like I could give you one, whenever you like. It would be great for your leg. What do you think?" Laura asked Phil.

I was betting the lovely Laura was good at a lot of things and I knew exactly what Phil was thinking.

"I'd enjoy that," he understated. "Would you

like to get a glass of wine with me?" Phil was hitting on her now, big-time. I think he was really interested in her. In fact, when I looked at him he still had the silly grin on his face that I had assumed was a grimace because of the pain in his leg. Now I saw that this might have been love at first sight for Phil. I decided I'd better help him out. After all, he was prepared to give me a helping hand in my quest for Prince Charming. I can be very subtle when I want to be and I could be a great help here to Phil in sussing out the situation.

"Are you single? Do you have a boyfriend? Are you available?" I decided not to mince my words. Get it all out in the open and let the girl know where she stood. Cut the crap and all the wondering where she stood.

I looked at Phil to see was he pleased with my very direct approach. He was sitting on the chair smiling. Open-legged and his two palms facing upwards. He looked like a primate, but a very handsome primate I had to say. She'd be a fool not to fall madly in love with him. Also, I liked this girl. She had been quick to help us and so far she had no annoying habits. It was important that I would like any partner Phil met. After all, we would be seeing a lot of each other.

"Yes. No. Yes. I am single. I don't have a boyfriend. I am available, but only to him." She was pointing directly at Phil I was pleased to see.

Phil put his hand out and took hers.

"Here, you sit down. You must be wrecked, what with dragging me out and rubbing my leg. I'd love a massage and whenever you can give me one would be terrific. Now you sit up here and I'll go and get some wine and we can have a chat. Get to know each other better. What do you think, Laura?"

"I'd love to."

I could see I was totally superfluous to requirements.

"Listen, I'm going to potter around here for a while so let's say we all meet up again in an hour?"

"You sure?" Phil said. "I was going to get you a glass of wine too, you know."

"Oh, yes, stay and we can all get to know each other." Laura, to give her her due, joined in even though I knew she couldn't wait to get her hands on Phil on his own.

"No. I want to have another look around. Now where will we meet up?"

"There's a big notice-board along the main corridor," Laura said. "You can't miss it. I just put an advertisement on it looking for somewhere to live. I'm only back from the States where I've been living for the past year and I badly need somewhere. At the moment I'm kipping down on a friend's couch and there's a limit to the length of time I can do that. I'm sure it will affect the friendship if I don't get something soon. Either of you don't know anywhere, do you?"

"No," I said quickly.

"Well, let's have a chat and I'll see if I can think of anywhere." Phil said.

"I'm not the easiest person to live with though. That's the big problem. I have a bit of a neatness thing going. I can't stand a mess. Most people don't relish neatness."

That was enough. Phil was now in love. It was official.

"Here, I'll leave you two to it and I'll have a look around. Talk to you in an hour."

I wandered over to the table where they were giving out the wine and nibbles. I hate drinking wine out of a plastic cup, but I'd rather drink it out of that than not drink it at all. So I forced myself.

"Red or white?" a young fella asked.

"White," I said, not looking up.

My head was buried in my bag searching for a few euros to drop into a tin box that was on the table. The food and drink were free, but you were expected to give a donation to the school building fund. It seemed they wanted to build a gym. I didn't know if I approved of the school having a gym. All the young kids would be turned into lollipops. Maybe it was a sophisticated way of the lollipop brigade infiltrating our young. Clever plan, if it was their plan.

I struck oil in my bag. It was all over my bag and

all over everything in my bag. The lid had loosened on a bottle of baby oil. I tightened the lid and put a well-oiled €10 note into the box. "Thanks," I said as I lifted my head to take the cup.

"That's OK. You're very welcome, Mrs Daniels. Are you having a nice evening? Are you joining a class?"

The gall of him! It was Charlie. He was all tarted up like a monkey in his dress suit and dicky bow. The brass neck of the little worm, talking to me like that! Who did he think he was? The cheek of him being nice to me! Asking me was I having a nice evening. I'd give him nice evening! The worm!

"Seems like a long time ago since Becca and Eve and I were in school here. It feels a bit weird to be back here working. I got a part-time job in the off-licence at weekends during college and that's how I'm here dishing out this stuff tonight. It's all supplied by the off-licence."

Had this guy no shame, talking away to me? My blood was boiling.

"Now, you listen here to me, you little worm you! I couldn't give a hang what you do in your spare time or any other time, spare or not. As long as it doesn't involve either of my daughters you can do what you like. Now, pour me another drop of wine into my cup and listen to me big-time, you little creep! If you ever so much as look at either Becca or Eve again I will make it my life's ambition to seek you out and make your miserable, selfish life an absolute nightmare. Hell hath no fury like a mother's wrath, Charlie, did you ever hear that?" I paraphrased. I was sure this ignorant worm wouldn't notice the changes.

"Oh, I thought that was 'a woman scorned'."

"Well, take a woman scorned and then take a woman scorned's mother and see which one you'd rather deal with. The scorned woman is easy pickings compared to her mother. Do you hear me, Charlie?"

"Yes, yes, I hear you, Mrs Daniels."

"Don't you 'Mrs Daniels' me. Don't ever ring my home again. Never try to get in touch with Becca again and yes, now that you ask, I am going to a class as a matter of fact. I am going to a martial arts course. It'll be of great use to me if someone ever upsets either of my girls again. What do you think?"

"Yes, yes. Whatever you like." The poor bastard was pulling at the collar of his shirt. He was hot under the collar.

I nearly felt sorry for him. Nearly, but not quite.

"I made a mistake with Becca," he said.

Can you believe he had the balls to say that?

"I only want to talk to her to see can we patch things up. I really like her and maybe we could try again."

"Try what exactly again? Kissing her sister? Oh,

yes, I know all about it. Sure maybe you could go for the hat trick and kiss the whole family, see if we're all the same. You can never make it up to Becca. You blew it. I only hope you know exactly what you're missing. Much as I detest you, Charlie, I really do hope all of this will stand to you and you've learnt something about people's feelings from it. You should have handled something as precious as Becca with care. You didn't. You don't get a second chance. Hard luck!"

"Will you tell her I was asking for her?"

"Are you a total idiot? Have you not been listening to a word I've said? Can I put it any plainer? Bugger off, Charlie! That plain enough for you?"

The poor kid! I let him have it. The poor worm was squirming. I knew we'd never hear from him again. That chapter in Becca's life was over. I turned on my heels and I have to say I felt a bit ashamed of myself. I was a big girl. He was only a kid. But Becca was my kid.

Today's List

To do

1. *Learn something from Laura – how to be nice and kind to a man.*

2. *Join an evening class that will be useful to me.*
3. *Give Gwen a quick ring just to make sure she is all right.*

Not to do
1. Don't get depressed just because Phil has met someone and won't be able to marry me when I'm fifty.

To ignore
1. My past record with men.

CHAPTER SIXTEEN

It wasn't as much fun going around peeping in doorways and dipping in and out of classes on my own, but I knew in my waters that Phil had met his life partner and who was I to be a gooseberry? I'd done gooseberry so often now, I was nearly a professional gooseberry. Next time I did gooseberry, I was going to ask for a fee. That's why I didn't want to do it on Phil. Phil was my friend and it's just a bit mean to be charging friends. I can never be accused of being mean.

I opened the door into the next class I thought I might like to join and went in.

I heard a loud voice booming from the top of the class. "Now, you have to be gentle with gooseberries!"

"Too bloody right," I said. "You should be very gentle with gooseberries."

The people watching the cookery demonstration all turned and smiled at me. They assumed I was another teacher and that this was a double act.

"They are hairy. You have to trim off both ends before you stew them."

I slithered into a seat and sank back into it.

"Now here's a gooseberry-pie I baked earlier," the demonstrator said in the best tradition of all cookery classes. "I will pass it among you and you can take a little taste each. Here's a bundle of forks. I don't have enough plates to go around so you'll have to eat it off the plate it's on. Just pass it on after you take a little sample. It's delicious. Gooseberries are very neglected and underrated."

I nodded energetically. The plate was passed from pillar to post. Each person licked their lips and passed the plate on. Each said how delicious it was. One man was ecstatic. He was going on a bit if you ask me. Then again, I hadn't tasted the pie yet. I was sure it was nice though.

"Orgasmic," he proclaimed to the whole class. "Pie like my mother used to make, Lord have mercy on her!"

"And what about the ones I make?" his wife snapped at him. The rest of us could see it coming a mile off.

"Well, yours are very nice too, dear. Just different, that's all. Anyway you never made gooseberry, did you? My mother, Lord have mercy on her soul, used to be able to bake anything anywhere."

He should've quit while he was ahead. But, oh no, he had to keep going.

"Your rhubarb is out on its own though," he said to his wife. "You should taste her rhubarb-tart!"

Ten points for a good recovery I was thinking and nearly went over to congratulate the man. Then he had to do it. He couldn't resist the temptation. Couldn't keep his big mouth shut.

"But my mother was the best cook ever – mouth-wateringly delicious."

If we all hadn't been looking at them so intently we'd never have noticed his wife's hand reach up and give him a right wallop across the back of the head, then quickly return back in her lap. The two of them acted as though nothing had happened.

To distract us all, a very kind man sitting beside me leaned over and asked: "Did everyone get some pie?"

They had all had a sample except me. I was starving.

"I didn't get any. Can I have just a little taste, please? It looks so lovely." And it did, look lovely. The smell of it was massive. My mouth was watering. I was lucky. The rest of the class had been very polite and they had only taken small bite-size bits. There was a good half of the pie left when it got to me.

"I'll just carry on here and when you have had

your taste if you just bring the plate back up to me. You'd be amazed at the number of plates I lose at these things."

"OK." I said, but I wasn't listening. It was truly the most amazing thing I have ever eaten. Your man was right; orgasmic was the only word for it. I had another small little piece. The demonstrator was whipping cream for all she was worth. Tiny beads of perspiration were forming on her upper lip. I was nearly going to go up and swab her all over like I'd seen on TV programmes. I think it was cookery programmes; then again maybe it was hospital programmes. I sat where I was. God, the pie was great. Fair play to the one doing the demonstration. She went over to a corner and wiped the sweat off with a tissue and then washed her hands really well. She searched in her bag and came out with a mask and put it on. I was enraptured now. Would she start requesting implements – spatula, tongs, fork?

I looked at the fork I was holding. Then I looked at the plate. It was empty. I looked to either side of me. There was no one sitting close enough to me that I could blame. I had eaten a whole half of a gooseberry-pie. I went up to hand over the plate. As I approached the demonstrator, she waved her hand at me to leave the plate at the sink. After all, she was in the middle of a very delicate operation.

I wondered if she had a Prince at home. Did she

bake little culinary delights for him every evening and did he rejoice in her delights and tell her how wonderfully delightful her delights were?

"Thanks, but there is no need for you to do that." The demonstrator was lifting off her mask and talking to me. I could see most of the class leaving. "I'm having a break now and I was going to do all that tidying up. I really do appreciate it, you know."

"What?"

"Well, you doing all the pots and dishes for me. It's very kind and nice of you. Most people wouldn't do it."

"What?" I looked at myself. She was right. I was standing there with a tea-towel in my hand, having just done all the dishes of the day. Old habits die hard.

I hung my head in shame and left the room without another word.

I checked the time. Half an hour to go before I was to meet up with Phil and Laura. I didn't want to meet them at all. Only that Phil had the car I would have gone home. One more class and that was it.

I stopped dead in my tracks as I entered the next room. I didn't even check it out for eligibles.

"Oh my God. *Oh! My! God!*"

All heads turned and looked at me. All male heads. I still didn't check if any of them were eligibles.

"It's! To! Die! For!"

All heads stayed turned, still looking at me.

"I have never seen anything like it in all my born days." I'm prone to exaggeration when I'm excited. I was very excited.

"*Wait!* Just give me a minute here. Let me have a look." I put my bag up onto a table and started taking the contents out of it. It was my Mary Poppins bag. Bottomless. Although mine never managed a lamp, like her one, I had been known to carry a torch which is one and the same thing if you ask me. Hairbrush, foundation, mascara, lipstick, tissues, tampons, mobile phone, keys, biros (4), purse, nail varnish (3), two cards to post since last week, stamps, face cream, three chocolate bar wrappers and finally at the bottom of the bag, my notebook. The one with all my lists. I did a quick check. I ran to the front of the room. There was a man standing there looking very worried. I think he was going to call security.

"Can I measure it?" I asked in all innocence.

The class laughed and I could hear one smart Alec in particular, "You have to measure us all!" Loud ignorant guffaw followed by another loud ignorant guffaw.

I took the measuring tape off the table and did the business. One way, the other way, the other way. It was perfect. Just perfect.

"Yes, yes, yes! I have found it. At last!" I jumped

around the room punching the air with delight, which was a bit silly after eating half a gooseberry-pie. I danced a few steps around it and put my arms right around it and kissed it on its side.

The class erupted. They thought I was some sort of exotic dancer. They whistled and clapped.

I was so chuffed that I stepped forward and bowed. I lifted my head and smiled at the sea of male faces. I zoned in on one. Feck. David. Feckin' Gwen's bloody brother. Now what the hell was a doctor doing at a woodwork class? I chose to ignore him. I was too mortified at what had happened at the party. He'd never remember me anyway. He kept staring at me; I think he was trying to work out what the hell I was doing and why the hell I was doing it at a woodwork class? And what substance I was on. He was looking at me very oddly. I was glad I was doing so well at ignoring him.

"Eh, would you like to sit down with the rest of the class?" the teacher said.

"No, thank you, I prefer it up here with this wonderful, to-die-for bathroom unit."

"Eh, er! Well, do you want to pull up a seat then?"

"Thank you. How long will it take me to build this?" I had my notebook out at the ready.

"About ten weeks. I'll give you all a list of materials and you can get them all in the builder's providers. You'll all want different measurements, depending on the size of the place you want to fit the unit."

"I'll be wanting that exact size."

"Well, I'll tell you what to get for that size then. Each week we will do a different part."

"Is there no way we could do it in less than ten weeks? I urgently need it."

"Only those who have done the course before or are very proficient at woodwork will manage to do it any quicker."

"Well, that's a bit mean, isn't it? I think that's a bit of preferential treatment to the ones that did the class last year. I'm just as entitled to have it finished in less than ten weeks."

"Yes, you are, but the fact is that you won't know what you're doing and will have to learn as you go along. Some of the others are old hands at this. David, for instance, has been in two previous classes."

All heads, except mine, turned to nod and wink at David.

"So when you come along next week we'll get cracking and do some joints."

Well, you can count me out of that, I immediately decided. I had never taken drugs in my life and I wasn't about to start now. I thought it was a bit irresponsible to have us smoking joints when we'd be working with sharp implements, saws and screwdrivers and of course the talented David's tongue.

"I will show any of you that are new to the class how to do a dovetail joint."

"Oh, right, those type of joints," says I, having already learned something. This was a good class.

The woodworker guy spelled out exactly what it took to build the magnificent bathroom cabinet. It seemed like a lot of hard work to me. I am a very intelligent person. I know my own limitations. His description of what to do went way beyond my limitations.

"How much would you sell me that one for?" I was wondering would it be cheaper to buy the demonstration model than enroll in the class to make it.

"Sorry, it's not for sale. It's an awkward shape and fits exactly into a space in my own bathroom. I only brought it to show you what we would be doing."

"Yeah, it's a very awkward shape all right."

I was deflated.

I decided not to enroll in the class.

It was time to meet up with Laura and Phil. I hoped I wouldn't feel too sick if they were still doing the lovey-dovey bit to each other. I also hoped they wouldn't have reached the touchy-feely stage.

Today's List

To do

1. Try to get the woodwork teacher on his own and ask him to build me a cabinet exactly like his. Offer my body. If he's not interested in mine offer Laura's or Phil's or both.
2. Clean out handbag.
3. Make sure my Prince is good with his hands – in more ways than one!

Not to do

1. Don't ever eat a gooseberry-pie again – I feel sick after it.

To ignore

1. David – bloody Gwen's bloody brother.

CHAPTER SEVENTEEN

They weren't anywhere to be seen.

I was left standing like a pilgarlick at the notice-board. I spent a few minutes using up the time wondering exactly what a pilgarlick was. I must've looked like an intelligent pilgarlick though because people kept coming up to me asking me questions. Not very intelligent questions, mind you.

"Can you tell me where the art class is, please?"

"Sorry, I don't know. But there is a chart just here that shows where everything is. Maybe you could get it off that." I decided to be nice to the poor lost soul.

"Good idea, thanks very much for your help."

"No problem. I hope you find it."

"Where's the gardening class?" another passer-by asked.

"I think it's along the corridor and to the right. Check the chart."

"OK, thanks."

"Can you tell me where the golf is?"

All these questions. They were really starting to piss me off, big-time.

"Sorry, I don't know. I'm only waiting for someone."

"Is the judo class along here?" Yet another one.

"Dunno, check the chart."

"Where's the computer class?"

"Hey, I'm only a pilgarlick. What do I know about computers or where their class is? Can you not follow the simple chart? You'll be useless in the computer class if you can't follow a simple chart of where each class is."

"I'm the teacher of the computer class so I doubt if I will be that useless. I only asked a simple question, but if you're going to take that attitude you can forget it. I thought you were an information person. Obviously I was wrong and the only information you have is the useless variety. Goodbye."

Ouch. That hurt. But still I wasn't going to be an information desk for anyone. I turned my back and ignored all the other questions that were coming at me from all angles.

I started reading all the notices that were on the

notice board. I was amazed at the things people put notices up for. All sorts looking for all sorts.

Wanted

Baby-sitter to look after 8-week-old baby
Every Wed. night
From 7.00 to 9.15
While mother attends the Looking After a
New Baby Class

Wanted

Someone to walk cocker spaniel every day.
Must be able to go for long, long walks as
dog is very energetic.

GARDENER
WANTED

TO MOW GRASS & DO WEEDING

GARDENER
AVAILABLE
AT REASONABLE RATES

WILL MOW GRASS & DO WEEDING

All of the notices had little flags of paper hanging

out of them with the phone numbers for the particular person who had put up the particular notice. They were easy enough to tear off. There were loads and loads of notices. Swapping books and stamps. Offering to clean houses, wanting houses to be cleaned. All of them looking for something. I searched my bag again and took out my notebook and red marker. There was only one space left for a notice to go – right in the middle:

WANTED
VERY URGENTLY

PRINCE
(not just any Prince but my Prince)

MUST BE CHARMING

PS.   FROGS NEED NOT APPLY

RING PRINCESS ON MOBILE BELOW

I found the last available thumbtack and stuck it into my notice and on to the board. The little flags with my mobile number looked very inviting. I felt good. Nothing like being pro-active to make you feel that you're doing something.

"What's up, Kelly?" Phil came around the corner beaming from ear to ear. He had his arm tightly around Laura's skinny waist. She had the perfect body. I wondered had she any cellulite and if not why not and what she had done to get rid of it. Maybe she never had any in the first place.

"Nothing much. I did all the rounds. I saw the cabinet of my dreams and, for one fleeting moment, it was in my grasp. Alas, it is no longer in my grasp or in my bathroom. Tell me, Laura, did you ever hear of cellulite? Did you have a good time?"

"Yes, I'd the best time ever. What did you say about cellulite?"

"Nothing."

"Oh, I thought you said something."

She had changed out of her sweats and into a pair of jeans that would give anyone else major urinary tract problems. Her top was cropped, of course and her boobs did as they were told and stayed firmly in place. She put her hand onto Phil's and she smiled an open happy smile at him. Only for the fact she was doing it to one of my best pals and he was loving every minute of it, I'd have been sick. With jealousy.

"Phil has offered to put me up for a while until I get fixed up in an apartment of my own. Isn't he just wonderful?"

Ah no, I hoped she wasn't just taking advantage of Phil and being nice to him to get a roof over her head.

"Don't worry, Kelly, I know what you're thinking,

but I'm not taking advantage of him just to have somewhere to stay. I told him I'd pay good rent and it would only be a temporary measure until I get somewhere else."

She must have read my mind. How dare she know what I was thinking?

"I wouldn't even think for a minute that you were taking advantage of him. Whatever will you think of next?"

I wondered would she stay over tonight in Phil's wonderful bed and would he do to her what he had done to me. I was thinking the two of them would have an even better time since one of them wouldn't be running off in the middle of it all. I bet she had Phil wrapped around her little finger and would be in keeping his back warm by midnight tonight.

"Phil has asked me to stay over tonight, but I'm not. I'll just go over for coffee to see the place and see my new room. I'll get my stuff from my friend's house and move in properly tomorrow or the next day."

I felt guilty.

"Well," I gave her a hug out of guilt for getting her so wrong and because for some reason, I genuinely liked the girl. She was easy to like. "It'll be great to have you around the place. Pity you aren't a slob."

Laura had her car with her so she agreed to

follow us first to my house to drop me off and then back to Phil's for a bit of how's you father, I suppose. I had to do my well-practiced gooseberry routine over at the cars. Phil and Laura were wrapped around each other. I stood there kicking stones and whistling while they had their first snog. Well, I assume it was the first one. Unless, of course, they had a sneaky one earlier and hadn't told me.

"Wow, Kelly, can you believe it?" Phil was elated and grinning from ear to ear when we got into the car. "Can you fucking believe it?"

"No, to be honest with you, Phil, I can't."

"We were supposed to be looking for a man for you and all of a sudden when I wasn't looking, a woman like Laura walks into my life and she's gorgeous. Do you believe in love at first sight, Kelly?"

"That's the second time I've been asked that question. I don't know what I believe any more."

"You were right too about you and me. I love you, but you were right that I'm not in love with you, that there is a difference. Right now I can hear fireworks! I'm just bursting. I'm madly in love and I just love it."

"I'm delighted for you, Phil." And I was.

My mobile rang. It was buried deep in the Mary Poppins bag. I just got to it before it rang out.

"Hello. Hello."

"Yes – hello."

"I can't hear you very well, where are you?"

"I can't hear you either. Hold on." I could only hear a very faint voice and it kept breaking up.

"Pull over to the side of the road, Phil, quick."

"Hang on, Kelly, I can't pull in here."

"Look, up there, pull in quick. Hello, are you still there?" I said the last bit into the phone. "Hang on a minute."

I leapt out of the car.

"Can you hear me now?"

"Not very well. I'll walk around a bit. Can you hear me now?"

"Yeah, it's a bit better, but not great."

"I better have the right person after all this. Is that Princess? The same Princess who put the wanted notice up on the school notice-board?"

"Yes." Oh, I was so silly to do the notice-board thing. I was even sillier to be standing on a grass verge leaning over to one side trying to hear, while traffic sped past me.

"Who's this?"

"This is your Prince. How are you?"

"I'm fine, but a bit nervous, to tell you the truth. Maybe it was a foolish thing to put a notice up at all. "

"I thought your notice was brilliant. I'm only sorry I didn't think of it myself."

"Yeah, I thought it was quite a good idea myself,

at the time." I giggled. "Now I'm not so sure though!"

"So! Tell me then, am I the first one to ring you?"

"Yes."

"OK – well then I have a great advantage."

"No. All Princes that phone me will be given the same chance."

"Well, Princess, tell me all about yourself."

"Nothing much to tell. I'm a mature Princess so if you're into the dolly-bird type you wouldn't like me. "

"I like the more mature style of Princess, thanks. So, what do you do when you're not doing your Sleeping Beauty routine or losing your slipper or sleeping on a pea?"

"Very funny. Probably the same type of thing you do when you're not beating off ugly sisters or dwarves."

"Are you single, divorced, married or what?"

"Single now after a divorce – what about you?"

"Single, always."

"Does my being divorced bother you?

"No, it's a fact of life nowadays. Some of my closest friends and family are divorced. It doesn't bother me at all, but it must've been tough for you. Have you children?"

"Two girls. Both at college. Both as well balanced, if not more well balanced, than their peers from so-called model families. It's weird, but if their dad had died everyone would have rallied around them. Grieved with them and helped them. But because he left, no one bothered their arses. Too embarrassed, I suppose. People don't know what to say. Funnily enough, all they have to say is something – anything at all would do. It's the ignoring everything that's the problem. Oh, I'm sorry, listen to me waffling on, I never do that normally. I especially never do it to people I don't know."

"Well, we could always do something about that. You could meet me tomorrow night and we could get to know each other."

"But, I don't know anything about you. I can't meet you until I know you a bit better. Your name isn't Dan by any chance, is it?"

"No, I told you my name is Prince. I'm single, early forties, gainfully employed, self-sufficient, never been married, never found the right Princess. I've been looking for her for ages. Seems like a lifetime. When I find her I'm not letting her go. Come on, what have you got to lose? I'm charming and we'll have a great time. As I'm the first one to answer your call for help, I think you should meet me sooner rather than later. Get the first one out of the way quickly. Why waste any time? I have a feeling we'll get on brilliantly."

I had the same feeling myself. I liked the way I could talk to this guy. I liked the way he listened. It was a pity the coverage on the mobile was so bad. I could have talked to him for ages.

"Hey, Princess, you're breaking up again. Will you meet me?"

"All right, all right. You win. I'll meet you. Where and what time? I hope I won't live to regret this."

"I promise you won't. What do you like to eat? Italian, Chinese, Thai?"

"Fish." I had a longing for fish ever since Clotilda had made Dan's favourite.

"Atlantis. The seafood restaurant."

"Brilliant. What time?"

"Eight o'clock."

"So how will I recognise you then? Please don't say you'll bring flowers and I'll bring a book. "

"Why not?"

"Long story. Remind me to tell you about it sometime."

"Well, firstly I'll be there on the dot of eight. I'm never late. I don't mind if you are though, I'll wait for you. Secondly, I'll wear a navy jacket and white shirt. Not sure about the color of my tie yet, but I'll definitely wear a tie. Other than that, what more can I tell you?"

Great. A chunky one, I hope. I have a weakness for a man in a white shirt.

"OK, my turn. I'll try to be on time, but will probably end up being a little bit late. I'll be wearing a red dress and red shoes. Probably a black jacket. Unless, of course I change my mind and wear something completely different."

I giggled.

He laughed. He seemed to have an easy sense of humor. Between that and the white shirt I was onto a winner. All I needed now was for him to be loving, kind, thoughtful and a bit of a stud in bed and I was sorted.

"Anyway, I have your mobile number if we can't find each other," he said. "I'd better give you mine, just in case."

I grabbed a bit of paper out of the Mary Poppins bag and wrote down the number.

"See you tomorrow then, Princess."

"Yeah, Prince, look after yourself till then."

"Goodnight."

"Night."

"What was all that about?" Phil had been trying to listen, but only heard bits and pieces.

"Guess who's got a hot date for tomorrow night?"

"Good for you."

I explained all about the notice-board.

"Way to go, Kelly! Brilliant idea."

"We'll see how brilliant it is after I meet him."

I only had the phone down when it rang again. Another Prince! Was I doing well or what?

"Hi. Where are you?"

"In Phil's car. I'm on my way home." It was only Becca.

"Right. Me and Eve are going to bed now. Any news?"

"Nothing much. I'll talk to you tomorrow. Goodnight. Tell Eve I said goodnight."

"Goodnight, Ma."

My phone was silent for the rest of the night. I wasn't disappointed. At least one Prince had called. The others would call at a later date. There were lots of things on in the community hall. All sorts of meetings and things. Loads of Princes dropping in and out of the place. There would be great opportunity for them all to see my notice. I made a note not to turn off my mobile phone.

We drove the rest of the way in a comfortable silence. I thinking about my hot date tomorrow night and Phil thinking about his tonight. Laura followed close behind no doubt thinking about her hot date too; well, at least I hoped she was.

"Come on in for a cup of coffee or something, will you, Phil? Eve and Becca are in bed and I don't feel like being alone. Come on – just a quick one?"

"You go on in and I'll check with Laura."

I was delighted when the two of them came into the house seconds after me. I got out some glasses and opened a couple of bottles of wine. I put on some good music and dimmed the lights so Laura, the self-confessed neatness freak, wouldn't notice that the place was very untidy. So it had worn off: Becca and Eve weren't keeping the place nice and clean any more. Everything was back to normal. Ah well, I suppose it had to end sometime.

Magazines and papers were flung around the room and there was a selection of bottles of different-coloured nail varnish and a bottle of nail-varnish remover and cotton balls lined up on the floor at the end of the couch. Becca and Eve never lifted things up with them when they went to bed. They went empty-handed up the stairs every night. I, on the other hand, went up the stairs every night laden like an ox with all the trappings they had left strewn around the place. My bedroom had an array of stuff all over it that I had carried up the stairs at night but hadn't gotten around to dumping in the right bedrooms.

I could see Laura looking around, itching to tidy up. If she offered I decided to let her do it. I was hoping she'd offer. She didn't. I was very disappointed.

"Nice wine."

"Mmm. It is nice, isn't it?" I was delighted I had got something right.

"Is this the one I gave you?" Phil had to ask.

"Yes."

"I told you it was better than that cheap vinegar you buy."

351

The wine was so nice we polished off the last two bottles left in the house.

I started searching in the drink cabinet.

"There has to be something in here to drink."

"Here, let me see." Laura was at my elbow. I was hoping she wouldn't see the cobwebs that had gathered in the corner of the press.

"Wow, that's the biggest cobweb I've ever seen!" she was truly amazed and pointing directly into the corner. "It's huge."

She must have seen very few cobwebs in her day and I was tempted to bring her up to my bedroom to see the mother and father of all cobwebs hanging delicately from the light shade and spreading down like a curtain along the ceiling. Every night as I lay in bed I watched it and reminded myself to get rid of it in the morning. Then when the mad dash of morning came, I forgot about it. It's been there so long now I'm sure it has some sort of legal rights to the place. I decided not to bring Laura up to see it because my legs were gone a bit funny and I didn't think I'd be able to make it up the stairs in any sort of a dignified fashion. I was trying to be dignified.

"Is there feck all to drink?" I asked. "There must be something to drink. Look! There are lots of ends of bottles in here. I'll make us a cocktail. A huge big cocktail. An enormous kick-ass cocktail." I fell backwards onto my bottom. My legs shot up in the air.

I was glad I had my trousers on. Dignity at all times.

"Brilliant," Laura said as she helped me up.

"Great idea." Phil was up on his feet now and was pulling out all the half-empty bottles.

"Go on, Kelly, get a bucket and we'll empty all the drink into it. Like a punch. We can scoop up the drink and drink it when we want one."

"But I've no bucket."

"A big bowl will do."

"What about a big pot?"

"That'll do."

We mixed up a lethal concoction, but it was delicious. Too delicious.

"OK, OK, it's Truth or Dare time." Laura was waving her drink around and was acting a bit silly from where I was sitting on a cushion on the floor. I was only sitting on the cushion because I had slid down off the armchair the last time I tried to re-fill my glass. I had decided to stay where I landed as it was nearer the pot of drink. I was feeling good and I had a lot of things I wanted to tell Phil about him being a wonderful friend.

"Phil, I don't know if I ever told you, and if I haven't, I should have. I'm very sorry if I never did. That is if I didn't. You are the best friend a person could ever have and I mean that. Laura, you have no idea what a wonderful friend Phil is. I hope you treat him very well because he deserves to be treated very well and if you don't you'll have me to answer to. Did I ever tell you, Phil, what a wonderful friend you are?"

"Yes, Kelly, you tell me often, ad nauseam and ad infinitum. You always tell me after you've had a lot to drink. Now come on and let's play Truth or Dare."

"Ladies first. Beauty before age and all that, so I'll go first." I slurred and started laughing loudly – too loudly – but I didn't notice. "Come on then, me first, ask me a question. Pick me. I want to go first." I was like a Christian to the lions. A lamb to the slaughter. A fucking eejit.

"Did you ever fancy Phil as more than a friend?" Laura asked the question she must have been dying to ask all night. Who could blame the girl? She seized an opportunity when it was handed to her on a platter.

"I can honestly say – hand on heart," I started.

"Wrong side, Kelly – your heart is on the other side." Phil was enjoying himself.

"Well, maybe I know something you don't and my heart, if I have one at all, is on that side. Granted, a different side to everyone else, but I think you should check that out first before you go making fun of me."

"I'm not making fun of you. So is your heart really in the wrong place?"

"No, my heart is in the right place all right, all the time. Anyway, getting back to the question. I have started the answer so I will finish it just to make sure there will be no confusion at a later stage. I will swear categorically that I, Kelly, have never fancied Phil as anything other than my friend."

"Did you ever sleep with him and I mean that in the biblical sense?"

"Hey, that's not fair!" Phil was alarmed. "That's not a question you can ask! That's not fair, Laura — it's just not a fair question. You can't ask her that. You can't ask any of us that. We are under the influence and we won't answer, will we, Kelly? That's not fair."

Phil runs out of vocabulary when he gets pissed. He has a very annoying habit of repeating himself when he gets pissed too.

"It is too a fair question!" Laura shouted. I think she was pissed too, but it was hard to tell because I only knew her a short time. I was guessing she always shouted when she got pissed, she being so quiet-spoken when she was sober.

"Yes. I have slept with Phil and I enjoyed every minute of it. Only once, mind you. He's good, very good, nod, nod, wink, wink." I started winking and nodding my head so much I thought it would fall off into the drink pot.

"Jesus, Kelly!" Phil was shocked.

"Jesus, Kelly!" Laura was shocked. She was also hurt. She had asked the question but couldn't handle the answer.

"So what do you two do then? Make do with each other when there is nothing else available? You're sick! Where's my coat, I'm going home!"

"You don't have one," Phil said, matter-of-fact.

"Coat? Home?"

"Neither."

Laura started to wail. She was very upset.

"Come here to me." Phil put his arm around her. "Kelly and I slept together once in all our lives. It was a foolish mistake. I thought I was in love with her, but I'm not and I know this is probably far too soon to say, but I know I'm in love with you. Do you believe in love at first sight, Laura? I never did until now."

"Oh, Phil, I think I do."

He leaned over and gently gave her a kiss. Both their eyes were closed. I had another drink.

"My turn to ask you a question, Kelly," Phil said with a smug smile. I think it was payback time.

"Who do you really, really fancy? I mean like rip-his-clothes-off fancy?"

"No one at the moment. Sad, isn't it? I was at a party recently and I could have fancied one of the guys there, but it was a disaster. Then when Graham was going all nicey-nicey I thought I felt a bit of a stirring, but that was only an act. So now I don't know."

"So it's not me then?"

"No, Phil, sorry."

He smiled. He looked directly into Laura's eyes.

"So then, Phil, who do you fancy?" I asked stupidly.

"Laura does it for me."

"Aaaaahhhh," I said. "Now, Laura, what do you think of that then?"

"I think it's wonderful because Phil does it for me too." She put her hand up to his face and traced her finger along his lips. They were gumming for each other and I was doing the gooseberry routine again.

"I'm off to bed. You'd better not drive. Stay in the spare room. See you in the morning." I dragged myself up the stairs, imagining all sorts of positions and propositions.

Today's List

To do
1. Too pissed to do list.
2. Oh, that rhymes.

Chapter Eighteen

I woke at about six in the morning. The room was spinning around and at the same time it was wobbling from side to side. If I'd stood out on the floor I'd have definitely fallen flat on my face. I stayed in bed. I was propped up on three pillows. I couldn't lie down flat because the room swayed very badly every time I lay down. Sitting up wasn't great either as the enormous cobweb kept coming for me. I kept ducking, but that only wrecked my poor head. My head was very sore. Like I had changed my parting in my hair after having it the same way for a hundred years. It was sore. My stomach was very tender and sickly. I needed to pee. I tried to get out of the bed. The bloody floor wouldn't keep still for me. I got down on my hands and knees and crawled along. The landing floor was in the same condition.

It was very dangerous. I'd have to get someone to have a look at it. I dragged myself along into the bathroom. I was spending a lot of time on the landing and in the bathroom these days. It was starting to worry me.

I mourned the loss of the cabinet I never had as I sat there on the bathroom floor. I mourned it every time I went into the bathroom. I was thinking it might be a good idea to ring the woodwork guy and try being nice to him. You never know, he could be on the brink of leaving his wife and family and home and be glad of another home to do all his DIY on. We could come to some sort of arrangement whereby he tended to all my woodwork needs and I gave him full run of my house to fit out whatever way he saw fit. Built-in everything. No hanky-panky. No need to complicate the situation.

"Ma, what are you doing on the bathroom floor?"

"Eve, why is it that you always have to know exactly what I'm doing all the time? Some time you'll have to just accept that your mother is just sitting down relaxing or reading a book or watching telly for the sheer escapism and pleasure of it all. I am sitting on the bathroom floor at this particular moment in time because I am dying and I thought here might be the least messiest place to do it."

"Well, no matter where you do it, me and Becca will have to clean up."

"What's going on?" Becca had heard the commotion.

"Ma – she's on the bathroom floor, dying."

"Did you have a drink?"

"I might have enjoyed a couple of beverages with my close friends, Phil and Laura."

"A couple of drinks? More than a couple I'm thinking."

"Be careful what you think. I can read thoughts. I read Laura's thoughts or she read mine. I can't remember."

"Who is Laura?"

"One of my closest friends. She and Phil are madly in love. Oh Eve, I have to tell you that I was a witness to love at first sight last night. It does exist you'll be pleased to hear, I'm sure. It happened to Phil and Laura. It definitely does exist. Go on, ask them – they're in the spare room, go on, go on."

"What? Phil and some strange friend are in our spare room?"

"Yeah. Shhhh, will you, you'll wake them. They are probably fast asleep in each other's arms by now. Don't be calling one of my best friends in the world strange. Laura's not that strange. Well, maybe a bit – she has no cellulite. That's certainly strange, isn't it?"

"You can't be serious. You let Phil and some woman we don't know stay here?"

"I do know Laura, she's one of my best cellulite-free friends."

"But we've never heard of her."

Becca knocked on the door of the spare room . . . Nothing. Not a sound from within.

She knocked again. A little bit harder this time. Still no answer. She opened the door slowly.

"Wakey-wakey!" I shouted from the bathroom floor.

"Shhh, Ma. Keep quiet!" said Becca.

"Who is this woman and where did you meet her? How come we haven't met her?" Eve was interrogating me. I didn't like it.

"Well, for goodness sake, I only just met the girl. I can't possibly make her do the whole meet-the-family-routine until I know her a bit better, now can I?"

"The spare room's empty. They've flown the coop if they were ever here in the first place."

"Jesus, I hope they didn't drive. They were in no fit state. One of you check and see are their cars still there."

I was still feeling a little bit wobbly and I wasn't quite sure, but something kept telling me I was talking a lot of rubbish.

"You're talking a lot of rubbish, Ma."

"They were here. Their cars are still here. They must've got a taxi." Becca was hanging out the window. Reporting back to base.

"Can you see them anywhere?" I asked.

"No, Ma, they must be gone in a taxi like Becca said."

"There's a note here on the landing window. *We're gone in a taxi – talk to you tomorrow, love Phil.* So that's it, they're gone."

"The cheek of them! Deserters! They just fecked off and left me here in this rotten state after me welcoming that girl into my home with open arms. Open arms and legs upwards." I was giggling big-time now. "Or should that be open legs and palms upwards?"

"How should I know?" said Eve. "I don't even know what you're talking about."

"Come on, Ma, you'll have to get back into bed. You can't stay on the bathroom floor."

"And pray tell why not? Oh, Jesus, the room is moving again. Oh, help me. Please do something. Oh, girls, help me!"

"Come on Ma, back into bed. You'll be OK in a while."

"Yeah, just have a lie down and you'll fall off to sleep and wake up feeling great. Well, maybe not great, but good anyway."

"Can you guarantee that?"

"It's a promise."

Becca tucked me into bed which must have been very hard for her because it was moving so much. Up and down and round and round.

I went into a deep sleep. When I woke I was still in a deep sleep only I was awake.

"Hi, Ma, are you all right?"

"No, Eve, I think I'm on the brink of dying. I feel really bad and it's not just a hangover."

"Come on, Ma, you're all right."

"No, I'm not all right. I'm really bad."

"Well, you're bad all right for drinking so much as to be sick."

Good aul' role reversal acting the maggot again.

"I think we'd better phone Dr Reid," said Becca anxiously.

"No, no, I don't want her coming near me. She'll only see the cut of the place."

"Eve and I will clean it before she gets here."

"She's one of the ever-increasing neatness freaks. I think they are taking over the whole world. My new pal Laura is one too."

Dr Reid was really lovely. She was immaculate and a nice gentle person too. She wore beautiful suits and matching shoes. I rarely got her to make house calls. I usually called to the surgery.

I felt a wave of nausea.

"Oh, Jesus, you better get her, I feel terrible. Turn the light down low, will you?"

"Is it upsetting you?"

"No, but the dirt of the kip is. I can't see it if the light is low and neither can the doctor."

Becca tucked me in and I felt much sicker. I thought I was going to faint. She put a damp cloth on my forehead.

The doctor arrived predictably enough before Eve and Becca had a chance to clean the black hole that is my bedroom.

"This way, doctor. We have the lights down low so mind your step."

"Ouch! Jesus! Ouch!" The doctor stubbed his toe on the door.

I heard a male voice cry out in agony.

"Who's that?" I shouted.

"It's the doctor, Eve said.

"But it's a man!"I shouted hoarsely.

"Yes, it's a locum. Dr Reid is away for a few days so Dr O'Brien is standing in for her."

"Hello, I'm Dr O'Brien. Can we please turn the lights on? I can't see a thing?"

"Jesus! No!"

"Please, I have to be able to see you to examine you."

"OK, turn up the lights, girls."

The lights came on full and strong. The cobweb moved dangerously close to Dr O'Brien's beautifully groomed hair.

"*Jesus! It's you!*" I shouted as I pulled at my hair, which was standing perpendicular to my head. I hauled at the sheet and dragged it up over my boobs.

I wiped my mouth and hoped I hadn't dribbled out onto the pillow during the night. I rolled my eyes around sideways to the pillow to see if I could see any dribbles. I couldn't. Not that that meant there were none there. It just meant my eyes weren't as flexible as I thought they were. I had to roll my eyes around in the other direction then to make them feel even again.

"When did she start rolling her eyes around like this?" David, Gwen's brother, Hugh and Ray's uncle, my arch-enemy asked.

"We didn't notice it until now."

"Ma, do you see who it is? It's Hugh and Ray's uncle. Do you remember him from the party?"

Becca tried to warn me.

"Yes, dear, I see him. I remember. Jesus, do I remember!" I said through clenched teeth.

"What's she trying to say? How long has her mouth been stiff like that?"

"Oh, that's OK. Don't mind that. She sometimes does that."

I could see the pile of ironing over in the corner vomiting down off my dressing-table. I jerked my head in that direction knowing that the two girls would pick up on it and hide the pile of unkempt-looking clothes.

"And the head jerking – has that been going on long?" the jerk of a doctor asked.

"Oh, she's been doing that for years," Eve said and followed the direction of the jerk – my head-movement jerk not the jerk of a doctor. She picked up a large towel and threw it over the ironing pile.

Becca, to give her her due in bucketfuls, was standing with an armload of shoes she had managed to pick up off the floor. She was kicking other stuff under the bed. I was very proud of both of them. I felt a tear in my eye.

"No need to cry. I'll just give you a stemital injection and you'll be fine."

"Oh, I'm dying. Could you not leave me alone to die in peace? Did you have to come along upsetting me? Trying to make me feel better and then looking at me and the state of the place and making me feel worse." I started to cry, big-time. Big, loud, awful crying. Nose-running and loud-noise type crying. I couldn't stop.

"There now. You'll be fine. I promise. Just let me give you this injection."

"OK." I went all submissive. I pulled out my arm and offered it up to him.

He didn't want my arm.

"It goes in your bum," he said gently.

I heard the girls giggling.

"Will you wait outside, you two?" I snapped at them. I would not give them the ultimate satisfaction of witnessing the most embarrassing moment in my entire life. It was bad enough they knew what was happening without seeing it too. I rolled over; he pulled the duvet down. I was wearing a skimpy thong so that was all he had to pull down. My bum was as good as bare.

"Just a little prick," he said.

"Oh, don't be so modest. I'm sure your prick it's perfectly adequate." I couldn't resist anything that would cover my own embarrassment.

He rubbed at my ass for a moment and then told me I could lie over on it again if I wanted to. He stood up straight and went straight into the bloody cobweb that he had managed to skillfully avoid up until now. It wrapped itself around him like a giant crochet shawl. He pulled and dragged and finally loosened himself from its grasp. He didn't say a word.

"Thanks," I said.

"Don't mention it. Take things easy. No more drinking and be careful what you eat."

"I have to go out tonight. I'll be all right to go, won't I?"

"I'm sure you'll be fine, but don't overdo it."

"Becca or Eve will pay you on the way out. Thanks again."

"Don't worry about it. Let's put it on the slate."

"No, I couldn't do that."

"Well, Kelly, I want to. Gwen was really upset. She told me about the narrow escape she had with

Graham. She said it was all down to you that she found out about him in time. I had warned her that he was only after her for her money. She wouldn't listen. It's hard to hear, particularly if you think you're in love. So, I owe you one. Graham was a real piece of work. The boys didn't like him either. I was with them a lot in the early days when Gwen's husband died. They were gutted. They're like sons to me. I tried to do the best I could for them, but it was really tough on the three of them. Gwen did a great job rearing the boys. I don't know how she didn't see through Graham though. I think he just swept her off her feet and she couldn't see any of his faults. It would have been a total disaster if she had married Graham. I think the boys were starting to cop on to him. They're no fools. She should be proud of them. So, I owe you one."

"They're fine lads – they seem to have captured my girl's hearts anyway."

"They seem like nice girls."

"They are, they are."

"Try to get some sleep then and you might be all right to out later on. It must be important to you. I hope you have a great time."

"Me too."

He left. I closed my eyes to the mess and the mortification and dosed off. I slept for the day.

Today's List

To do
1. *Remove all cobwebs from the house.*
2. *Make room in a press to keep the ironing in.*
3. *Get Eve and Becca to lift up their mess every night.*
4. *Give Gwen a ring and see how she is.*
5. *Have a great time with my Prince.*

Not to do
1. *Don't ever drink again.*
2. *Don't judge a book by its cover. David isn't as bad as I first thought.*
3. *Don't mess it up with my Prince.*

CHAPTER NINETEEN

"Ma," Becca gave me a gentle nudge through the duvet. "Here's a cup of tea for you. Come on sit up. You'll feel better after it."

"Go away."

"You told me to call you at six if you slept all day so you could see if you were able to go out or if you wanted to cancel."

"Oh, God. You're cruel. Is it six already? I could sleep on broken bottles. I wonder should I cancel going out tonight? I hope my red dress is clean? What have I let myself in for? Oh girls, I have definitely lost the plot, big-time."

I pulled myself upright and started sipping the tea. It tasted lovely. I felt much better.

"I feel better after that, thanks. Ah, to hell with it! Sure I may as well go. What have I got to lose? Are ye with me or agin' me? Will you help me to get ready? I look a fright and look at the state of my hair. Do you think I'm mad going out to meet someone I don't know? I must have been mad to put up that notice."

"Stop fussing. What harm can it do? You're going to meet him in a crowded place. Anyway, you said he sounded nice."

"No, I didn't. What I said was that he sounded normal but that I could hardly hear him."

"You'll be fine, Ma. Now sit up straight and close your eyes tight and keep them closed till we tell you to open them."

"What?"

"Go on, you heard me."

"Keep them closed." I could hear Eve was in the room now too.

I heard the light click on.

"Open them now."

I was stunned. The room gleamed. It shone. No cobwebs. No mess.

"All the ironing is done and a load of washing on. We spent nearly all day doing it."

"You're the best. Thanks a million." They really are the best children ever. I always knew they were terrific and sometimes they bloody well showed me how truly terrific they could be. I felt a little tear coming on. I wiped it away.

"Then we slipped into town and . . ."

They both reached under the bed and picked up bags and bags. Well, they deserved a treat after all the work they had done.

"Good on you! Show me what wonderful things you bought yourselves."

A magnificent white linen dress, trimmed with coffee-colored stitching. Coffee and white shoes and matching bag and a coffee pashmina. Neither of my children would wear any of these.

"They're beautiful, but where did you get them? You'll never wear this lot. They are classy and classic. I love them. But aren't they a bit too old for you?"

"They're not for us. They're for you."

"But how could you afford them?"

"The money you gave us from the divorce is too much for us," said Eve. "We wanted to spend some of it on you. We knew you'd be stuck for tonight so here you are."

"I'll run the bath and you can have a good soak," said Becca.

They were some kids. They were my kids.

I soaked. I rubbed. I lathered. I shaved. I exfoliated, I cleansed, I toned, I did it all and I enjoyed every bit of it.

They did my nails, a pearly white color that I'd never have dreamed of wearing, but it looked fantastic. Then they did my make-up – not a hint of green eye-shadow anywhere to be seen. They even made my hair look as though I had just walked out of one of the top salons in Dublin. I felt like a real woman. They had bought me new underwear. A fabulous, creamy lace, platform bra and matching thong. My cellulite would have a field-day in the thong. I slipped on the dress, shoes and shawl and though I say so myself I looked like a millionaire in the outfit. No need to phone a friend or ask the audience, I knew I looked terrific. It was a perfect fit too. My two girls were charmed with themselves.

"Now, you can't go driving yourself and you only up out of your sick bed," said Becca. "We've rung a taxi and he'll be here any minute. You wait downstairs and we'll just make your bed and change the sheets and then the whole house will have been done. Go on, shoo!"

"Out of the way. Skidaddle!"

I glided down the stairs with the confidence of a woman who has confidence. I was gliding and I was doing it very well.

The taxi pulled up and I kissed my two Fairy Godmothers goodbye and off Cinderella went in her carriage.

"*Don't drink too much!*" Becca shouted after me.

"*Don't drink at all!*" Eve shouted even louder.

"*Have fun, Ma!*" They shouted in unison.

I felt nervous but excited. I knew my Prince wouldn't recognise me because I was wearing the wrong clothes, even if they were the right clothes. I had the advantage. I was early too, another advantage. I would be able to spot him coming into the restaurant. He wouldn't know who I was until I introduced myself.

There was a terrific atmosphere in the place. I took a quick look around. It was the best seafood restaurant in Dublin. The décor was very modern with stainless steel and glass all over the place. There were huge fish tanks built into the walls. I was hoping we wouldn't be sitting too near one of the tanks. I couldn't bear to have all the fish watching me eating one of their friends or relations. Maybe even their mother.

Oh God! I couldn't believe it. He was here already. I spotted him and I saw him looking over at me. There was no going back now. He had a navy suit on and a white shirt. His tie was definitely chunky. Navy and grey. Nice. He looked lovely. He was older than I had imagined. But he was cute. I must be a mad bitch altogether to be doing this, I thought. I nearly didn't go over to him. But he was very cute. He had brown hair graying at the sides and thinning at the top. I sat on the seat opposite him. He had blue eyes and a very surprised expression on his face.

"Hi." I spoke very softly, as I didn't want the whole restaurant to know we were just meeting this second.

"Hi?"

"I'm Princess. You're obviously Prince."

"No. I'm King."

"King? Have you been promoted without my say so?"

"Promoted? No?"

"You said you were King not Prince. If this is a joke, I'm not getting it."

"Look, Princess or whatever your name is, I'm really not into this. You have some nerve all the same coming onto men who are trying to have a quiet evening. You should try and come up with a more original name than Princess though."

"What?"

"I told you I'm not interested."

"What? You read my notice. You called me, remember?"

"I never read any of those type of notices. Call-girls, no matter what they call themselves or how classy they look, are still call-girls. I am not interested in paying for sex and I never called anyone. Now will you please leave my table? I'm waiting on my wife? I'll have to call the waiter if you don't leave."

"I don't believe this. Are you or are you not Prince?"

"For the last time, how many times do I have to tell, you my name is King, George King. Not Prince."

"George, what's going on? Who's this?"

"Hello, darling. She was just leaving. A case of mistaken identity, dear."

I stood up. I didn't have to sit here and listen to this. I only got as far as standing up though. I stood still and couldn't move. How dare he think I was some sort of a call-girl? The bloody nerve of him, making arrangements to meet me and then insulting me! He must get his jollys making gobshites out of people. I could feel the tears coming to my eyes. Why was all of human nature letting me down? Was everything against me?

Well, that was it. No more. I was done with kissing frogs and I was done with looking for a Prince. There is no such thing. It's all a shagging fairytale. There isn't one decent Prince left. They are extinct. We should have been told when they were only an endangered species. We could have saved them. I could have put Dan on the case and we'd be up to our whatsits in Princes now. But it was too late. Fair fucks to Cinderella and Snow White and the rest of the gang who managed to grab a Prince while they were still around.

So that was it. No Prince. I wasn't going to settle for second best, so it looked like there would be no man in my life, for the rest of my life. Oh, I'd still have my male friends, but no one male that would go beyond friendship. I could live with that. Better to be with none than one who'd give me a dog's life. Although, have you seen the way some people treat their dogs? Beauty parlours and the likes. How bad would that be? Just not good enough. Not good enough for me, anyway. I felt deflated and let down by males everywhere. I felt humiliated. The bloody nerve of this guy! I was better off before when I didn't want any man in my life and I was determined I was going to return to that way of living. Enjoy myself by myself. I didn't need a man. The humiliation of the guy thinking I was a tart had chased away all my confidence but not my sense of right and wrong.

"I'm so sorry," I said to his wife. "Your husband rang me and arranged to meet me here tonight. I don't know why he wanted to meet me if he knew you were going to be here. Perhaps to humiliate me. Well, it worked. You'd want to be careful – if he rang me, God knows how many more he rang. He's a worm."

I marched out. I left the two of them sitting, dumbfounded. I stopped at the doorway. I could hear their raised voices.

"What is she talking about?" the wife was shouting.

"I haven't a bloody clue. She just sat down and started calling me Prince."

"Did you ring her, you creep? You promised you'd never have an affair again after the last one. You promised. Well, at least this time I didn't catch you with your trousers down. At least I was spared that embarrassment this time!"

In exaggerated movements, she lifted up the glass vase off the table. Slowly she took out the single red

Jacinta McDevitt

rose that was in it. She put the vase back down on the table. She held the rose so close to her husbands face that he could smell it. She snapped the stem. It was like an explosion. The whole restaurant was dumbfounded, watching the side-show. She pulled at his breast pocket and shoved the rose into it. Once again she lifted the vase off the table. Once again she pulled at his breast pocket, where the rose was snuggled. She upended the vase into his pocket. The water went everywhere. She pressed his pocket flat against his chest. He was sitting open-mouthed and open-legged. Dripping water. She turned and headed straight for me. I was afraid I was next on her agenda. He leapt up and followed his wife. I opened the door wide. They went straight out.

"I swear to God I never saw her before in my life," he was shouting as they breezed past me.

"Tell it to my lawyer!" she shouted back at him.

I couldn't believe it. I was still standing there like a doorman. It had started to rain. I closed the door and went over to ask the waiter to ring me a taxi. I was going home to my house and I was never coming out again.

A little clock chimed. Eight chimes. The door opened.

I looked right at him as he came into the restaurant. He didn't see me. He was distracted, brushing rain off his navy jacket. He straightened up his chunky tie. It was pink and navy and white. It was really

378

nice. He looked wonderful. He searched along the tables. His eyes rested on a woman in a red dress and red shoes. She was with a gang of women.

I decided to make a dash for the door and get a taxi around the corner. Get the hell out of here and quick. I watched as he was led to his table. It was in the corner. It was set for two. I had to do a runner. Leg it, quick. But he looked so forlorn sitting there with his expectations at their highest. My heart went out to him. But I wasn't going to fall for that doe-eyed expression or that gentle, kind manner. I headed for the door. Something made me turn and look back. He still hadn't seen me. He was fixing his tie again. Now fixing his hair. Making sure everything was right. I couldn't watch the poor bastard. I had my hand on the doorknob. I was all set to leave. I don't know how, but next thing I knew, I was standing at his table.

"Hi, David."

"Eh, Kelly. So what are you doing here? How's the tummy? The injection did the trick, I bet."

"Yes. It did."

"So where's the hot date you were talking about earlier?"

"Well, David, eh, I don't think you're going to believe this, but I think it's eh, you."

"Me?"

"Are you waiting on a Princess?"

"All my life."

"Well, I'm waiting on my Prince."

"Eh. Er. So, you're the one who put up the wanted notice?"

"The very one."

He laughed, a lovely gentle, sexy laugh. Not mocking me.

"Sit down, Kelly, sit down. So what exactly do Princesses drink these days?"

"Water will do. After last night I don't want to get into that condition again. So, what do you think? Will I stay or do you want me to go?"

I was sure he would want me to go. I was sure he was pissed off with me. Every time he saw me something crazy happened. He never saw my calm self. He had never seen the normal me. Or maybe he had. Maybe all the mishaps and disasters are the normal me, warts and all. If he only knew what had happened to the poor bastard a few minutes ago.

I wanted to go, but then again I wanted to stay. I only wanted to go because I thought he didn't want me to stay. I really wanted to stay so much.

"I really want to stay," I whispered. I know, a bit obvious. I'll have to work on not being too obvious.

"I'd love you to stay. We can have a meal together as friends at least."

"That'd be lovely."

We talked non-stop about everything and anything. He told me all about his life and loves and why he had become a doctor and I told him all about my life and loves and the tribulations of being a mother.

The waiter kept coming over, interrupting us, to ask if we were ready to order.

"Just a few more minutes," David said every time. Each time we went to read the menu we got as far as the starters and then got distracted by each other.

Finally we both scanned the menu quickly and ordered just to get rid of the guy.

I have no idea what I ordered or ate. I can only tell you it was the most mouth-wateringly, delicious, orgasmic meal I have ever had. There could have been a million flies in my soup, if I had soup, and I wouldn't have noticed. The whole school of fish could have watched and cheered from the water-tanks as I tucked into their teacher. We never even noticed how late it was getting. We got the hint that it was time to leave when we saw the staff lifting chairs out of the way to clean the floor.

"I'd better get a taxi home."

"No, please don't. Please, let me give you a lift."

My mobile rang. I was hoping it wouldn't be another Prince. I was pretty happy with my present quota of Princes. My Prince insisted on paying the bill. I was happy with that. It meant I could ask him out next to return the compliment. No sitting around waiting on the phone for this girl.

"Hi, Ma, how's it going?"

"Wonderful. I've loads to tell you when I get home."

"It'll have to wait until tomorrow. We're going to a dance in college and we're staying over in one of the girl's flats. Is that OK? See you in the morning or, more likely, the afternoon. Have a good time!

"You too. Enjoy it."

We talked all the way home. I won't bore you with the details. Although, I have to tell you there wasn't one boring detail about the man.

"How come you're in a woodwork class?" I was dying to know.

"I bought a little cottage a few years ago and it needed a lot of work done to it. I found it hard to get anyone to do it. I started doing a few bits and pieces and I liked doing it. I needed to know a bit more, so I went to a woodwork class. I enjoy it now. Some day I hope that I'll have renovated the whole cottage myself. I want to restore it to the way it was originally. I'm really enjoying doing it and I've got more than half it done already. You should come down with me for the weekend and see what you think."

"I'd love to. Maybe I could give you a hand although I'm hopeless at DIY. I'm more your DDIY person. Don't Do It Yourself."

"Well how good are you at watching and making the odd cup of tea now and again?"

"I think I could manage that."

"I'll make you that bathroom cabinet you were swooning over if you want," he offered. "I'd have to measure and come and fit it and it might take a couple of days. I have a few days off next week. If you want me to do it, I'll do it then for you."

"Oh, you are so charming!"

We were sitting in the driveway.

"Kelly, do you believe in love at fourth sight or maybe it was third?"

"I believe in love – isn't that enough for you?"

He leaned over and kissed me. A soft kiss at first and then a more passionate, I want you, here and now, type of kiss.

It was lovely: fireworks were raging all around the place and I was terrified of a fire.

"Do you want to come in for coffee?" I asked, hoping.

"I was hoping you'd ask."

The place was sparkling. Eve and Becca were the best kids in the world. I searched and searched but I could find no coffee.

"Sorry, but I'm all out of coffee – will tea do?" I was shaking. I have to be honest (well, amn't I always, God help me?), tea was the last thing on my mind.

I flicked on the kettle. I felt his arms around my waist. He started kissing my neck. The bloody fireworks started again.

"Do you hear them?" I whispered.

"The fireworks? Of course I do."

We managed to make it to the top of the stairs still fully clothed, but only just.

I stood on the landing and looked at my Prince. I wanted him so much. He put his arms around me and kissed me a slow lingering kiss. He kissed my neck. I felt his hand move up along my leg, up under my dress and around by my bum. He'd had the pleasure of seeing my bum before. He must have liked what he saw and wanted to see a lot more.

He pulled my dress up over my head and tossed it over the banisters. He stood looking at me as if I was the most beautiful thing he'd ever seen. I was delighted my new underwear gave me such a good figure. It was sexy too. Becca and Eve had done me proud. He held me again and buried his face in my boobs. He unfastened the hooks at the back of my bra and threw my bra on top of my dress. He let the full of my breasts rest in his hands while he rubbed my nipples. Then flicked his tongue across the nipples.

We were still on the landing. It was featuring hugely in my life lately. I opened the door of my bedroom. It was cobwebless. I wondered if he'd notice. I was thinking he wouldn't. Well, not until tomorrow morning anyway.

I was dying for him to make love to me, but he was into foreplay. I was loving every minute of that too. I ripped off his shirt and felt his strong muscles.

I opened his belt and then the fly of his trousers. His clothes lay in a pile on the floor. I wanted him all for myself for always. I wanted to devour him. I was madly in love. The best and only way to make love is when you're in love. There is no comparison. I felt sorry for anyone that hadn't been made love to by someone who loves them. I knew with every touch, every kiss that this wonderful, kind, loving Prince truly loved me.

We loved each other over and over, long into the night and the following morning. I felt so loved and special. That's the way he made me feel, special. He was a wonderful lover and knew all the little nooks and crannies that got me going. He held me in his arms and told me I was beautiful and that he loved being with me. He wondered how silly we had been that we hadn't seen it earlier. I couldn't answer. I guess I had been just too busy with frogs.

My mobile rang. "Hi, is that the Princess that put the ad up on the notice board looking for her Prince Charming?"

"Yes."

"Well, I think I'm your Prince, all right."

"Oh, I'm sorry, but my Prince has already come."

Today's List

To do
1. *Enjoy every single moment of being with David.*
2. *Handle him with care.*
3. *Carpe diem.*

Not to do.
1. *Don't waste a single moment.*

To ignore
1. *Any more phone calls from princes – they are only fake.*

CHAPTER TWENTY

In fairytales a year passes in the turning of a page. I was living a fairytale and I was loving every single second of it.

It was February. February 14th. It was Valentine's Day again. The sun was shining. Thank God. It confirmed that the whole world was in happy mode. I wanted everyone to be happy today.

Men were walking along the pavement carrying large bouquets of flowers, Babys' Breath and roses. Some had boxes of chocolates under their oxters. Others had both.

This morning David had brought me my breakfast in bed. He had also given me a dozen of the reddest roses I had ever seen. No Babies' Breath. He had also given me hand-made chocolates and a very funny card about frogs and toads. I gave him

a single red rose and a romantic card. Becca and Eve
got red roses and cards. We were a happy lot.

Now it was early afternoon and I was standing
on the steps of the Registry Office. I was all togged
out in a short deep-cream lace dress. My shoes
matched to perfection, as usual. Little flowers were
caught in around my hair, which was more blonde
and more spiky than last Valentine's Day.

David was beside me. He looked so handsome.
He was all togged out for the day. Eve and Becca
were on either side of us. They were breathtakingly
beautiful. Becca in a pink dress and pink suede
boots. Eve in a blue dress and blue suede boots.
Both of them had their hair piled high on their
heads. They were having great craic.

"David, get a photo with me and Becca and Ray
and Hugh, will you?" Eve, of course, wanted to
capture all the happiness for a later date when we
might need it. She was so happy these days I thought
she'd burst.

"Ok. Here, come on. Ah, you look like a line of
soldiers. Will you relax and put an arm around each
other. Like this."

He grabbed me and gave me a big hug.

"Come on, Dad, put that woman down and get
on with the photo. I can't stop laughing." Becca was
always smiling lately.

They had started calling David 'Dad'. At first it

was a great joke – they enjoyed slagging him and he loved the banter with them. But little by little the joke had stuck and he was glad it had. He deserved the title. He had done more with them in a year than Graham had in a lifetime.

We were getting our photograph taken after the wedding.

Joan and Christopher were all tanned and radiant. They had found the perfect villa and opened a health and beauty salon in the sun. They had flown over for the wedding.

Dan and Tilda were doing the proud-parents routine with Gary and his new sister, Rosie, who was a miniature of her mother. Gary had taken to Rosie immediately. He loved doing the big-brother bit and he had finally given up sucking his mother's tit.

Gwen and I had become great pals. She looked happy and content with her new bloke. I had introduced her to the gym and she met a Jim there and they were so happy together. He adored her for herself and not for her money.

"Smile," the photographer shouted, so we all obeyed. "Now can I have one with the bride and groom only, please."

David and I watched the photographer set the camera. He lined everything up to perfection. Then he took a picture of the happy couple, Phil and Laura.

The bride was stunning in a long, tailored off-white dress with deeper cream trimmings and tiny pearls scattered here and there in clusters all over the dress. Her shoes matched the dress and she had her hair piled high and decorated with roses and pearls. The groom was, as usual, impeccable. His suit was so dark it looked black, but every now and again the light caught it and you could see it was brown. His shirt was the same colour as the bride's dress and his tie was deep cream. He looked fantastic.

I had never been Best Person at a wedding before, but I had my speech in my pocket and I had done all my duties to perfection. A good night and a good life was ahead for all of us. I just knew it. I felt it in my waters and they never let me down. I turned to look at all the happy faces and was just in time to see Eve and Becca catch Laura's bouquet between them. They didn't fight over it. They just winked at each other and slipped their hands into Hugh and Ray's hands. I had another little feeling in my waters: a double wedding.

For today, everything was wonderful. We were happy and whatever sadness or worries might come our way in the future we'd weather them together. We'd just hold firm and hang on to each other. Now, at last, I had someone who really loved me, to hold on to. I put my arm around his waist and gave him a squeeze.

He squeezed me back, pecked me on the lips and said, "I'm so glad you came looking for me."

Then he gently slipped his hand into mine, where it seemed to belong. Had there been a sunset I just know we would have walked off hand and hand into it. But, as it was the middle of a February afternoon, in Dublin, we just sauntered over to the limo that was to take us to the wedding reception. We had booked a suite to stay in tonight. I had ordered champagne to be sent to the room later.

David held the door open for me and I climbed in. He followed and touched my face gently as he sat down beside me. I put my head on his chest and felt his heart beat. I lifted my head to look at him and he kissed me, a gentle, loving kiss. A kiss of promises and hopes.

"You know what happens now?" he said.

"What?" I whispered.

"We all live happily ever after."

My Prince smiled at me and I could see all the laughter-lines and the worry-lines crinkle up. I could see genuine kindness and love. A generosity of spirit I had never known before.

"I love you so much," I said.

"I love you millions," he replied.

I felt a little sigh coming on. I sighed a lovely, gentle, happy sigh.

Today's List

To do

1. Get rings made a tiny bit bigger.
2. Final fitting for bridesmaids – check what day Eve and Becca can go together.
3. Pack for honeymoon – St Lucia, here I come – make sure Eve and Becca have their flight times and tickets for joining us for the third week – get David to check Hugh and Ray have theirs.
4. Find out if pregnancy test is foolproof.
5. Get wedding dress taken out a little.

Not to do

1. Don't panic – I'm too old to panic – just because I'm marrying the man of my dreams in two weeks time is no reason to panic.
3. Don't worry over pregnancy – there will be a doctor in the house.

Note

1. Open the champagne tonight and tell David about the baby. He's going to be so charmed.
2. We'll tell Becca and Eve tomorrow. I know they're just going to love having a baby brother or sister.

To ignore

1. The begrudgers.